Henrik Ibsen, William Archer, Eleanor Marx Aveling, Frances Archer

Ibsen's Prose Dramas

Vol. 6

Henrik Ibsen, William Archer, Eleanor Marx Aveling, Frances Archer

Ibsen's Prose Dramas
Vol. 6

ISBN/EAN: 9783337376536

Printed in Europe, USA, Canada, Australia, Japan

Cover: Foto ©Andreas Hilbeck / pixelio.de

More available books at **www.hansebooks.com**

PEER GYNT

A DRAMATIC POEM

BY

HENRIK IBSEN

AUTHORISED TRANSLATION

BY

WILLIAM AND CHARLES ARCHER

LONDON:

WALTER SCOTT, Ltd., 24 WARWICK LANE.

CHARLES SCRIBNER'S SONS,

743 & 745 BROADWAY, NEW YORK.

1892.

TO

HENRIK IBSEN.

Vagliami 'l lungo studio, e 'l grande amore,
Che m' han fatto cercar lo tuo volume.

W. A.
C. A.

INTRODUCTION.

HENRIK IBSEN was in his thirty-seventh or thirty-eighth year when he wrote *Peer Gynt,* published in Copenhagen in 1867. He had left Norway in the spring of 1864, having by that time produced his historical and legendary tragedies in prose, and his fascinating, if somewhat juvenile, *Love's Comedy,* written in rhymed decasyllables. Proceeding to Rome, he there (or, more precisely, at Ariccia, under the Alban Mount) wrote the satiric tragedy, *Brand,* which at once made him famous throughout Scandinavia. *Brand* was published in 1866, while the poet, who had now wandered still further southward, to Ischia and Sorrento, was writing *Peer Gynt.* The production of two such poems within the space of two consecutive years is surely unique in the history of letters. It is unique, at any rate, in Ibsen's record, for he is, as a rule, an extremely deliberate worker.

Unlike *Brand,* which is entirely of the poet's own invention, *Peer Gynt* has its roots in Norwegian Folk-lore. In the invaluable collections of popular tales made by P. C. Asbjörnsen and Jörgen Moe,[1] we find the germs of several scenes and

---

[1] *Norske Folkeeventyr, samlede ved P. C. Asbjörnsen og Jörgen Moe,* Christiania, 1842; second (enlarged) ed., Christiania, 1852; third ed., 1866; fourth, 1868; fifth, 1874. Many of these translated by Sir George Webbe Dasent, *Popular Tales from the Norse,* Edinburgh, 1859; second ed. (enlarged), same place and date. See also *Tales from the Fjeld, a second series of Tales from the Norse of P. C. Asbjörnsen,* by G. W. Dasent, London, 1874. Also *Norske Huldre-Eventyr og Folkesagn,* by P. C. Asbjörnsen, Christiania, 1848 and 1859; third ed., Christiania, 1870. Also *Norske Folke-og Huldre-Eventyr, i Udvalg ved P. Chr. Asbjörnsen,* Copenhagen, 1879, translated under the title of *Round the Yule Log,* by H. L. Brækstad, London, 1881.

incidents. The very name "Peer Gynt" is suggested by
Asbjörnsen's "Reindeer-hunting in the Rondë Hills;"[1] and in the
same group of tales occurs the adventure of Gudbrand Glesnë
on the Gendin-Edge, which Peer Gynt works up so unblushingly
in Act I., Sc. 1. The text of both these tales will be found in
the Appendix, and the reader will recognise how very slight are
the hints which set the poet's imagination to work. The
encounter with the Sæter-Girls (Act II., Sc. 3), and the struggle
with the Boyg (Act II., Sc. 7), are foreshadowed in Asbjörnsen,
and the concluding remark of Anders Ulvsvolden evidently
suggested to Ibsen the idea of incarnating Fantasy in Peer
Gynt, as in Brand he had given us incarnate Will. But the
Peer Gynt of the drama has really nothing in common with the
Peer Gynt of the story, and the rest of the characters are not
even remotely suggested. Many scattered traits and allusions,
however, are borrowed from other legends in the same store-
house of grotesque and marvellous imaginings. Thus the story
of the devil in the nutshell (Act I., Sc. 3) appears in Asbjörnsen
under the title of "The Boy and the Devil."[2] The appearance
of the Green-Clad One with her Ugly Brat, who offers Peer
Gynt a goblet of beer (Act III., Sc. 3), is obviously suggested
by an incident in "Berthe Tuppenhaug's Stories."[3] Old
Berthe,[4] too, supplies the idea of correcting Peer Gynt's eye-
sight according to the standard of the hill-trolls (Act II., Sc. 6),
as well as the germ of the fantastic yarn-ball episode in the
last Act (Sc. 6). The castle, "East of the Sun and West of the
Moon" (Act III., Sc. 4), gives its title to one of Asbjörnsen's
stories,[5] which may be read in English in Mr. Andrew Lang's
Blue Fairy Book; and "Soria Moria Castle" is the title of
another legend.[6] Herr Passarge (in his *Henrik Ibsen*, Leipzig,
1883) goes so far as to trace the idea of Peer Gynt's shrinking

---

[1] *Norske Huldre-Eventyr og Folkesagn*, Christiania, 1848, p. 47.
See also Copenhagen edition, 1879, p. 154.

[2] *Norske Folke-og Huldre-Eventyr*, Copenhagen, 1879, p. 44.

[3] *Ibid.*, p. 134.

[4] *Ibid.*, pp. 130, 139.　　　　　[5] *Ibid.*, p. 243.

[6] Not included in the Copenhagen 1879 edition. See edition,
Christiania, 1866, p. 115.

from the casting-ladle, even though hell be the alternative (Act V., Sc. 7, etc.), to Asbjörnsen's story of "The Smith whom they dared not let into Hell;"[1] but the circumstances are so different, and Ibsen's idea is such an inseparable part of the ethical scheme of the drama, that we can scarcely take it to have been suggested by this (or any other) individual story. At the same time there is no doubt that "Folk-Lore of *Peer Gynt*" might form the subject of a much more extended study than our space or our knowledge admits of. The whole atmosphere of the first three acts and of the fifth is that of the Norwegian "Folk and Fairy Tales." A careful study of Asbjörnsen and Moe would probably reveal many direct suggestions besides those above enumerated. It must be remembered, too, that in the early sixties Ibsen was commissioned by the Norwegian Government to visit Romsdal and Söndmöre for the purpose of collecting folk-songs and legends, so that he must have come in direct personal contact with the mythopœic faculty of the peasantry in its very stronghold. To these journeys, no doubt, we are mainly indebted for the local colour of *Brand* and *Peer Gynt.*

What are we to say, now, of the drift, the interpretation, of *Peer Gynt?* The first thing to be said is that a complete understanding of its manifold satiric and symbolic bearings is by no means necessary to its enjoyment as a work of pure imagination. Rather we would counsel the reader, in the first instance, to skip the remaining pages of this introduction, to ignore the footnotes referring back to them, and, heedless of its ethical and political intentions, to take the poem as it comes, simply, as a dramatic romance or phantasmagoria of purely-human humour and pathos. Reading it in this way, he will naturally find a good deal that is obscure; but if the sheer interest, the pure poetry, of the thing does not carry him past these obscurities, then the poem, or at any rate this translation, is clearly not one of the books which are his by elective affinity. If the poem bites upon his mind at all, he will, even in reading it merely for its story, gain some general con-

---

[1] Copenhagen 1879 edition, p. 141.

ception of its symbolic scheme. At a second reading, with
the aid of such side-lights as we can here afford him, he will
probably find many of the obscurities vanish. But he must
not seek in *Peer Gynt* for a clear, consistent, cut-and-dried
allegory, with a place for everything and everything in its place.
It is not an allegory, but a phantasmagory. Its chief fascina-
tion, to our thinking (apart from its aforesaid charm as a mere
romance), lies in the multiplicity of meaning which may be read
into it. The poet, no doubt, had his own more or less distinct
and definable purpose in every scene, and this purpose it is
interesting to decipher. But *Peer Gynt* takes its place, as we
hold, on the summits of literature, precisely because it means
so much more than the poet consciously intended. Is not this
one of the characteristics of the masterpiece, that every one can
read in it his own secret? In the material world (though
Nature is very innocent of symbolic intention) each of us finds
for himself the symbols that have relevance and value for him;
and so it is with the poems which are instinct with true vitality.

The conscious and deliberate meanings of *Peer Gynt* fall
under three heads. First we have "allgemein-menschlich"
satire and symbolism, bearing upon human nature in general,
irrespective of race or nationality. Next we have satire upon
Norwegian human nature in particular, upon the religious and
political life of Norway as a nation. Lastly, we find a certain
number of local and ephemeral references—what, in the slang
of our stage, are called "topical allusions." The English reader
would scarcely thank us if we attempted to identify and
elucidate all the sub-intentions of this third order. It will be
enough if we point out some of the most obvious as they occur.

In order to provide the reader with a clue to the complex
meanings of *Peer Gynt*, on its higher lines or planes of significance, we cannot do better than quote some paragraphs from
the admirable summary of the drama given by Mr. P. H.
Wicksteed in his *Four Lectures on Henrik Ibsen.*[1] Mr.
Wicksteed is in such perfect sympathy with Ibsen in the stage
of his development marked by *Brand* and *Peer Gynt*, that he

---

[1] London: Sonnenschein, 1892.

has understood these poems, to our thinking, at least as well as any other commentator, whether German or Scandinavian. He writes as follows :—

"In *Brand* the hero is an embodied protest against the poverty of spirit and half-heartedness that Ibsen rebelled against in his country-men. In *Peer Gynt* the hero is himself the embodiment of that spirit. In *Brand* the fundamental antithesis, upon which, as its central theme, the drama is constructed, is the contrast between the spirit of com-promise on the one hand, and the motto 'everything or nothing' on the other. And Peer Gynt is the very incarnation of a compromising dread of decisive committal to any one course. In *Brand* the problem of self-realisation and the relation of the individual to his surroundings is obscurely struggling for recognition, and in *Peer Gynt* it becomes the formal theme upon which all the fantastic variations of the drama are built up. In both plays alike the problems of heredity and the influence of early surroundings are more than touched upon; and both alike culminate in the doctrine that the only redeeming power on earth or in heaven is the power of love.

"Peer Gynt, as already stated, stands for the Norwegian people, much as they are sketched in *Brand*, though with more brightness of colouring. Hence his perpetual 'hedging' and determination never so to commit himself that he cannot draw back. Hence his frag-mentary life of smatterings. Hence his perpetual brooding over the former grandeur of his family, his idle dreams of the future, and his neglect of every present duty. Hence his deep-rooted selfishness and cynical indifference to all higher motives; and hence, above all, his sordid and superstitious religion; for to him religion is the apotheosis of the art of 'hedging.'

"But Ibsen's allegories are never stiffly or pedantically worked out. His characters, though typical, are personal. We could read *Brand*, and could feel the tragedy and learn the lessons of the drama without any knowledge whatever of the circumstances or feelings under which it was written, or the references to the Norwegian character and conduct with which it teems.

"So, too, with *Peer Gynt*. We may forget the national significance of the sketch, except where special allusions recall it to our minds, and may think only of the universal problems with which the poem deals, and which will retain their awful interest when Ibsen's polemic against his countrymen has sunk into oblivion. The study of *Peer Gynt* as an occasional poem should be strictly subsidiary and introductory to its study as the tragedy of a lost soul.

"What is it to be one's self? God *meant something* when he made each one of us. For a man to embody that meaning of God in his words and deeds, and so become in his degree a 'word of God made flesh,' is to be himself. But thus to be himself he must slay himself. That is to say, he must slay the craving to make himself the centre round which others revolve, and must strive to find his true orbit and

b

swing, self-poised, round the great central light. But what if a poor
devil can never puzzle out what on earth God *did* mean when he made
him? Why, then, he must *feel* it. But how often your 'feeling'
misses fire! Ay! there you have it. The devil has no stauncher ally
than *want of perception!* [Act V., Sc. 9.]

" But, after all, you may generally find out what God meant you for
if you will face facts. It is easy to find a refuge from facts in lies, in
self-deception, and in self-sufficiency. It is easy to take credit to yourself for what circumstances have done for you, and lay upon circumstances what you owe to yourself. It is easy to think you are realising
yourself by refusing to become a 'pack-horse for the weal and woe of
others' [Act IV., Sc. 1], keeping alternatives open and never closing
a door behind you, or burning your ships, and so always remaining the
master of the situation and self-possessed. If you choose to do these
easy things you may always 'get round' your difficulties [Act II., Sc.
7], but you will never get through them. You will remain master of
the situation indeed, but the situation will become poorer and narrower
every day. If you never commit yourself, you never express yourself,
and your self becomes less and less significant and decisive. Calcu-
lating selfishness is the annihilation of self."

The significance of the drama in relation to the poet's
countrymen is well indicated by Herr Jæger in his valuable
biographical study.[1]

"The contest,"[2] he says, "did not end with *Brand*. The following
year Ibsen stepped forward once more, armed with a new dramatic
poem. *Peer Gynt* stands in the closest connection with *Brand*. If
Brand is the antithesis of the typical Norwegian, Peer Gynt is the
man himself; the former represents what the Norwegian nation lacks,
the latter what it is. Already in Brand's sketch of the Norwegian
people we have the outlines of Peer Gynt's portrait. In the following
verses, for instance, we find all the essential traits :—

> ' Go but around in this our land,
>   and question every man you meet,
>   you'll find each one has learnt to bo
>   a little bit of everything.
>
>   .   .   .   .   .   .
>
>   In all he's but a little bit ;
>   his faults, his merits, go not far ;
>   a fraction he in great and small,
>   a fraction, both in ill and good ;
>   and, what's the worst, the fraction's parts,
>   each of them murders all the rest.'

---

[1] *Henrik Ibsen*, 1828-1888. *Et Literært Livsbillede.* Copenhagen,
1888.

[2] That is, the satiric war which the poet was waging.

" Peer Gynt, then, is the nation thrown into relief as a single typical figure ; all the defects which Ibsen saw in his fellow-countrymen are to be found in him ; he is half-heartedness, want of character, egoism personified. . . . At the same time, *Peer Gynt* could never have been the complete and living work it is had the poet adhered strictly and exclusively to the conception of his hero as a national type. In this case, too, he began by conceiving an abstraction, and ended by pourtraying a living, individual character.

" Peer Gynt is not the Norseman in general, but the Norseman of a particular epoch, to wit, the end of the romantic period. Attacks on the outworks of romanticism are to be found even in *Brand*—the sheriff's enthusiasm for the age of King Bele, for example. In *Peer Gynt* the blow is aimed at the very heart of the system. Similar types from the transition period between romanticism and our modern world are to be found in several other literatures. In Turgenieff's *Rudin*, for example, and in Spielhagen's *Problematische Naturen* . . . we find personages who have this in common with Peer Gynt, that they are visionaries, incapable of playing their part in the life of reality. Ibsen, however, has gone his own way ; while the others went to the cultured classes for their typical figures, he has taken his from among the people. Peer Gynt is not, like the others, a product of the romanticism of culture, but of the national, popular romanticism, on which the cultured variety was based. Thus not only the name, Peer Gynt, but various details of the story are taken partly from Asbjörnsen and Moe's *Folke-eventyr*, partly from Asbjörnsen's *Huldre-eventyr;* and the poet expressly indicates [Act II., Sc. 2] that the germ of Peer Gynt's fantasy-spinning was im-planted by the fairy-tales on which, so to speak, his mother had brought him up. . . . This up-bringing on legends has borne fruit ; from the very beginning of our acquaintance with him he is a visionary, who walks about in a day-dream instead of setting to work at anything. When he tells the story of Gudbrand-Glesnö's ride[1] along the Gendin-Edge on the reindeer's back, he fully and firmly believes that it was he himself to whom it happened, though his ideas of the Gendin-Edge are so incorrect that it is plain he has never even seen it. Shortly after, he falls into a muse over a strangely-shaped cloud, and forgets both his neighbours' sneers and the wedding guests in dreaming that he is riding upon it, an Emperor. And when, for once in a way, he works him-self up to the point of action, the motive is that which usually actuates weak characters—namely, pique. His flight with Ingrid is a mere piece of bravado, and is indeed in itself an act as rash, as romantic, as meaningless as any visionary of them all could desire.

" There is a moment when he feels that the life of deeds is better than that of dreams ; the moment, namely, when he is being hunted by the whole parish like a wild beast [Act II., Sc. 3]. But this improvement does not last long ; he is soon so deep again in his fantastic world that he cannot distinguish between his real experiences

[1] See Appendix.

and those he has only dreamt of, but mixes them all up in one hotch-
potch. [Act II., Sc. 4.]

"Whenever he is confronted by the earnest things of real life he
has recourse to the plan his mother has taught him ; he takes refuge in
his fantastic world, to

> "'forget what's awry and crooked,
> and all that is sharp and sore.'

He invariably 'goes roundabout'—never straight through. Not even
by his mother's death-bed [Act III., Sc. 4] will he look the truth in the
face, but spirits her and himself away from it in a tissue of inventions.
What a difference between Brand's hard but honest behaviour towards
his dying mother, and the pitiful fantasy-mongering with which Peer
Gynt lies his mother away from life. There can be no doubt that
Ibsen conceived Åse's death-scene as a contrast and a parallel to the
death of Brand's mother.

"The double existence which Peer Gynt thus leads necessarily
develops in his character the half-heartedness of the true romanticist ;
it develops cowardice and impotence, egoism and bungling ; it opens
an impassable gulf between desire and action, between willing a thing
and carrying it out ; its motto is the characteristic—

> "'Ay, think of it,—wish it done—*will* it to boot,—
> But *do* it—! No, that's past my understanding.'—[Act III., Sc. 1.]

"All that Peer Gynt does is only half done ; he rubs out with one
hand what he has done with the other, and accordingly he is and
remains characterless and effaced, and must end in the casting-ladle
[Act V., Sc. 7], like everyone who has made of himself, not a personality,
but only an egoist, the caricature of a personality—who has not 'been
himself,' but has only been 'to himself—enough' [Act II., Sc. 6].
In reading *Peer Gynt* one is reminded involuntarily of H. C. Örsted's
maxim : 'Forget thyself, but never lose thy self.' It is in Peer Gynt's
nature that he should completely reverse this maxim in practice ; he
loses his self, though he has never forgotten himself.

"Thus the figure, which was originally conceived as a national type,
underwent a transformation into a personage typical of a special period,
the latest phase of which Ibsen himself had lived through, and with
which, in producing *Brand* and *Peer Gynt*, he finally and decisively
broke.

"Directly satirical sallies are obviously much rarer in *Peer Gynt*
than in *Brand*. The first three acts contain only one instance, a hit at
Norwegian chauvinism in the patriotic maxim of the Old Man of the
Dovre—

> "'The cow gives cakes and the bullock mead ;
> ask not if its taste be sour or sweet;
> the main matter is, and you mustn't forget it,
> it's all of it home-brewed.'—[Act II., Sc. 6.]

"A similar satirical passage addressed specially to the ' Målstrævers'[1] is introduced into the scene in the mad-house at Cairo [Act IV., Sc. 13], where Huhu deplores the extinction of the language of the orang-outangs. The characters of the two other madmen, who are brought forward in this scene, are satiric references to conditions then existing in the north. The Fellah with the royal mummy on his back is—like Trumpeterstråle—a cut at the Swedes, the mummy being Charles the Twelfth. Like the Fellah, it is implied, the Swedes are extremely proud of their 'Hero-king,' and yet during the Dano-German war they showed not the smallest sign of having anything in common with him, unless it were that they, like him, 'kept still and completely dead.' In the delusion of the minister Hussein, who imagines himself a pen, there is a general reference to the futile address- and note-mongering which went on in Norwegian-Swedish officialdom during the Dano-German war, and a more special one to an eminent Swedish statesman, who, during the war, had been extremely proud of his official notes, and had imagined that by means of them he might exercise a decisive influence on the course of events.

"General political and psychological considerations, however, and not special and occasional satiric objects, were those which mainly influenced the poet during the production of *Peer Gynt*; and accordingly, in drawing in the hero a transition-figure characteristic of our century, he created a type, which has relevance far beyond the limits whether of Norway or of Scandinavia."

Readers who desire further assistance in solving the riddles of *Peer Gynt* will find an elaborate, not to say laborious, commentary on the poem in Passarge's *Henrik Ibsen: ein Beitrag zur neusten Geschichte der norwegischen National-literatur* (Leipzig, 1883). Passarge quotes largely from Valfrid Vasenius's *Henrik Ibsen: ett Skaldeporträtt* (Stockholm, 1882), which may also be consulted, not without profit, by those who read Swedish. Both Passarge and Vasenius, however, attempt to compress the

---

[1] "Målstræver" may be translated "language reformer." It was the name given to a party which desired to substitute a language compounded from the various local dialects, for the Norwegian of the bourgeoisie and of literature, which they called Danish, and declared to be practically a foreign tongue to the peasants and the lower classes generally. The peasants, they argued (like Huhu's orang-outangs), lived and died "uninterpreted." The movement attained no little force in the sixties and seventies, and a considerable literature sprang up in the so-called "mål," the work of such men as Ivar Åsen, A. O. Vinje, and Kristofer Janson. Some of the dialect poems which the movement produced, more especially those of Ivar Åsen, are highly esteemed even by the opponents of the "Målstræv."

poem into a mould of scholastic psychology and ethics which it bursts on every hand. The phrase " ondoyant et divers " might have been invented to characterise *Peer Gynt*. A more profitable commentary, both from the literary-historical and the philosophic point of view, will be found in Auguste Ehrhard's *Henrik Ibsen et le Théâtre Contemporain* (Paris, 1892), probably the most thorough-going and competent piece of Ibsen criticism which has yet appeared. M. Ehrhard (in a passage suggested by Henrik Jæger's essay on " *Synnöve Solbakken* and its Period " in his *Norske Forfattere*) tries to show that Ibsen deliberately intended *Peer Gynt* as a satiric counterblast to Björnson's first and most characteristic peasant-novel. In this, to our thinking, he goes too far. *Synnöve Solbakken* is no doubt a typical production of the period of national romanticism, against which (as we have seen above) *Peer Gynt* marks the reaction. But the analogies on which M. Ehrhard founds his theory that Peer and Solveig are designed as counterparts to Thorbjörn and Synnöve seem to us fortuitous where they are not purely fanciful. Again, the French critic accepts with too great facility Herr Georg Brandes's very inadequate interpretation of the Boyg[1] as representing " Akkordens Ånd," the spirit of compromise, and his criticism of the yarn-ball scene (Act V., Sc. 6.) as an utter-

---

[1] Deeming it unnecessary to trouble the English reader with niceties of pronunciation, we have represented the " Böig " of the original by the more easily pronouncible " Boyg." The root-idea seems to be that of bending, of sinuousness; compare Norwegian *bóie*, German *biegen*, to bend. The German translator, both in the folk-tale and in the drama, renders " Böigen " by " der Krumme." So far as we are aware, the name occurs in no other folk-tale save that of *Peer Gynt*. It is not generic, but denotes an individual troll-monster. We may pretty safely conjecture that the idea of this vague, shapeless, ubiquitous, inevitable, invulnerable Thing was what chiefly fascinated the poet's imagination in the legend of Peer Gynt. There are no doubt many possible sub-intentions in the Boyg as presented by Ibsen, and we may, if we please, understand it as the Spirit of Compromise among other things. But the key to its primary significance is unquestionably to be found in Act IV., Sc. 12.

ance of personal self-reproach on Ibsen's part, Peer Gynt being
"too miserable a creature" ever to have experienced such an
emotion. Herr Brandes is justly esteemed one of the most
competent of living critics, but his treatment of *Peer Gynt*[1]
is decidedly perfunctory. Yet again, the reader must judge for
himself how much weight to attach to M. Ehrhard's suggestion
that Ibsen had Goethe's *Faust* distinctly present to his mind
in conceiving *Peer Gynt.* To our thinking, the analogies on
which he dwells are, as in the case of *Synnöve Solbakken*, either
fanciful or fortuitous. The redemption of the hero through a
woman's love is the only real point of similarity; and this we
take to be a mere commonplace of romanticism, which Ibsen,
though he satirised it, had by no means finally outgrown when
he wrote *Peer Gynt.* Peer's return to Solveig is (in the original)
a passage of the most poignant lyric beauty, but it is surely a
shirking, not a solution, of the ethical problem. It would be
impossible to the Ibsen of to-day, who knows (none better) that
"No man[2] can save his brother's soul, or pay his brother's
debt." Or are we, with Mr. George Bernard Shaw,[3] to read the
situation ironically, and understand that "With this crowningly
unreal self-realisation Peer Gynt is left to face the Button-
Moulder as best he can"? Perhaps; but it is to be noted that
the poet gives Solveig the last word.

The principles which have guided us in the following transcript
demand a few words of explanation, not to say apology. *Peer
Gynt* is written from first to last in rhymed verse. Six or eight
different measures are employed in the various scenes, and the
rhymes are exceedingly rich and complex. The frequency of
final light syllables in Norwegian, resulting from the number of
inflexions in *e, en, et, er, es, ene, ende,* etc., implies an exceptional
abundance of double rhymes, and Ibsen has taken full advantage of this peculiarity. In the short first scene of the second

[1] See his *Æsthetiske Studier,* ed. 1888, p. 330, and *Det Moderne
Gjennembruds Mænd,* 1883, Essay on Ibsen, *passim.*
[2] "No, nor woman neither."
[3] Mr. Shaw's *Quintessence of Ibsenism* (London, 1891) contains a
summary but very suggestive exegesis of *Peer Gynt.*

Act, for example, twenty-five out of the forty lines end in double rhymes, and there are three sets of three lines ending in the same double rhyme.[1] The tintinnabulation of these double rhymes, then, gives to most of the scenes a metrical character which it might puzzle Mr. Swinburne himself to reproduce in English. Moreover, the ordinary objections to rhymed translations seemed to apply with exceptional force in the case of *Peer Gynt*. The characteristic quality of its style is its vernacular ease and simplicity. It would have been heart-breaking work (apart from its extreme difficulty) to substitute for this racy terseness the conventional graces of English poetic diction, padding here and perverting there. From such a task even a master of rhymes and metres might well have shrunk, as from a "labor improbus" in a double sense; and we were the less tempted to essay it as we knew ourselves no masters either of metre or rhyme. To a prose translation, on the other hand, the objections seemed even greater. It is possible to give in prose some faint adumbration of epic dignity and even of lyric loveliness; but we had here no epic, no lyric, to deal with; not even a poetic drama, like *Tasso* or *Hernani*, based on a single rhetorical convention. We found (though the statement may at first seem paradoxical) that the same vernacular simplicity of style which forbade a translation in rhyme, militated no less strongly against a translation in prose. The characteristic quality of the poet's achievement lay precisely in his having given to the most easy and natural dialogue (natural in expression, however fantastic in idea) new beauty, aptitude, and elevation by the aid of rhythm and rhyme. Entirely to

[1] Brott—og brott igjen os binder——
Djævelen stå i alt som minder——
Djævelen stå i alle kvinder——

Uden en. Hvem er den enö——
Fort! Til faer din! Kjære, venö——
Ti! Du kan umuligt menö——

Godt! så se da hvem som vinder——
Djævelen stå i alt som minder——
Djævelen stå i alle kvinder——

eliminate these graces of form was to reduce the poem to prose indeed. It seemed little better than casting a silver statue into the crucible and asking the world to divine from the ingot something of the sculptor's power. A prose translation, in short, could not but strip Fantasy of its pinions, rob Satire of its barbs. We put the matter to the test ; for one of us made a complete translation in prose, with some vague intention of publishing it along with the original text—the Norwegian on one page, the English on the next. It was found, however, that the expense of such a publication would be prohibitive ; and we rejected at once all idea of publishing the English alone, our own dissatisfaction with it being reinforced by Henrik Ibsen's express declaration that he would rather let *Peer Gynt* remain untranslated than see it rendered in prose. But, as there is no copyright between England and the Scandinavian kingdoms, it was not in Ibsen's power to lay upon others the injunction which to us was absolutely binding. We knew that, in one form or another, the poem was certain ere long to be translated ; and, placing this consideration before the poet, we suggested to him a middle course between prose and rhyme, a translation as nearly as possible in the metres of the original, but with the rhymes suppressed. To this compromise he readily assented, and the following pages are the result.

We had no precedent—within our knowledge, at any rate— to guide us, and were forced to lay down our own laws. Even at the risk of falling between two stools, we proposed to ourselves a dual purpose. We sought to produce a translation which should convey to the general reader some faint conception of the movement and colour, the wit and pathos, of the original, and at the same time a transcript which should serve the student as a "crib" to the Norwegian text. We knew of several people who had applied themselves to the study of Norwegian (a very easy language) with the express purpose of reading *Peer Gynt* and *Brand* in the original ; we held it certain that, for some years at any rate, an increasing number would follow their example ; and we felt bound to do all in our power to assist so excellent a movement. This, then, the reader must be good enough to bear in mind : that the following version is designed to facilitate, not to supersede, the study of the original, for all who would really master a poem which we, its translators, are the first to declare essentially untranslatable. But, apart from our desire to provide a "crib" to *Peer Gynt*, we felt that, in taking the liberty of suppressing the rhymes, we abjured our right to any other liberty whatsoever. A rhymed paraphrase of a great poem may have a beauty of its own ; an unrhymed version must be no paraphrase but a faithful transcript, else "the ripple of laughing rhyme" has been sacrificed in vain. Our fundamental principle, then, has been to represent the original *line for line;* and to this principle we have adhered with the utmost fidelity. There are probably not fifty cases in the whole poem in which a word has been transferred from one line to another, and then only some pronoun or auxiliary verb. It is needless to say that in adhering to this principle we have often had to resist temptation. Many cases presented themselves in which greater clearness, grace, and vigour might easily have been attained by transferring a word or phrase from this line to that, or even altering the sequence of a whole group of lines. In no case have we yielded to such temptation, feeling that, our rule once relaxed, we should insensibly but inevitably lapse into mere paraphrase. Temptation beset us with especial force in the less vital passages of the poem. The first scene of the fourth Act, for example, is written in a spirit of reckless whimsicality, not to say sheer burlesque, and the style becomes in places decidedly flaccid. In these places it would have been easy to give our rendering some approach to grace and point by disregarding inversions and other defects of expression, justified in the original by the wit and spirit of the rhymes, but of course deprived in our transcript of any such excuse. Here, as else-where, we were proof against temptation ; it is for our readers to decide whether our constancy was heroic or pedantic.

It would be folly to pretend either that we have reproduced every word of the original, or that we have avoided all necessity for "padding." The chief drawback of our line-for-line principle is that it has debarred us from eking out the deficiency of one line with the superfluity of the next. We trust, however, that few essential ideas, or even words, of the original will be found quite unaccounted-for ; while with regard to padding, to *cheville*, we have tried, where we found it absolutely forced upon us, to use only such mechanical parts of speech as introduced no new idea into the context.   Only in the rarest cases have we made use of an epithet not supplied us in the original.   For example, we have had no scruple (on occasion) in saying "very true" or "true indeed" where Ibsen said only "true"; we may sometimes, but not often, have said "milk-white" or "sky-blue" where he said only "white" or "blue"; we have never (to the best of our belief) made a horse "white" or a rose "red" when its colour was undetermined in the original.   We have found by experiment that the fact of writing in measure has frequently enabled us to keep much closer to the original than would have been possible in prose. This is not in reality so strange as it may at first sight appear. A prose translation of verse can avoid paraphrase only at the cost of grotesque inelegance ; whereas in rendering metre into metre, we are working under the same laws which govern the original, and are therefore enabled in many cases to adopt identical forms of expression which would be quite inadmissible in prose.

Thirty out of the thirty-eight scenes into which the five acts are divided are written almost entirely in an irregular measure of four accents, evidently designed to give the greatest possible variety and suppleness to the dialogue.   The four accents constitute almost the only assignable law of this measure, the feet being of any length, from two to four syllables, and of all possible denominations—iambics, trochees, dactyls, anapæsts, amphibrachs.   The effect is at first rather baffling to the unaccustomed ear ; but when one gets into the swing of the rub-a-dub rhythm, if we may venture to call it so, the feeling of ruggedness vanishes, and the verse is found to be capable of poignantly pathetic, as well as of buoyantly humorous, expression.   We pick out at random two specimens of this metre—the first from Act I., Sc. 3, where Peer Gynt first sees Solveig ; the second from Act III., Sc. 3, where Solveig comes to Peer Gynt's hut in the forest :—

Hvor lýs ! | Nej, skúlde | du sét | en slíg !
Skótted ned | paa skóen | og det hví- | de spréde !
Og saa hóldt | hun i mó- | derens skjør- | teflíg,
og bár | en sálme- | bog svøbt i | et klæde.

Nætterne | túnge og | dágene | tómme
bár mig det | búd at | nú fik jeg | kómme.
Det blév som | lívet var | slúkknet der- | néde ;
jeg kúnde ik- | ke hjérte- | fyldt lé el- | ler græde ;
jeg vídste ik- | ke trýggt hvad | sínd du | áatte ;
jeg vídste | kun trýggt hvad | jeg skúlde | og máatte.

We have not attempted to reproduce each line of this measure
accurately, foot for foot, holding it enough to observe the law
of the four accents. On the average, probably, our lines will be
found somewhat longer than those of the original, for we have
throughout been conscious of a tendency to increase the
proportion of three-syllable to two-syllable feet. Where the
four-accent rule is obviously departed from, it will generally be
found to be in obedience to the original ; for Ibsen now and
then (but very rarely) introduces a line or couplet of three or
of five accents.

Of the eight scenes in which this measure is not employed,
three—Act I. Sc. 1, Act II. Sc. 1, and Act IV. Sc. 7—are in a
perfectly regular trochaic measure of four accents, the lines
containing seven or eight syllables, according as the rhymes
are single or double. For example :

Først saa | rénder | dú till- | fjelds
máaneds- | vís i | trávle | áannen,
fór at | véjde | rén paa | sáannen,
kómmer | hjém med | róven | pels,
úden | býrse, | úden | vildt ;—
óg till- | slút med | áabne | øjne
méner | dú at | sáa mig | bildt
índ de | værste | skýtter- | løgne.

In dealing with this measure, we have not thought it necessary
to follow the precise arrangement of the original in the alternation of seven and eight syllable lines. In other words, we
have sometimes represented a seven-syllable line by one of eight

syllables, an eight-syllable line by one of seven. In the short first scene of the second act, however, every line represents accurately the length of the corresponding line in the original.

The fourth scene of Act II. is written in lines of three accents, consisting for the most part of trochees, dactyls, and amphibrachs. For example :

> Flúgt over | Géndin | éggen.
> Dígt og for- | bándet | løgn !
> óppover | brátteste | væggen
> med brúden | —og drúkken | et døgn ;
> jáget af | høg og | glénter,
> trúet af | tróld og | sligt,
> túret med | gálne | jénter ; —
> løgn og for | bándet | digt !

The last scene of the third Act—Åse's death-scene—is written in lines of three accents with alternate double and single rhymes, the normal lines consisting of three amphibrachs, or two amphibrachs and a trochee, alternating with an amphibrach and two iambics, thus :

> Nu, móer, vil | vi sámmen | snákke ;
> men báre | om løst | og fást, —
> og glémme | det vránge | og skákke
> og ált som | er sáart | og hvásst.

In rendering this scene we have been careful to preserve the alternation of strong with light endings, which gives it its metrical character.

Two scenes—Act IV. Sc. 1, and Act V. Sc. 2—consist of four-accent iambic lines, differing from the octosyllabic verse of *Marmion* or *The Giaour* chiefly in the greater prevalence of double and even treble rhymes. For example :

> Det gýnt- | ske sélv | det ér | den hær
> af øn- | sker lýst- | er óg | begjǽr, —
> det gýnt- | ske sélv, | det ér | det háv
> af índ- | fald fór- | dringér | og kráv,
> kort ált | som nétt- | opp mít | bryst hǽver,
> og gjør | at jég | som sáa- | dan léver.

Finally, the sixth scene of Act V. consists mainly of eight-line lyrical stanzas, with two accents in each line, Peer Gynt's interspersed remarks being in trochaic verses, like those of Act I., Sc. 1. In such intercalated passages, so to speak, as the rhapsodies of Huhu and the Fellah in Act IV., Sc. 13, and the Pastor's speech at the grave in Act V., Sc. 3, we have accurately reproduced the measures of the original. The Pastor's speech is the only passage in the whole poem which is couched in iambic pentameters.

In dealing with idioms and proverbial expressions, our practice has not been very consistent. We have sometimes, where they seemed peculiarly racy and expressive, translated them literally; in other cases we have had recourse to the nearest English equivalent, even where the metaphor employed is quite different. In the latter instances we have usually given the literal rendering of the phrase in a footnote.

W. A.

C. A.

PEER GYNT.

CHARACTERS.

ÅSE,[1] a peasant's widow.

PEER GYNT,[2] her son.

TWO OLD WOMEN with corn-sacks. ASLAK, a smith. WEDDING-GUESTS. A MASTER-COOK, A FIDDLER, etc.

A MAN AND WIFE, newcomers to the district.

SOLVEIG and LITTLE HELGA, their daughters.

THE FARMER AT HEGSTAD.

INGRID, his daughter.

THE BRIDEGROOM and HIS PARENTS.

THREE SÆTER-GIRLS. A GREEN-CLAD WOMAN.

THE OLD MAN OF THE DOVRË.

A TROLL-COURTIER. SEVERAL OTHERS. TROLL-MAIDENS and TROLL-URCHINS. A COUPLE OF WITCHES. BROWNIES, NIXIES, GNOMES, etc.

AN UGLY BRAT. A VOICE IN THE DARKNESS. BIRD-CRIES.

KARI, a cottar's wife.

Master COTTON, Monsieur BALLON, Herren VON EBERKOPF and TRUMPETERSTRÅLE, gentlemen on their travels. A THIEF and A RECEIVER.

ANITRA, daughter of a Bedouin chief.

ARABS, FEMALE SLAVES, DANCING-GIRLS, etc.

THE MEMNON-STATUE (singing). THE SPHINX AT GIZEH (*muta persona*).

PROFESSOR BEGRIFFENFELDT, Dr. phil., director of the madhouse at Cairo.

HUHU, a language-reformer from the coast of Malabar. HUSSEIN, an eastern Minister. A FELLAH, with a royal mummy.

SEVERAL MADMEN, with their KEEPERS.

A NORWEGIAN SKIPPER and HIS CREW. A STRANGE PASSENGER.

A PASTOR. A FUNERAL-PARTY. A PARISH-OFFICER. A BUTTON-MOULDER. A LEAN PERSON.

(The action, which opens in the beginning of the present century, and ends towards our own days, takes place partly in Gudbrandsdale, and on the mountains around it, partly on the coast of Morocco, in the desert of Sahara, in a madhouse at Cairo, at sea, etc.)

---

[1] Pronounce *Oase*. The letter å is pronounced like the *o* in "home."

[2] Pronounce *Pair Günt*—the G hard, the y like the German modified *ü*.

PEER GYNT.

ACT FIRST.

SCENE FIRST.

(A wooded hillside near Âse's *farm. A river rushes down
the slope. On the further side of it an old mill shed.
It is a hot day in summer.)*
*(*PEER GYNT, *a strongly-built youth of twenty, comes down
the pathway. His mother,* Âse, *a small, slightly-
built woman, follows him, scolding angrily.)*

ÂSE.

Peer, you're lying!

PEER
(without stopping).

No, I am not!

ÂSE.

Well then, swear that it is true!

PEER.

Swear? Why should I?

ÅSE.

See, you dare not!
It's a lie from first to last.

PEER
(*stopping*).

It is true—each blessed word!

ÅSE
(*confronting him*).

Don't you blush before your mother?
First you skulk among the mountains
monthlong in the busiest season,
stalking reindeer in the snows;
home you come then, torn and tattered,
gun amissing, likewise game;—
and at last, with open eyes,
think to get me to believe
all the wildest hunters'-lies!—
Well, where did you find the buck, then?

PEER.

West near Gendin.[1]

ÅSE
(*laughing scornfully*).

Ah! Indeed!

PEER.

Keen the blast towards me swept;
hidden by an alder-clump,
he was scraping in the snow-crust
after lichen——

[1] Pronounce *Yendeen*.

ÅSE
(*as before*).

Doubtless, yes!

PEER.

Breathlessly I stood and listened,
heard the crunching of his hoof,
saw the branches of one antler.
Softly then among the boulders
I crept forward on my belly.
Crouched in the moraine I peered up;—
such a buck, so sleek and fat,
you, I'm sure, have ne'er set eyes on.

ÅSE.

No, of course not!

PEER.

Bang! I fired!
Clean he dropped upon the hillside.
But the instant that he fell
I sat firm astride his back,
gripped him by the left ear tightly,
and had almost sunk my knife-blade
in his neck, behind his skull—
when, behold! the brute screamed wildly,
sprang upon his feet like lightning,
with a back-cast of his head
from my fist made knife and sheath fly,
pinned me tightly by the thigh,
jammed his horns against my legs,
clenched me like a pair of tongs; --
then forthwith away he flew
right along the Gendin-Edge!

ÅSE
(*involuntarily*).

Jesus save us——!

PEER.

Have you ever
chanced to see the Gendin-Edge?
Nigh on four miles long it stretches
sharp before you like a scythe.
Down o'er glaciers, landslips, scaurs,
down the toppling grey moraines,
you can see, both right and left,
straight into the tarns that slumber,
black and sluggish, more than seven
hundred fathoms deep below you.

Right along the Edge we two
clove our passage through the air.

Never rode I such a colt!
Straight before us as we rushed
'twas as though there glittered suns.
Brown-backed eagles that were sailing
in the wide and dizzy void
half-way 'twixt us and the tarns,
dropped behind, like motes in air.

Ice-floes on the shores broke crashing,
but no murmur reached my ears.
Only sprites of dizziness[1] sprang,
dancing, round;—they sang, they swung,
circle-wise, past sight and hearing!

ÅSE
(*dizzy*).

Oh, God save me!

---

[1] This is the poet's own explanation of this difficult passage.
"Ilvirvlens vætter," he writes, is equivalent to "Svimmelhedens
ånder"—*i.e.*, spirits of dizziness or vertigo.

PEER.

All at once,
at a desperate, break-neck spot,
rose a great cock-ptarmigan,
flapping, cackling, terrified,
from the crack where he lay hidden
at the buck's feet on the Edge.
Then the buck shied half around,
leapt sky-high, and down we plunged
both of us into the depths!

(ASE *totters, and catches at the trunk of a tree.*
PEER GYNT *continues :*)

Mountain walls behind us, black,
and below a void unfathomed!
First we clove through banks of mist,
then we clove a flock of sea-gulls,
so that they, in mid-air startled,
flew in all directions, screaming.
Downward rushed we, ever downward.
But beneath us something shimmered,
whitish, like a reindeer's belly.—
Mother, 'twas our own reflection
in the glass-smooth mountain tarn,
shooting up towards the surface
with the same wild rush of speed
wherewith we were shooting downwards.

ÅSE
(*gasping for breath*).

Peer! God help me——! Quickly, tell——!

PEER.

Buck from over, buck from under,

in a moment clashed together,
scattering foam-flecks all around.
　　　There we lay then, floating, plashing,—
But at last we made our way
somehow to the northern shore;
buck, he swam, I clung behind him :—
I ran homewards——

ÅSE.

But the buck, dear?

PEER.

He's there still, for aught I know ;—
　　　(*Snaps his fingers, turns on his heel, and adds :*)
catch him, and you're welcome to him !

ASE.

And your neck you haven't broken?
Haven't broken both your thighs?
and your backbone, too, is whole?
Oh, dear Lord—what thanks, what praise,
should be thine who helped my boy !
There's a rent, though, in your breeches ;
but it's scarce worth talking of
when one thinks what dreadful things
might have come of such a leap——!
　　　(*Stops suddenly, looks at him open-mouthed and
　　　　　wide-eyed ; cannot find words for some time,
　　　　　but at last bursts out :*)
Oh, you devil's story-teller,
Cross of Christ, how you can lie !
All this screed you foist upon me,
I remember now, I knew it

when I was a girl of twenty.
Gudbrand Glesnë[1] it befell,
never you, you——

PEER.

Me as well.
Such a thing can happen twice.

ÅSE
(*exasperated*).

Yes, a lie, turned topsy-turvy,
can be prinked and tinselled out,
decked in plumage new and fine,
till none knows its lean old carcass.
That is just what you've been doing,
vamping up things, wild and grand,
garnishing with eagles' backs
and with all the other horrors,
lying right and lying left,
filling me with speechless dread,
till at last I recognised not
what of old I'd heard and known !

PEER.

If another talked like that
I'd half kill him for his pains.

ÅSE
(*weeping*).

Oh, would God I lay a corpse ;
would the black earth held me sleeping !
Prayers and tears don't bite upon him.—
Peer, you're lost, and ever will be !

[1] See Introduction, p. vi., and Appendix.

PEER.

Darling, pretty little mother,
you are right in every word ;—
don't be cross, be happy——

ÅSE.

Silence !

Could I, if I would, be happy,
with a pig like you for son ?
Think how bitter I must find it,
I, a poor defenceless widow,
ever to be put to shame !

(*Weeping again.*)

How much have we now remaining
from your grandsire's days of glory ?
Where are now the sacks [1] of coin
left behind by Rasmus Gynt ?
Ah, your father lent them wings,—
lavished them abroad like sand,
buying land in every parish,
driving round in gilded chariots.
Where is all the wealth he wasted
at the famous winter-banquet,
when each guest sent glass and bottle
shivering 'gainst the wall behind him ?

PEER.

Where's the snow of yester-year ?

ÅSE.

Silence, boy, before your mother !
See the farmhouse ! Every second
window-pane is stopped with clouts.

[1] Literally, "bushels."

Hedges, fences, all are down,
beasts exposed to wind and weather,
fields and meadows lying fallow,
every month a new distraint——

PEER.

Come now, stop this old-wife's talk!
Many a time has luck seemed drooping,
and sprung up as high as ever!

ÅSE.

Salt-strewn is the soil it grew from.
Lord, but you're a rare one, you,—
just as pert and jaunty still,
just as bold as when the Pastor,
newly come from Copenhagen,
bade you tell your Christian name,
and declared that such a headpiece
many a Prince down there might envy;
till the cob your father gave him,
with a sledge to boot, in thanks
for his pleasant, friendly talk.—
Ah, but things went bravely then!
Provost,[1] Captain, all the rest,
dropped in daily, ate and drank,
swilling, till they well-nigh burst.
But 'tis need that tests one's neighbour.
Still it grew and empty here
from the day that "Gold-bag Jon"[2]
started with his pack, a pedlar.
(Dries her eyes with her apron.)

[1] An ecclesiastical dignitary—something equivalent to a rural dean.
[2] "Jon med Skjæppen"—literally, "John with the Bushel"—a nick-
name given him in his days of prosperity, in allusion to his supposed
bushels of money.

Ah, you're big and strong enough,
you should be a staff and pillar
for your mother's frail old age,—
you should keep the farm-work going,
guard the remnants of your gear ;—

(*Crying again.*)

oh, God help me, small's the profit
you have been to me, you scamp !
Lounging by the hearth at home,
grubbing in the charcoal embers ;
or, round all the country, frightening
girls away from merry-makings—
shaming me in all directions,
fighting with the worst rapscallions——

PEER
(*turning away from her*).

Let me be.

ÅSE
(*following him*).

Can you deny
that you were the foremost brawler
in the mighty battle royal
fought the other day at Lundë,
when you raged like mongrels mad ?
Who was it but you that broke
Blacksmith Aslak's arm for him,—
or at any rate that wrenched one
of his fingers out of joint ?

PEER.

Who has filled you with such prate ?

ÅSE

(*hotly*).

Cottar Kari heard the yells!

PEER

(*rubbing his elbow*).

Maybe, but 'twas I that howled.

ÅSE.

You?

PEER.

Yes, mother,—*I* got beaten.

ÅSE.

What d'you say?

PEER.

He's limber, *he* is.

ÅSE.

Who?

PEER.

Why Aslak, to be sure.

ÅSE.

Shame—and shame; I spit upon you!
Such a worthless sot as that,
such a brawler, such a sodden
dram-sponge to have beaten you!
(*Weeping again.*)
Many a shame and slight I've suffered;
but that this should come to pass
is the worst disgrace of all.

What if he be ne'er so limber,
need you therefore be a weakling?

PEER.

Though I hammer or am hammered,—
still we must have lamentations.
            (*Laughing.*)
Cheer up, mother——

ÅSE.

            What?   You're lying
now again?

PEER.

            Yes, just this once.
Come now, wipe your tears away;—
            (*Clenching his left hand.*)
see,—with this same pair of tongs,
thus I held the smith bent double,
while my sledge-hammer right fist——

ÅSE.

Oh, you brawler!   You will bring me
with your doings to the grave!

PEER.

No, you're worth a better fate;
better twenty thousand times!
Little, ugly, dear old mother,
you may safely trust my word,—
all the parish shall exalt you;
only wait till I have done
something—something really grand!

ÂSE

(*contemptuously*).

You!

PEER.

Who knows what may befall one!

ÂSE.

Would you'd get so far in sense
one day as to do the darning
of your breeches for yourself!

PEER

(*hotly*).

I will be a king, a kaiser!

ÂSE.

Oh, God comfort me, he's losing
all the wits that he had left!

PEER.

Yes, I will! Just give me time!

ÂSE.

Give you time, you'll be a prince,
so the saying goes, I think!

PEER.

You shall see!

ÂSE.

Oh, hold your tongue!
You're as mad as mad can be.—
Ah, and yet it's true enough,—
something might have come of you,

had you not been steeped for ever
in your lies and trash and moonshine.
Hegstad's girl was fond of you.
Easily you could have won her
had you wooed her with a will——

PEER.

Could I?

ÅSE.

The old man's too feeble
not to give his child her way.
He is stiff-necked in a fashion;
but at last 'tis Ingrid rules;
and where *she* leads, step by step,
stumps the gaffer, grumbling, after.
(*Begins to cry again.*)
Ah, my Peer!—a golden girl—
land entailed on her! Just think,
had you set your mind upon it,
you'd be now a bridegroom brave,—
you that stand here grimed and tattered!

PEER
(*briskly*).

Come, we'll go a-wooing, then!

ÅSE.

Where?

PEER.

At Hegstad!

ÅSE.

Ah, poor boy;
Hegstad way is barred to wooers!

PEER.

How is that?

ÅSE.

Ah, I must sigh!
Lost the moment, lost the luck——

PEER.

Speak!

ÅSE
(*sobbing*).

While in the Wester-hills
you in air were riding reindeer,
here Mads Moen's[1] won the girl!

PEER.

What!   That women's-bugbear!   He——!

ÅSE.

Ay, she's taking him for husband.

PEER.

Wait you here till I have harnessed
horse and waggon——

(*Going.*)

ÅSE.

Spare your pains.
They are to be wed to-morrow——

PEER.

Pooh; this evening I'll be there!

_____
[1] Pronounce *Maass Moo-en.*

ÅSE.

Fie now! Would you crown our miseries
with a load of all men's scorn?

PEER.

Never fear; 'twill all go well.
              (*Shouting and laughing at the same time.*)
Mother, jump! We'll spare the waggon;
'twould take time to fetch the mare up——
              (*Lifts her up in his arms*).

ÅSE.

Put me down!

PEER.

              No, in my arms
I will bear you to the wedding!
              (*Wades out into the stream.*)

ÅSE.

Help! The Lord have mercy on us!
Peer! We're drowning-——

PEER.

              I was born
for a braver death——

ÅSE.

              Ay, true;
sure enough you'll hang at last!
              (*Tugging at his hair.*)
Oh, you brute!

PEER.

Keep quiet now;
here the bottom's slippery-slimy.

ÅSE.

Ass!

PEER.

That's right, don't spare your tongue;
that does no one any harm.
Now it's shelving up again——

ÅSE.

Don't you drop me!

PEER.

Heisan! Hop!
Now we'll play at Peer and reindeer;—
(*Curvetting.*)
I'm the reindeer, you are Peer!

ÅSE.

Oh, I'm going clean distraught!

PEER.

There see; now we've reached the shallows;—
(*Wades ashore.*)
come, a kiss now, for the reindeer;
just to thank him for the ride——

ÅSE
(*boxing his ears*).

This is how I thank him!

PEER.

Ow!

That's a miserable fare!

ÅSE.

Put me down!

PEER.

First to the wedding.
Be my spokesman.   You're so clever;
talk to him, the old curmudgeon;
say Mads Moen's good for nothing——

ÅSE.

Put me down!

PEER.

And tell him then
what a rare lad is Peer Gynt.

ÅSE.

Truly, you may swear to that!
Fine's the character I'll give you.
Through and through I'll show you up;
all about your devil's pranks
I will tell them straight and plain——

PEER.

Will you?

ÅSE
(*kicking with rage*).

I won't stay my tongue
till the old man sets his dog
at you, as you were a tramp!

PEER.

Hm; then I must go alone.

ÂSE.

Ay, but I'll come after you!

PEER.

Mother dear, you haven't strength------

ÂSE.

Strength?　When I'm in such a rage,
I could crush the rocks to powder!
Hu! I'd make a meal of flints!
Put me down!

PEER.

You'll promise then-----

ÂSE.

Nothing!　I'll to Hegstad with you!
They shall know you, what you are!

PEER.

Then you'll even have to stay here.

ÂSE.

Never!　To the feast I'm coming!

PEER.

That you shan't.

ÂSE.

What will you do?

PEER.

Perch you on the mill-house roof.

(*He puts her up on the roof.* ÅSE *screams.*)

ÅSE.

Lift me down !

PEER.

Yes, if you'll listen——

ÅSE.

Rubbish !

PEER.

Dearest mother, pray——

ÅSE
(*throwing a sod of grass at him*).

Lift me down this moment, Peer !

PEER.

If I dared, be sure I would.

(*Coming nearer.*)

Now remember, sit quite still.
Do not sprawl and kick about ;
do not tug and tear the shingles,—
else 'twill be the worse for you ;
you might topple down.

ÅSE.

You beast !

PEER.

Do not kick !

ÅSE.

I'd have you blown,
like a changeling, into space !¹

PEER.

Mother, fie !

ÅSE.

Bah !

PEER.

Rather give your
blessing on my undertaking.
Will you?   Eh?

ÅSE.

I'll thrash you soundly,
hulking fellow though you be !

PEER.

Well, good-bye then, mother dear !
Patience; I'll be back ere long.

(*Is going, but turns, holds up his finger warningly,
and says:*)

Careful now, don't kick and sprawl !

(*Goes.*)

ÅSE.

Peer !—God help me, now he's off;
Reindeer-rider ! Liar ! Hei !
Will you listen !—No, he's striding
o'er the meadow——! (*Shrieks.*)   Help ! I'm dizzy !

(TWO OLD WOMEN, *with sacks on their backs, come
down the path to the mill.*)

¹ It is believed in some parts of Norway that "changelings" (elf-
children left in the stead of those taken away by the fairies) can, by
certain spells, be made to fly away up the chimney.

FIRST WOMAN.

Christ, who's screaming?

ÂSE.

It is I!

SECOND WOMAN.

Åse! Well, you *are* exalted!

ÂSE.

This won't be the end of it;—
soon, God help me, I'll be heaven-high!

FIRST WOMAN.

Bless your passing!

ÂSE.

Fetch a ladder;
I must be down! That devil Peer——

SECOND WOMAN.

Peer! Your son?

ÂSE.

Now you can say
you have seen how he behaves.

FIRST WOMAN.

We'll bear witness.

ÂSE.

Only help me;
straight to Hegstad I will hasten——

SECOND WOMAN.

Is he there?

FIRST WOMAN.

You'll be revenged, then;
Aslak Smith will be there too.

ÅSE
(*wringing her hands*).

Oh, God help me with my boy;
they will kill him ere they're done!

FIRST WOMAN.

Oh, that lot has oft been talked of;
comfort you : what must be must be!

SECOND WOMAN.

She is utterly demented.
                    (*Calls up the hill.*)
Eivind, Anders!   Hei!   Come here!

A MAN'S VOICE.

What's amiss?

SECOND WOMAN.

Peer Gynt has perched his
mother on the mill-house roof!

———————————

SCENE SECOND.

(*A hillock, covered with bushes and heather. The high-
road runs behind it ; a fence between.*)
(PEER GYNT *comes along a footpath, goes quickly up to the
fence, stops, and looks out over the stretch of country
below.*)

PEER.

There it lies, Hegstad.   Soon I'll have reached it.
(*Puts one leg over the fence ; then hesitates.*)
Wonder if Ingrid's alone in the house now ?
(*Shades his eyes with his hand, and looks out.*)
No; to the farm guests are swarming like gnats.—
Hm, to turn back now perhaps would be wisest.
(*Draws back his leg.*)
Still they must titter behind your back,
and whisper so that it burns right through you.
(*Moves a few steps away from the fence, and begins
absently plucking leaves.*)
Ah, if I'd only a good strong dram now.
Or if I could pass to and fro unseen.—
Or were I unknown.—Something proper and strong
were the best thing of all, for the laughter don't bite then.

(*Looks around suddenly as though afraid; then
hides among the bushes.   Some* WEDDING-[1]
GUESTS *pass by, going downwards towards the
farm.*)

[1] "Sendingsfolk," literally, "folks with presents."   When the Norwegian peasants are bidden to a wedding-feast, they bring with them
presents of eatables.

A MAN

(in conversation as they pass).

His father was drunken, his mother is weak.

A WOMAN.

Ay, then it's no wonder the lad's good for nought.

> (*They pass on. Presently* PEER GYNT *comes forward, his face flushed with shame. He peers after them.*)

PEER

(softly).

Was it me they were talking of?

> (*With a forced shrug.*)

　　　　　　　　　Oh, let them chatter!
After all, they can't sneer the life out of my body.

> (*Casts himself down upon the heathery slope; lies for some time flat on his back with his hands under his head, gazing up into the sky.*)

What a strange sort of cloud! It is just like a horse.
There's a man on it too—and saddle—and bridle.—
And after it comes an old crone on a broomstick.

> (*Laughs quietly to himself.*)

It is mother. She's scolding and screaming: You beast!
Hei you, Peer Gynt—— (*His eyes gradually close.*) Ay,
　　now she is frightened.—
Peer Gynt he rides first, and there follow him many.—
　　His steed it is gold-shod and crested with silver.
Himself he has gauntlets and sabre and scabbard.
　　His cloak it is long, and its lining is silken.
Full brave is the company riding behind him.
　　None of them, though, sits his charger so stoutly.

None of them glitters like him in the sunshine.—
   Down by the fence stand the people in clusters,
lifting their hats, and agape gazing upwards.
   Women are curtseying.   All the world knows him,
Kaiser Peer Gynt, and his thousands of henchmen.
   Sixpenny pieces and glittering shillings
over the roadway he scatters like pebbles.
   Rich as a lord grows each man in the parish.
High o'er the ocean Peer Gynt goes a-riding.
   Engelland's Prince on the seashore awaits him;
there too await him all Engelland's maidens.
   Engelland's nobles and Engelland's Kaiser,
see him come riding and rise from their banquet.
   Raising his crown, hear the Kaiser address him——

ASLAK THE SMITH
(*to some other young men, passing along the road*).

Just look at Peer Gynt there, the drunken swine——!

PEER
(*starting half up*).

What, Kaiser——!

THE SMITH
(*leaning against the fence and grinning*).

Up with you, Peer, my lad!

PEER.

What the devil?   The Smith!   What do you want here?

THE SMITH
(*to the others*).

He hasn't got over the Lundë-spree yet.

PEER

(*jumping up*).

You'd better be off!

THE SMITH.

I am going, yes.
But tell us, where have you dropped from, man?
You've been gone six weeks.　Were you troll-taken, eh?

PEER.

I have been doing strange deeds, Aslak Smith!

THE SMITH

(*winking to the others*).

Let us hear them, Peer!

PEER.

They are nought to you.

THE SMITH

(*after a pause*).

You're going to Hegstad?

PEER.

No.

THE SMITH.

Time was
they said that the girl there was fond of you.

PEER.

You grimy crow——!

THE SMITH

(*falling back a little*).

Keep your temper, Peer!

'Though Ingrid has jilted you, others are left ;—
think—son of Jon Gynt!   Come on to the feast ;
you'll find there both lambkins and widows well on——

PEER.

To hell——!

THE SMITH.

You will surely find one that will have you.—
Good evening!   I'll give your respects to the bride.—

(They go off, laughing and whispering.)

PEER

(looks after them a while, then makes a defiant
motion and turns half round).

For my part, may Ingrid of Hegstad go marry
whoever she pleases.   It's all one to me.

(Looks down at his clothes.)

My breeches are torn.   I am ragged and grim.—
If only I had something new to put on now.

(Stamps on the ground.)

If only I could, with a butcher-grip,
tear out the scorn from their very vitals !

(Looks round suddenly.)

What was that?   Who was it that tittered behind there?
Hm, I certainly thought——   No no, it was no one.—
I'll go home to mother.

(Begins to go upwards, but stops again and listens
towards Hegstad.)

They're playing a dance !

(Gazes and listens ; moves downwards step by step ;
his eyes glisten ; he rubs his hands down his
thighs.)

How the lasses do swarm!   Six or eight to a man!
Oh, galloping death,—I must join in the frolic!—
But how about mother, perched up on the mill-house———

> (*His eyes are drawn downwards again; he leaps
> and laughs.*)

Hei, how the Halling[1] flies over the green!
Ay, Guttorm, he *can* make his fiddle speak out!
It gurgles and booms like a foss[2] o'er a scaur.
And then all that glittering bevy of girls!—
Yes, galloping death, I must join in the frolic!

> (*Leaps over the fence and goes down the road.*)

SCENE THIRD.

(*The farm-place at Hegstad.   In the background, the
dwelling-house.*   A THRONG OF GUESTS.   *A lively
dance in progress on the green.*   THE FIDDLER *sits on
a table.*   THE MASTER COOK[3] *is standing in the doorway.*   COOKMAIDS *are going to and fro between the
different buildings.   Groups of* ELDERLY PEOPLE *sit
here and there, talking.*)

A WOMAN
(*joins a group that is seated on some logs of wood*)

The bride?   Oh yes, she is crying a bit;
but that, you know, isn't worth heeding.

THE MASTER-COOK
(*in another group*).

Now then, good folk, you must empty the barrel.

---

[1] A somewhat violent peasant dance.
[2] Foss (in the North of England "force")—a waterfall.
[3] A sort of master of ceremonies.

A MAN.

Thanks to you, friend; but you fill up too quick.

A LAD
(*to the* FIDDLER, *as he flies past, holding* A GIRL *by the hand*).

To it now, Guttorm, and don't spare the fiddlestrings!

THE GIRL.

Scrape till it echoes out over the meadows!

OTHER GIRLS
(*standing in a ring round a lad who is dancing*).

That's a rare fling!

A GIRL.

He has legs that can lift him!

THE LAD
(*dancing*).

The roof here is high,[1] and the walls wide asunder!

THE BRIDEGROOM
(*comes whimpering up to his* FATHER, *who is standing talking with some other men, and twitches his jacket*).

Father, she will not; she is so proud!

HIS FATHER.

What won't she do?

THE BRIDEGROOM.

She has locked herself in.

[1] To kick the rafters is considered a great feat in the Halling-dance. The boy means that, in the open air, his leaps are not limited even by the rafters.

HIS FATHER.

Well, you must manage to find the key.

THE BRIDEGROOM.

I don't know how.

HIS FATHER.

You're a nincompoop!

(*Turns away to the others.   The* BRIDEGROOM
drifts across the yard.)

A LAD
(*comes from behind the house*).

Wait a bit, girls!   Things 'll soon be lively!
Here comes Peer Gynt.

THE SMITH
(*who has just come up*).

Who invited him?

THE MASTER-COOK.

No one.

(*Goes towards the house.*)

THE SMITH
(*to the girls*).

If he should speak to you, never take notice!

A GIRL
(*to the others*).

No, we'll pretend that we don't even see him.

PEER GYNT
(*comes in heated and full of animation, stops right
in front of the group, and claps his hands*).

Which is the liveliest girl of the lot of you?

A GIRL
(*as he approaches her*).

I am not.

ANOTHER
(*similarly*).

I am not.

A THIRD.

No; nor I either.

PEER
(*to a fourth*).

You come along, then, for want of a better.

THE GIRL.

Haven't got time.

PEER
(*to a fifth*).

Well then, you!

THE GIRL
(*going*).

I'm for home.

PEER.

To-night? are you utterly out of your senses?[1]

---

[1] A marriage party among the peasants will often last several days.

THE SMITH
(*after a moment, in a low voice*).

See, Peer, she's taken a greybeard for partner.

PEER
(*turns sharply to an elderly man*).

Where are the unbespoke girls?

THE MAN.

Find them out.
(*Goes away from him.*)

(PEER GYNT *has suddenly become subdued. He
glances shyly and furtively at the group. All
look at him, but no one speaks. He approaches
other groups. Wherever he goes there is silence;
when he moves away they look after him and
smile.*)

PEER
(*to himself*).

Mocking looks; needle-keen whispers[1] and smiles.
They grate like a sawblade under the file!

(*He slinks along close to the fence.* SOLVEIG, *leading
little* HELGA *by the hand, comes into the yard,
along with her* PARENTS.)

A MAN
(*to another, close to* PEER GYNT).

Look, here are the new folk.

THE OTHER.

The ones from the west?

---

[1] Literally, "thoughts."

THE FIRST MAN.

Ay, the people from Hedal.

THE OTHER.

Ah yes, so they are.

PEER
(*places himself in the path of the new-comers, points
to* SOLVEIG, *and asks the* FATHER :)

May I dance with your daughter?

THE FATHER
(*quietly*).

You may so; but first
we must go to the farm-house and greet the good people.

(*They go in.*)

THE MASTER-COOK
(*to* PEER GYNT, *offering him drink*).

Since you *are* here, you'd best take a pull at the liquor.

PEER
(*looking fixedly after the new-comers*).

Thanks; I'm for dancing; I am not athirst.

(*The* MASTER-COOK *goes away from him.* PEER
GYNT *gazes towards the house and laughs.*)

How fair!   Did ever you see the like?
Looked down at her shoes and her snow-white apron—!
And then she held on to her mother's skirt-folds,
and carried a psalm-book wrapped up in a kerchief—!
I must look at that girl.

(*Going into the house.*)

A LAD

(coming out of the house, with several others).

Are you off so soon, Peer,
from the dance?

PEER.

No, no.

THE LAD.

Then you're heading amiss!

(Takes hold of his shoulder to turn him round.)

PEER.

Let me pass!

THE LAD.

I believe you're afraid of the Smith.

PEER.

I afraid!

THE LAD.

You remember what happened at Lundë?

(They go off, laughing, to the dancing-green.)

SOLVEIG

(in the doorway of the house).

Are you not the lad that was wanting to dance?

PEER.

Of course it was me; don't you know me again?
(Takes her hand.)
Come, then!

SOLVEIG.

We mustn't go far, mother said.

PEER.

Mother said!   Mother said!   Were you born yesterday?[1]

SOLVEIG.

Now you're laughing——!

PEER.

              Why sure, you are almost a child.
Are you grown up?

SOLVEIG.

              I read with the pastor last spring.[2]

PEER.

Tell me your name, lass, and then we'll talk easier.

SOLVEIG.

My name is Solveig.   And what are you called?

PEER.

Peer Gynt.

SOLVEIG
(*withdrawing her hand*).

Oh heaven!

PEER.

              Why, what is it now?

---

[1] Literally, "last year."

[2] "To read with the pastor," the preliminary to confirmation, is currently used as synonymous with "to be confirmed."

SOLVEIG.

My garter is loose; I must tie it up tighter.

(*Goes away from him.*)

THE BRIDEGROOM
(*pulling at his* MOTHER'S *gown*).

Mother, she will not——!

HIS MOTHER.

She will not?   What?

THE BRIDEGROOM.

She won't, mother——

HIS MOTHER.

What?

THE BRIDEGROOM.

Unlock the door.

HIS FATHER
(*angrily, below his breath*).

Oh, you're only fit to be tied in a stall!

HIS MOTHER.

Don't scold him.   Poor dear, he'll be all right yet.

(*They move away.*)

A LAD
(*coming with a whole crowd of others from the
dancing-green*).

Peer, have some brandy?

PEER.

No.

THE LAD.

Only a drain?

PEER
(*looking darkly at him*).

Got any?

THE LAD.

Well, I won't say but I have.
(*Pulls out a pocket-flask and drinks.*)
Ah! How it stings your throat!—Well?

PEER.

Let me try it.

(*Drinks.*)

ANOTHER LAD.

Now you must try mine as well, you know.

PEER.

No!

THE LAD.

Oh, nonsense; now don't be a fool.
Take a pull, Peer!

PEER.

Well then, give me a drop.
(*Drinks again.*)

A GIRL.
(half aloud).

Come, let's be going.

· PEER.

Afraid of me, wench?

A THIRD LAD.

Who isn't afraid of *you?*

A FOURTH.

At Lundë
you showed us clearly what tricks you could play.

PEER.

I can do more than that, when once I get started!

THE FIRST LAD
(whispering).

Now he's getting into swing!

SEVERAL OTHERS
(forming a circle around him).

Tell away! Tell away!
What can you——?

PEER.

To-morrow——!

OTHERS.

No now, to-night!

A GIRL.

Can you conjure, Peer?

PEER.

I can call up the devil!

A MAN.

My grandam could do that before I was born!

PEER.

Liar! What *I* can do, that no one else can.
I one day conjured him into a nut.
It was worm-bored, you see!

SEVERAL
(*laughing*).

Ay, that's easily guessed!

PEER.

He cursed, and he wept, and he wanted to bribe me
with all sorts of things——

ONE OF THE CROWD.

But he had to go in?

PEER.

Of course. I stopped up the hole with a peg.
Hei! If you'd heard him rumbling and grumbling!

A GIRL.

Only think!

PEER.

It was just like a humble-bee buzzing.

THE GIRL.

Have you got him still in the nut?

PEER.

Why, no ;
by this time that devil has flown on his way.
The grudge the Smith bears me is all *his* doing.

A LAD.

Indeed ?

PEER.

I went to the smithy, and begged
that he would crack that same nutshell for me.
He promised he would !—laid it down on his anvil ;
but Aslak, you know, is so heavy of hand ;—
for ever swinging that great sledge-hammer——

A VOICE FROM THE CROWD.

Did he kill the foul fiend ?

PEER.

He laid on like a man.
But the devil showed fight, and tore off in a flame
through the roof, and shattered the wall asunder.

SEVERAL VOICES.

And the Smith——?

PEER.

Stood there with his hands all scorched.
And from that day onwards, we've never been friends.

(*General laughter.*)

SOME OF THE CROWD.

That yarn is a good one.

OTHERS.

About his best.

PEER.

Do you think I am making it up?

A MAN.

Oh no,
that you're certainly not; for I've heard the most on't
from my grandfather[1]——

PEER.

Liar!   It happened to me!

THE MAN.

Yes, like everything else.

PEER
(*with a fling*).

I can ride, I can,
clean through the air, on the bravest of steeds!
Oh, many's the thing I can do, I tell you!
(*Another roar of laughter.*)

ONE OF THE GROUP.

Peer, ride through the air a bit!

MANY.

Do, dear Peer Gynt——!

PEER.

You may spare you the trouble of begging so hard.
I will ride like a hurricane over you all!
Every man in the parish shall fall at my feet!

[1] See Introduction, p. vi.

AN ELDERLY MAN.

Now he is clean off his head.

ANOTHER.

The dolt!

A THIRD.

Braggart!

A FOURTH.

Liar!

PEER
(*threatening them*).

Ay, wait till you see!

A MAN
(*half drunk*).

Ay, wait; you'll soon get your jacket dusted!

OTHERS.

Your back beaten tender!   Your eyes painted blue!

(*The crowd disperses, the elder men angry, the younger laughing and jeering.*)

THE BRIDEGROOM
(*close to* PEER GYNT).

Peer, is it true you can ride through the air?

PEER
(*shortly*).

It's all true, Mads!   You must know I'm a rare one!

THE BRIDEGROOM.

Then have you got the Invisible Cloak too?

PEER.

The Invisible Hat, do you mean? Yes, I have.

(Turns away from him. SOLVEIG *crosses the yard, leading little* HELGA.)

PEER
(goes towards them; his face lights up).

Solveig! Oh, it is well you have come!
(Takes hold of her wrist.)
Now will I swing you round fast and fine!

SOLVEIG.

Loose me!

PEER.

Wherefore?

SOLVEIG.

You are so wild.

PEER.

The reindeer is wild, too, when summer is dawning.
Come then, lass; do not be wayward now!

SOLVEIG
(withdrawing her arm).

Dare not.

PEER.

Wherefore?

SOLVEIG.

No, you've been drinking.
(Moves off with HELGA.)

PEER.

Oh, if I had but my knife-blade driven
clean through the heart of them,—one and all!

THE BRIDEGROOM
(*nudging him with his elbow*).

Peer, can't you help me to get at the bride?

PEER
(*absently*).

The bride? Where is *she?*

THE BRIDEGROOM.

In the store-house.

PEER.

Ah.

THE BRIDEGROOM.

Oh, dear Peer Gynt, you must try at least!

PEER.

No, you must get on without my help.
(*A thought strikes him; he says softly but sharply:*)
Ingrid! The store-house!
(*Goes up to* SOLVEIG.)
Have you thought better on't?
(SOLVEIG *tries to go; he blocks her path.*)
You're ashamed to, because I've the look of a tramp.

SOLVEIG
(*hastily*).

No, that you haven't; that's not true at all!

PEER.

Yes! And I've taken a drop as well;
but that was to spite you, because you had hurt me.
Come then!

SOLVEIG.

Even if I would now, I daren't.

PEER.

Who are you frightened of?

SOLVEIG.

Father, most.

PEER.

Father? Ay, ay; he is one of the quiet ones!
One of the godly, eh?—Answer, come!

SOLVEIG.

What shall I say?

PEER.

Is your father a psalm-singer? [1]
And you and your mother as well, no doubt?
Come, will you speak?

SOLVEIG.

Let me go in peace.

PEER.

No!
(In a low but sharp and threatening tone.)
I can turn myself into a troll!
I'll come to your bedside at midnight to-night.

[1] Literally, "A reader."

If you should hear some one hissing and spitting,
you mustn't imagine it's only the cat.
It's me, lass! I'll drain out your blood in a cup,
and your little sister, I'll eat her up;
ay, you must know I'm a were-wolf at night;—
I'll bite you all over the loins and the back——

> (*Suddenly changes his tone, and entreats, as if in dread:*)

Dance with me, Solveig!

SOLVEIG

(*looking darkly at him*).

Then you were grim.[1]

(*Goes into the house.*)

THE BRIDEGROOM

(*comes sidling up again*).

I'll give you an ox if you'll help me!

PEER.

Then come!

> (*They go out behind the house. At the same moment a crowd of men come up from the dancing green; most of them are drunk. Noise and hubbub.* SOLVEIG, HELGA, *and their* PARENTS *appear among a number of elderly people in the doorway.*)

THE MASTER-COOK

(*to the* SMITH, *who is the foremost of the crowd*).

Keep peace now!

---

[1] In the original "Nu var du styg," literally "Now you were ugly."

THE SMITH
(*pulling off his jacket*).

No, we must fight it out here.[1]
Peer Gynt or I must be taught a lesson.[2]

SOME VOICES.

Ay, let them fight for it !

OTHERS.

No, only wrangle !

THE SMITH.

Fists must decide ; for the case is past words.

SOLVEIG'S FATHER.

Control yourself, man !

HELGA.

Will they beat him, mother ?

A LAD.

Let us rather tease him with all his lies !

ANOTHER.

Kick him out of the company !

A THIRD.

Spit in his eyes !

A FOURTH
(*to the* SMITH).

You're not backing out, Smith ?

---

[1] Literally, "Here shall judgment be called for."
[2] Literally, " Must be bent to the hillside," made to bite the dust —
but not in the sense of being killed.

THE SMITH
(*flinging away his jacket*).

The jade shall be slaughtered!

SOLVEIG'S MOTHER
(*to* SOLVEIG).

There, you can see how that windbag is thought of.

ÅSE
(*coming up with a stick in her hand*).

Is that son of mine here? Now he's in for a drubbing!
Oh! how heartily I will dang him!

THE SMITH
(*rolling up his shirt-sleeves*).

That switch is too light for a carcass like his.

SOME OF THE CROWD.

The Smith will dang him!

OTHERS.

Bang him!

THE SMITH
(*spits on his hands and nods to* ÅSE).

Hang him!

ÅSE.

What? Hang my Peer? Ay, just try if you dare;—
Åse and I,[1] we have teeth and claws!—
Where is he? (*Calls across the yard:*) Peer!

[1] A peasant idiom.

THE BRIDEGROOM
(*comes running up*).

   Oh, God's death on the cross!
Come father, come mother, and——!

HIS FATHER.

     What is the matter?

THE BRIDEGROOM.

Just fancy, Peer Gynt——!

    ÅSE
   (*screams*).

    Have they taken his life?

THE BRIDEGROOM.

No, but Peer Gynt——! Look, there on the hillside——!

   THE CROWD.

With the bride!

    ÅSE
  (*lets her stick sink*).

Oh, the beast!

   THE SMITH
  (*as if thunderstruck*).

    Where the slope rises sheerest
he's clambering upwards, by God, like a goat!

   THE BRIDEGROOM
   (*crying*).

He's shouldered her, mother, as I might a pig!

ÅSE

(shaking her fist up at him).

Would God you might fall, and——!

(Screams out in terror.)

Take care of your footing!

THE HEGSTAD FARMER

(comes in, bare-headed and white with rage).

I'll have his life for this bride-rape yet!

ÅSE.

Oh no, God punish me if I let you!

ACT SECOND.

SCENE FIRST.

(*A narrow path, high up in the mountains. Early morning.*)
(PEER GYNT *comes hastily and sullenly along the path.* INGRID, *still wearing some of her bridal ornaments, is trying to hold him back.*)

PEER.

Get you from me!

INGRID
(*weeping*).

After this, Peer?
Whither?

PEER.

Where you will for me.

INGRID
(*wringing her hands*).

Oh, what falsehood!

PEER.

Useless railing.
Each alone must go his way.

INGRID.

Sin—and sin again unites us!

PEER.

Devil take all recollections!
Devil take the tribe of women—
all but *one*—— !

INGRID.

Who is that one, pray?

PEER.

'Tis not you.

INGRID.

Who is it then?

PEER.

Go!　Go thither whence you came!
Off!　To your father!

INGRID.

Dearest, sweetest——

PEER.

Peace!

INGRID.

You cannot mean it, surely,
what you're saying?

PEER.

Can and do.

INGRID.

First to lure—and then forsake me!

PEER.

And what terms have you to offer?

INGRID.

Hegstad Farm, and more besides.

PEER.

Is your psalm-book in your kerchief?
Where's the gold-mane on your shoulders?
Do you glance adown your apron?
Do you hold your mother's skirt-fold?
Speak!

INGRID.

No, but——

PEER.

Went you to the Pastor[1]
this last spring-tide?

INGRID.

No, but Peer——

PEER.

Is there shyness in your glances?
When I beg, can you deny?

INGRID.

Heaven! I think his wits are going!

PEER.

Does your presence sanctify?[2]
Speak!

[1] See note on page 36.
[2] "Blir der Helg når en dig ser?" literally, "Does it become a holy-day (or holy-tide) when one sees you?"

INGRID.

No, but——

PEER.

What's all the rest then?
(*Going.*)

INGRID
(*blocking his way*).

Know you it will cost your neck
should you fail me?

PEER.

What do I care?

INGRID.

You may win both wealth and honour
if you take me——

PEER.

Can't afford.

INGRID
(*bursting into tears*).

Oh, you lured me——!

PEER.

You were willing.

INGRID.

I was desperate!

PEER.

Frantic I.

INGRID
(*threatening*).

Dearly shall you pay for this!

PEER.

Dearest payment cheap I'll reckon.

INGRID.

Is your purpose set?

PEER.

Like flint.

INGRID.

Good! we'll see, then, who's the winner!
(*Goes downwards.*)

PEER
(*stands silent a moment, then cries:*)

Devil take all recollections!
Devil take the tribe of women!

INGRID
(*turning her head, and calling mockingly upwards:*)

All but *one!*

PEER.

Yes, all but *one.*

(*They go their several ways.*)

——————

SCENE SECOND.

(Near a mountain tarn; the ground is soft and marshy round about. A storm is gathering.)

(ÅSE enters, calling and gazing around her despairingly, in every direction. SOLVEIG has difficulty in keeping up with her. SOLVEIG'S FATHER and MOTHER, with HELGA, are some way behind.)

ÅSE

(tossing about her arms, and tearing her hair).

All things are against me with wrathful might!
Heaven, and the waters, and the grisly mountains!
Fog-scuds from heaven roll down to bewilder him!
The treacherous waters are lurking to murder him!
The mountains would crush him with landslip and rift!—
And the people too! They're out after his life!
God knows they shan't have it! I can't bear to lose him!
Oh, the oaf! to think that the fiend should tempt him!

(Turning to SOLVEIG.)

Now isn't it clean unbelievable this?
He, that did nought but romance and tell lies;—
he, whose sole strength was the strength of his jaw;
he, that did never a stroke of true work;—
he——! Oh, a body could both cry and laugh!—
Oh, we clung closely in sorrow and need.
Ay, you must know that my husband, he drank,
loafed round the parish to roister and prate,
wasted and trampled our gear under foot.
And meanwhile at home there sat Peerkin and I—
the best we could do was to try to forget;
for ever I've found it so hard to bear up.

It's a terrible thing to look fate in the eyes;
and of course one is glad to be quit of one's cares,
and try all one can to keep thought far away.
Some take to brandy, and others to lies;
and we—why we took to fairy-tales
of princes and trolls and of all sorts of beasts;
and of bride-rapes as well. Ah, but who could have dreamt
that those devil's yarns would have stuck in his head?

(In a fresh access of terror.)

Hu! What a scream! It's the nixie or droug![1]
Peer! Peer!—Up there on that hillock——!

*(She runs to the top of a little rise, and looks out
      over the tarn. SOLVEIG'S FATHER and MOTHER
      come up.)*

ÅSE.

Not a sign to be seen!

THE FATHER
(quietly).

It is worst for him!

ÅSE
(weeping).

Oh, my Peer! Oh, my own lost lamb!

THE FATHER
(nods mildly).

You may well say lost.

ÅSE.

Oh no, don't talk like that!
He is so clever. There's no one like him.

---

[1] A malevolent water-monster.

THE FATHER.

You foolish woman !

ÅSE.

Oh ay; oh ay;
foolish I am, but the boy's all right!

THE FATHER
(*still softly and with mild eyes*).

His heart is hardened, his soul is lost.

ÅSE
(*in terror*).

No, no, he can't be so hard, our Lord!

THE FATHER.

Do you think he can sigh for his debt of sin ?

ÅSE
(*eagerly*).

No, but he can ride through the air on a buck, though!

THE MOTHER.

Christ, are you mad ?

THE FATHER.

Why, what do you mean ?

ÅSE.

Never a deed is too great for him.
You shall see, if only he lives so long——

THE FATHER.

Best if you saw him on the gallows hanging.

ÂSE
(*shrieks*).

Oh, cross of Christ!

THE FATHER.

In the hangman's hands,
it may be his heart would be turned to repentance.

ÂSE
(*bewildered*).

Oh, you'll soon talk me out of my senses!
We must find him!

THE FATHER.

To rescue his soul.

ÂSE.

And his body!
If he's stuck in the swamp, we must drag him out;
if he's taken by trolls, we must ring the bells for him.

THE FATHER.

Hm!—Here's a sheep-path——

ÂSE.

The Lord will repay you
your guidance and help!

THE FATHER.

It's a Christian's duty.

ÂSE.

Then the others, fie! they are heathens all;
there wasn't one that would go with us——

THE FATHER.

They knew him too well.

ÅSE.

He was too good for them!
(*Wrings her hands.*)
And to think—and to think that his life is at stake!

THE FATHER.

Here are tracks of a man.

ÅSE.

Then it's here we must search!

THE FATHER.

We'll scatter around on this side of our sæter.[1]

(*He and his wife go on ahead.*)

SOLVEIG
(*to* ÅSE).

Say on; tell me more.

ÅSE
(*drying her eyes*).

Of my son, you mean?

SOLVEIG.

Yes;—

Tell everything!

ÅSE
(*smiles and tosses her head*).

Everything?—Soon you'd be tired!

SOLVEIG.

Sooner by far will you tire of the telling
than I of the hearing.

---

[1] *Sæter*—a châlet, or small mountain farm, where the cattle are sent
to pasture in the summer months.

SCENE THIRD.

(Low, treeless heights, close under the mountain moorlands ;
peaks in the distance.   The shadows are long ; it is
late in the day.)
(PEER GYNT comes running at full speed, and stops short
on the hillside.)

PEER.

The parish is all at my heels in a pack !
Every man of them armed or with gun or with club.
Foremost I hear the old Hegstad-churl howling.—
Now it's noised far and wide that Peer Gynt is abroad!
It is different, this, from a bout with a smith !
This is life !   Every limb grows as strong as a bear's.
          (Strikes out with his arms and leaps in the air.)
To crush, overturn, stem the rush of the foss !¹
To strike !   Wrench the fir-tree right up by the root !
This is life !   This both hardens and lifts one high !
To hell then with all of the savourless lies !

THREE SÆTER GIRLS²
(rush across the hillside, screaming and singing).

Trond of the Valfjeld !³   Bård and Kårë !
Troll-pack !   To-night would you sleep in our arms ?

PEER.

To whom are you calling ?

¹ See note, p. 29.
² See Introduction, p. vi., and Appendix.
³ Pronounce *Vaal-fyeld.*

THE GIRLS.

To the trolls! to the trolls!

FIRST GIRL.

Trond, come with kindness!

SECOND GIRL.

Bård, come with force!

THIRD GIRL.

The cots in the sæter are all standing empty!

FIRST GIRL.

Force is kindness!

SECOND GIRL.

And kindness is force!

THIRD GIRL.

If lads are awanting, one plays with the trolls!

PEER.

Why, where are the lads, then?

ALL THREE
(*with a horse-laugh*).

They cannot come hither!

FIRST GIRL.

Mine called me his sweetheart and called me his darling.
Now he has married a grey-headed widow.

SECOND GIRL.

Mine met a gipsy-wench north on the upland.
Now they are tramping the country together.

THIRD GIRL.

Mine put an end to our bastard brat.
Now his head's grinning aloft on a stake.

ALL THREE.

Trond of the Valfjeld!   Bård and Kårë!
Troll-pack!   To-night would you sleep in our arms?

PEER
(*stands, with a sudden leap, in the midst of them*).

I'm a three-headed troll, and the boy for three girls!

THE GIRLS.

Are you *such* a lad, eh?

PEER.

You shall judge for yourselves!

FIRST GIRL.

To the hut!   To the hut!

SECOND GIRL.

We have mead!

PEER.

Let it flow!

THIRD GIRL.

No cot shall stand empty this Saturday night!

SECOND GIRL
(*kissing him*).

He sparkles and glisters like white-heated iron.

THIRD GIRL
(*doing likewise*).

Like a baby's eyes from the blackest tarn.

PEER

(dancing in the midst of them).

Heavy of heart and wanton of mind.
The eyes full of laughter, the throat of tears!

THE GIRLS

(making mocking gestures towards the mountain-tops,
screaming and singing).

Trond of the Valfjeld! Bård and Kårë!
Troll-pack!—To-night will you sleep in our arms?

　　　　(They dance away over the heights, with PEER GYNT
　　　　in their midst.)

SCENE FOURTH.

(Among the Rondë mountains. Sunset. Shining snow-
peaks all around.)
*(*PEER GYNT *enters, dizzy and bewildered.)*

PEER.

Tower over tower arises!
Hei, what a glittering gate!
Stand! Will you stand! It's drifting
further and further away!
High on the vane the cock stands
lifting his wings for flight;—
blue spread the rifts and bluer,
locked is the fell and barred.—
　　　What are those trunks and tree-roots,
that grow from the ridge's clefts?
They are warriors heron-footed!
Now they, too, are fading away.

5

A shimmering like rainbow-streamers
goes shooting through eyes and brain.
What is it, that far-off chiming?
What's weighing my eyebrows down?
Hu, how my forehead's throbbing—
a tightening red-hot ring——!
I cannot think who the devil
has bound it around my head!

(Sinks down.)

Flight o'er the Edge of Gendin—
stuff and accursed lies!
Up o'er the steepest hill-wall
with the bride,—and a whole day drunk;
hunted by hawks and falcons,
threatened by trolls and such,
sporting with crazy wenches :—
lies and accursed stuff!

(Gazes long upwards.)

Yonder sail two brown eagles.
Southward the wild geese fly.
And here I must splash and stumble
in quagmire and filth knee-deep!

(Springs up.)

I'll fly too! I will wash myself clean in
the bath of the keenest winds!
I'll fly high! I will plunge myself fair in
the glorious christening-font!
I will soar far over the sæter;
I will ride myself pure of soul;
I will forth o'er the salt sea waters,
and high over Engelland's prince!
Ay, gaze as ye may, young maidens;

my ride is for none of you ;
you're wasting your time in waiting—!
Yet maybe I'll swoop down, too.—
    What has come of the two brown eagles—?
They've vanished, the devil knows where!—
    There's the peak of a gable rising ;
it's soaring on every hand ;
it's growing from out the ruins ;—
see, the gateway is standing wide!
Ha-ha, yonder house, I know it ;
it's grandfather's new-built farm!
Gone are the clouts from the windows ;
the crazy old fence is gone.
The lights gleam from every casement ;
there's a feast in the hall to-night.
    There, that was the provost clinking
the back of his knife on his glass ;—
there's the captain flinging his bottle,
and shivering the mirror to bits.—
Let them waste ; let it all be squandered!
Peace, mother ; what need we care!
'Tis the rich Jon Gynt gives the banquet ;
hurrah for the race of Gynt!
What's all this bustle and hubbub?
Why do they shout and bawl?
The captain is calling the son in ;—
oh, the provost would drink my health.
In then, Peer Gynt, to the judgment ;
it rings forth in song and shout :
Peer Gynt, thou art come of great things,
and great things shall come of thee!

    (*Leaps forward, but runs his head against a rock ;
      falls, and remains stretched on the ground.*)

SCENE FIFTH.

(*A hillside, wooded with great soughing trees. Stars are gleaming through the leaves; birds are singing in the tree-tops.*)

(*A* GREEN-CLAD WOMAN *is crossing the hillside;* PEER GYNT *follows her, with all sorts of lover-like antics.*)

THE GREEN-CLAD ONE
(*stops and turns round*).

Is it true?

PEER
(*drawing his finger across his throat*).

As true as my name is Peer;—
as true as that you are a lovely woman!
Will you have me? You'll see what a fine man I'll be;
you shall neither tread the loom nor turn the spindle.
You shall eat all you want, till you're ready to burst.
I never will drag you about by the hair——

THE GREEN-CLAD ONE.

Nor beat me?

PEER.

No, can you think I would?
We kings' sons never beat women and such.

THE GREEN-CLAD ONE.

You're a king's son?

PEER.

Yes.

THE GREEN-CLAD ONE.

I'm the Dovrë-King's daughter.

PEER.

Are you?   See there, now, how well that fits in!

THE GREEN-CLAD ONE.

Deep in the Rondë has father his palace.

PEER.

My mother's is bigger, or much I'm mistaken.

THE GREEN-CLAD ONE.

Do you know my father?   His name is King Brosë.[1]

PEER.

Do you know my mother?   Her name is Queen Åsë.

THE GREEN-CLAD ONE.

When my father is angry the mountains are riven.

PEER.

They reel when my mother by chance falls a-scolding.

THE GREEN-CLAD ONE.

My father can kick e'en the loftiest roof-tree.[2]

PEER.

My mother can ride through the rapidest river.

---

[1] Pronounce Broasë.
[2] Kicking the rafters is a much-admired exploit in peasant dancing.
See note, page 30.

THE GREEN-CLAD ONE.

Have you other garments besides those rags?

PEER.

Ho, you should just see my Sunday clothes!

THE GREEN-CLAD ONE.

My week-day gown is *of* gold and silk.

PEER.

It looks to me liker tow and straws.

THE GREEN-CLAD ONE.

Ay, there is *one* thing you must remember :—
this is the Rondë-folk's use and wont :
all our possessions have twofold form.
When you shall come to my father's hall,
it well may chance that you're on the point
of thinking you stand in a dismal moraine.

PEER.

Well now, with us it's precisely the same.
Our gold will seem to you litter and trash!
And you'll think, mayhap, every glittering pane
is nought but a bunch of old stockings and clouts.

THE GREEN-CLAD ONE.

Black it seems white, and ugly seems fair.

PEER.

Big it seems little, and dirty seems clean.

THE GREEN-CLAD ONE
(*falling on his neck*).

Ay, Peer, now I see that we fit, you and I!

PEER.

Like the leg and the trouser, the hair and the comb.

THE GREEN-CLAD ONE
(*calls away over the hillside*).

Bridal-steed! Bridal-steed! Come, bridal-steed mine!

(*A gigantic pig comes running in with a rope's end
for a bridle and an old sack for a saddle.
PEER GYNT vaults on its back, and seats the
GREEN-CLAD ONE in front of him.*)

PEER.

Hark-away! Through the Rondë-gate gallop we in!
Gee-up, gee-up, my courser fine!

THE GREEN-CLAD ONE
(*tenderly*).

Ah, but lately I wandered and moped and pined—.
One never can tell what may happen to one!

PEER
(*thrashing the pig and trotting off*).

You may know the great by their riding-gear!

SCENE SIXTH.

*(The Royal Hall of the King of the Dovrë-Trolls. A
great assembly of* TROLL-COURTIERS, GNOMES, *and*
BROWNIES. THE OLD MAN OF THE DOVRË *sits on
the throne, crowned, and with his sceptre in his hand.
His* CHILDREN *and* NEAREST RELATIONS *are ranged
on both sides.* PEER GYNT *stands before him.
Violent commotion in the hall.)*

THE TROLL-COURTIERS.

Slay him ! a Christian-man's son has deluded
the Dovrë-King's loveliest maid !

A TROLL-IMP.

May I hack him on the fingers ?

ANOTHER.

May I tug him by the hair ?

A TROLL-MAIDEN.

Hu, hei, let me bite him in the haunches !

A TROLL-WITCH
(with a ladle).

Shall he be boiled into broth and bree ?

ANOTHER TROLL-WITCH
(with a chopper).

Shall he roast on a spit or be browned in a stewpan ?

THE OLD MAN OF THE DOVRË.

Ice to your blood, friends !
(*Beckons his counsellors nearer around him.*)
                    Don't let us talk big.
We've been drifting astern in these latter years;
we can't tell what's going to stand or to fall,
and there's no sense in turning recruits away.
Besides the lad's body has scarce a blemish,
and he's strongly-built too, if I see aright.
It's true, he has only a single head;
but my daughter, too, has no more than one.
Three-headed trolls are going clean out of fashion;
one hardly sees even a two-header now,
and even those heads are but so-so ones.
                    (*To* PEER GYNT.)
It's my daughter, then, you demand of me?

PEER.

Your daughter and the realm to her dowry, yes.

THE OLD MAN.

You shall have the half while I'm still alive,
and the other half when I come to die.

PEER.

I'm content with that.

THE OLD MAN.

                    Ay, but stop, my lad ;—
you also have some undertakings to give.
If you break even one, the whole pact's at an end,
and you'll never get away from here living.
First of all you must swear that you'll never give heed
to aught that lies outside the Rondë-hills' bounds;
day you must shun, and deeds, and each sunlit spot.

PEER.

Only call me king, and that's easy to keep.

THE OLD MAN.

And next—now for putting your wits to the test.

(*Draws himself up in his seat.*)

THE OLDEST TROLL-COURTIER
(*to* PEER GYNT).

Let us see if you have a wisdom-tooth
that can crack the Dovrë-King's riddle-nut!

THE OLD MAN.

What difference is there 'twixt trolls and men?

PEER.

No difference at all, as it seems to me.
Big trolls would roast you and small trolls would claw you;—
with us it were likewise, if only they dared.

THE OLD MAN.

True enough; in that and in more we're alike.
Yet morning is morning, and even is even,
and there *is* a difference all the same.—
Now let me tell you wherein it lies:
Out yonder, under the shining vault,
among men the saying goes: "Man, be thyself!"
At home here with us, 'mid the tribe of the trolls,
the saying goes: "Troll, to thyself be—enough!"

THE TROLL-COURTIER
(*to* PEER GYNT).

Can you fathom the depth?

PEER.

It strikes me as misty.

THE OLD MAN.

My son, that " Enough," that most potent and sundering
word, must be graven upon your escutcheon.

PEER

(*scratching his head*).

Well, but——

THE OLD MAN.

It *must*, if you here would be master!

PEER.

Oh well, let it pass; after all, it's no worse——

THE OLD MAN.

And next you must learn to appreciate
our homely, everyday way of life.
　　(*He beckons; two* TROLLS *with pigs'-heads, white night-
　　caps, and so forth, bring in food and drink.*)
The cow gives cakes and the bullock mead;
ask not if its taste be sour or sweet;
the main matter is, and you mustn't forget it,
it's all of it home-brewed.[1]

PEER

(*pushing the things away from him*).

The devil fly off with your home-brewed drinks!
I'll never get used to the ways of this land.

---

[1] See Introduction, p. xii.

THE OLD MAN.

The bowl's given in, and it's fashioned of gold.
Whoso owns the gold bowl, him my daughter holds dear.

PEER
(*pondering*).

It is written : Thou shalt bridle the natural man ;—
and I daresay the drink may in time seem less sour.
So be it!
(*Complies.*)

THE OLD MAN.

Ay, that was sagaciously said.
You spit?

PEER.

One must trust to the force of habit.

THE OLD MAN.

And next you must throw off your Christian-man's garb ;
for this you must know to our Dovrë's renown :
here all things are mountain-made, nought's from the dale,
except the silk bow at the end of your tail.

PEER
(*indignant*).

I haven't a tail !

THE OLD MAN.

Then of course you must get one.
See my Sunday-tail, Chamberlain, fastened to him.

PEER.

I'll be hanged if you do !   Would you make me a fool?

THE OLD MAN.

None comes courting my child with no tail at his rear.

PEER.

Make a beast of a man !

THE OLD MAN.

                    Nay, my son, you mistake ;
I make you a mannerly wooer, no more.
A bright orange bow we'll allow you to wear,
and that passes here for the highest of honours.

PEER
(*reflectively*).

It's true, as the saying goes : Man's but a mote.
And it's wisest to follow the fashion a bit.
Tie away !

THE OLD MAN.

        You're a tractable fellow, I see.

THE COURTIER.

Just try with what grace you can waggle and whisk it !

PEER
(*peevishly*).

Ha, would you force me to go still further ?
Do you ask me to give up my Christian faith ?

THE OLD MAN.

No, that you are welcome to keep in peace.
Doctrine goes free ; upon that there's no duty ;
it's the outward cut one must tell a troll by.
If we're only at one in our manners and dress,
you may hold as your faith what to us is a horror.

PEER.

Why, in spite of your many conditions, you are
a more reasonable chap than one might have expected.

THE OLD MAN.

We troll-folk, my son, are less black than we're painted ;[1]
that's another distinction between you and us.—
But the serious part of the meeting is over ;
now let us gladden our ears and our eyes.
Music-maid, forth !   Set the Dovrë-harp sounding !
Dancing-maid, forth !   Tread the Dovrë-hall's floor !
(Music and a dance.)

THE COURTIER.

How like you it ?

PEER.

Like it ?   Hm——

THE OLD MAN.

Speak without fear !
What see you ?

PEER.

Why, something unspeakably grim :[2]
a bell-cow with her hoof on a gut-harp strumming,
a sow in socklets a-trip to the tune.

THE COURTIERS.

Eat him !

[1] Literally, "Better than our reputation."
[2] "Ustyggelig stygt." "Ustyggelig" seems to be what Mr.
Lewis Carroll calls a portmanteau word, compounded of "usigelig"=
unspeakable, and "styg"=ugly. The words might be rendered
"beyond grimness grim."

THE OLD MAN.

His sense is but human, remember!

TROLL-MAIDENS.

Hu, tear away both his ears and his eyes!

THE GREEN-CLAD ONE
(*weeping*).

Hu-hu! And this we must hear and put up with,
when I and my sister make music and dance.

PEER.

Oho, was it you? Well, a joke at the feast,
you must know, is never unkindly meant.

THE GREEN-CLAD ONE.

Can you swear it was so?

PEER.

　　　　Both the dance and the music
were utterly charming, the cat claw me else.

THE OLD MAN.

This same human nature's a singular thing;
it sticks to people so strangely long.
If it gets a gash in the fight with us,
it heals up at once, though a scar may remain.
My son-in-law, now, is as pliant as any;
he's willingly thrown off his Christian-man's garb,
he's willingly drunk from our chalice of mead,
he's willingly tied on the tail to his back,—
so willing, in short, did we find him in all things,
I thought to myself the old Adam, for certain,

had for good and all been kicked out of doors;
but lo! in two shakes he's atop again!
Ay ay, my son, we must treat you, I see,
to cure this pestilent human nature.

PEER.

What will you do?

THE OLD MAN.

In your left eye,[1] first,
I'll scratch you a bit, till you see awry;
but all that you see will seem fine and brave.
And then I'll just cut your right window-pane out——

PEER.

Are you drunk?

THE OLD MAN
(*lays a number of sharp instruments on the table*).

See, here are the glazier's tools.
Blinkers you'll wear, like a raging bull.
Then you'll recognise that your bride is lovely,—
and ne'er will your vision be troubled, as now,
with bell-cows harping and sows that dance.

PEER.

This is madman's talk!

THE OLDEST COURTIER.

It's the Dovrë-King speaking;
it's he that is wise, and it's you that are crazy!

---

[1] See Introduction, p. vi.

THE OLD MAN.

Just think how much worry and mortification
you'll thus escape from, year out, year in.
You must remember, your eyes are the fountain
of the bitter and searing lye of tears.

PEER.

That's true; and it says in our sermon-book:
If thine eye offend thee, then pluck it out.
But tell me, when will my sight heal up
into human sight?

THE OLD MAN.

Nevermore, my friend.

PEER.

Indeed!   In that case, I'll take my leave.

THE OLD MAN.

What would you without?

PEER.

I would go my way.

THE OLD MAN.

No, stop!   It's easy to slip in here,
but the Dovrë-King's gate doesn't open outwards.

PEER.

You wouldn't detain me by force, I hope?

THE OLD MAN.

Come now, just listen to reason, Prince Peer!
You have gifts for trolldom.   He acts, does he not,
even now in a passably troll-like fashion?
And you'd fain be a troll?

6

PEER.

Yes, I would, sure enough.
For a bride and a well-managed kingdom to boot,
I can put up with losing a good many things.
But there is a limit to all things on earth.
The tail I've accepted, it's perfectly true;
but no doubt I can loose what the Chamberlain tied.
My breeches I've dropped; they were old and patched;
but no doubt I can button them on again.
And lightly enough I can slip my cable
from these your Dovrefied ways of life.
I am willing to swear that a cow is a maid;
an oath one can always eat up again;—
but to know that one never can free oneself,
that one can't even die like a decent soul;
to live as a hill-troll for all one's days—
to feel that one never can beat a retreat,—
as the book has it, *that's* what your heart is set on;
but that is a thing I can never agree to.

THE OLD MAN.

Now, sure as I live, I shall soon lose my temper;
and then I am not to be trifled with.
You pasty-faced loon! Do you know who I am?
First with my daughter you make too free——

PEER.

There you lie in your throat!

THE OLD MAN.

You must marry her.

PEER.

Do you dare to accuse me——?

THE OLD MAN.

What?   Can you deny
that you lusted for her in heart and eye?

PEER
(*with a snort of contempt*).

No more?   Who the deuce cares a straw for that?

THE OLD MAN.

It's ever the same with this humankind.
The spirit you're ready to own with your lips,
but in fact nothing counts that your fists cannot handle.
So you really think, then, that lust matters nought?
Wait; you shall soon have ocular proof of it——

PEER.

You don't catch me with a bait of lies!

THE GREEN-CLAD ONE.

My Peer, ere the year's out, you'll be a father.

PEER.

Open doors! let me go!

THE OLD MAN.

In a he-goat's skin,
you shall have the brat after you.

PEER
(*mopping the sweat off his brow*).

Would I could waken!

THE OLD MAN.

Shall we send him to the palace?

PEER.

You can send him to the parish!

THE OLD MAN.

Well well, Prince Peer; that's your own look-out.
But one thing's certain, what's done is done;
and your offspring, too, will be sure to grow;
such mongrels shoot up amazingly fast——

PEER.

Old man, don't act like a headstrong ox!
Hear reason, maiden! Let's come to terms.
You must know I'm neither a prince nor rich;—
and whether you measure or whether you weigh me,
be sure you won't gain much by making me yours.

(THE GREEN-CLAD ONE *is taken ill, and is carried
out by* TROLL-MAIDS.)

THE OLD MAN
(*looks at him for a while in high disdain; then says:*)

Dash him to shards on the rock-walls, children!

THE TROLL-IMPS.

Oh dad, mayn't we play owl-and-eagle first!
The wolf-game! Grey-mouse and glow-eyed cat!

THE OLD MAN.

Yes, but quick. I am worried and sleepy. Good-night!
(*He goes.*)

PEER
(*hunted by the* TROLL-IMPS).

Let me be, devil's imps!
(*Tries to escape up the chimney.*)

THE IMPS.

Come brownies !   Come nixies !
Bite him behind !

PEER.

Ow !

(*Tries to slip down the cellar trap-door.*)

THE IMPS.

Shut up all the crannies !

THE TROLL-COURTIER.

Now the small-fry are happy !

PEER

(*struggling with a little* IMP *that has bit himself
fast to his ear*).

Let go will you, beast !

THE COURTIER
(*hitting him across the fingers*).

Gently, you scamp, with a scion of royalty !

PEER.

A rat-hole—— !

(*Runs to it.*)

THE IMPS.

Be quick, Brother Nixie, and block it !

PEER.

The old one was bad, but the youngsters are worse !

THE IMPS.

Slash him !

PEER.

Oh, would I were small as a mouse!
(*Rushing around.*)

THE IMPS
(*swarming round him*).

Close the ring! Close the ring!

PEER
(*weeping*).

Would that I were a louse!

(*He falls.*)

THE IMPS.

Now into his eyes!

PEER
(*buried in a heap of* IMPS).

Mother, help me, I die!

(*Church-bells sound far away.*)

THE IMPS.

Bells in the mountain! The Black-Frock's cows!

(THE TROLLS *take to flight, amid a confused uproar
of yells and shrieks. The palace collapses;
everything disappears.*)

SCENE SEVENTH.

(*Pitch darkness.*)
(PEER GYNT *is heard beating and slashing about him with
  a large bough.*)

PEER.

Answer!   Who are you?

A VOICE IN THE DARKNESS.

Myself.

PEER.

Clear the way!

THE VOICE.

Go roundabout, Peer!   The hill's roomy enough.

PEER
(*tries to force a passage at another place, but strikes
  against something*).

Who are *you?*

THE VOICE.

Myself.   Can you say the same?

PEER.

I can say what I will; and my sword can smite!
Mind yourself!   Hu, hei, now the blow falls crushing!
King Saul slew hundreds; Peer Gynt slew thousands!
(*Cutting and slashing.*)
Who *are* you?

THE VOICE.

Myself.

PEER.

That stupid reply
you may spare ; it doesn't clear up the matter.
What are you?

THE VOICE.

The great Boyg.[1]

PEER.

Ah, indeed!
The riddle was black ; now I'd call it grey.
Clear the way then, Boyg!

THE VOICE.

Go roundabout, Peer!

PEER.

No, through!
(Cuts and slashes.)
There he fell!
(Tries to advance, but strikes against something.)
Ho ho, are there more here?

THE VOICE.

The Boyg, Peer Gynt! the one only one.
It's the Boyg that's unwounded, and the Boyg that was hurt,
it's the Boyg that is dead, and the Boyg that's alive.

---

[1] See Introduction, pp. vi. and xiv., and Appendix.

PEER
(*throws away the branch*).

The weapon is troll-smeared;[1] but I have my fists!
(*Fights his way forward.*)

THE VOICE.

Ay, trust to your fists, lad, trust to your body.
Hee-hee, Peer Gynt, so you'll reach the summit.

PEER
(*falling back again*).

Forward or back, and it's just as far ;—
out or in, and it's just as strait ![2]
He is *there !*   And *there !*   And he's round the bend!
No sooner I'm out than I'm back in the ring.—
Name who you are !   Let me see you !   What are you?

THE VOICE.
The Boyg.

PEER
(*groping around*).

Not dead, not living; all slimy; misty.
Not so much as a shape !   It's as bad as to battle
in a cluster of snarling, half-wakened bears !
(*Screams.*)
Strike back at me, can't you !

THE VOICE.
                            The Boyg isn't mad.

PEER.
Strike !

—————
[1] Rendered harmless by magical anointing.
[2] " Atter og fram, det er lige langt ;—
       ud og ind, det er lige trangt ! "

THE VOICE.

The Boyg strikes not.

PEER.

Fight! You shall!

THE VOICE.

The great Boyg conquers, but does not fight.

PEER.

Were there only a nixie here that could prick me!
Were there only as much as a year-old troll!
Only something to fight with.   But here there is nothing.—
Now he's snoring!   Boyg!

THE VOICE.

What's your will?

PEER.

Use force!

THE VOICE.

The great Boyg conquers in all things without it.[1]

PEER

(*biting his own arms and hands*).

Claws and ravening teeth in my flesh!
I must feel the drip of my own warm blood.
      (*A sound is heard like the wing-strokes of great birds.*)

BIRD-CRIES.

Comes he now, Boyg?

---

[1] "Med lempe," literally "by gentleness" or "easy-goingness."
"Quiescence" is somewhere near the idea.

THE VOICE.

Ay, step by step.

BIRD-CRIES.

All our sisters far off!   Gather here to the tryst!

PEER.

If you'd save me now, lass, you must do it quick!
Gaze not adown so, lowly and bending.—
Your clasp-book!   Hurl it straight into his eyes!

BIRD-CRIES.

He totters!

THE VOICE.

We have him.

BIRD-CRIES.

Sisters!   Make haste!

PEER.

Too dear the purchase one pays for life
in such a heart-wasting hour of strife.
(*Sinks down.*)

BIRD-CRIES.

Boyg, there he's fallen!   Seize him!   Seize him!
(*A sound of bells and of psalm-singing is heard far away.*)

THE BOYG
(*shrinks up to nothing, and says in a gasp:*)

He was too strong.   There were women behind him.

SCENE EIGHTH.

(*Sunrise. The mountain-side in front of* ÅSE'S *sæter. The door is shut; all is silent and deserted.*)
(PEER GYNT *is lying asleep by the wall of the sæter.*)

PEER
(*wakens, and looks about him with dull and heavy eyes. He spits*).

What wouldn't I give for a pickled herring!
      (*Spits again, and at the same moment catches sight of* HELGA, *who appears carrying a basket of food.*)
Ha, child, are you there?   What is it you want?

HELGA.

It is Solveig——

PEER
(*jumping up*).

Where is *she?*

HELGA.

             Behind the sæter.

SOLVEIG
(*unseen*).

If you come nearer, I'll run away!

PEER
(*stopping short*).

Perhaps you're afraid I might take you in my arms?

SOLVEIG.

For shame!

PEER.

Do you know where I was last night?—
Like a horse-fly the Dovrë-King's daughter is after me.

SOLVEIG.

Then it was well that the bells were set ringing.

PEER.

Peer Gynt's not the lad they can lure astray.—
What do you say?

HELGA
(*crying*).

Oh, she's running away!
(*Running after her.*)

Wait!

PEER
(*catches her by the arm*).

Look here, what I have in my pocket!
A silver button, child!   You shall have it,—
only speak for me!

HELGA.

Let me be; let me go!

PEER.

There you have it.

HELGA.

Let go; there's the basket of food.

PEER.

God pity you if you don't——!

HELGA.

Uf, how you scare me!

PEER
(*gently; letting her go*).

No, I only meant : beg her not to forget me!

(HELGA *runs off*.)

ACT THIRD.

SCENE FIRST.

(*Deep in the pine-woods. Grey autumn weather. Snow is falling.*)
(PEER GYNT *stands in his shirt-sleeves, felling timber.*)

PEER
(*hewing at a large fir-tree with twisted branches*).

Oh ay, you are tough, you ancient churl;
but it's all in vain, for you'll soon be down.

(*Hews at it again.*)

I see well enough you've a chain-mail shirt,
but I'll hew it through, were it never so stout.—
Ay, ay, you're shaking your twisted arms;
you've reason enough for your spite and rage;
but none the less you must bend the knee——!

(*Breaks off suddenly.*)

Lies! 'Tis an old tree, and nothing more.
Lies! It was never a steel-clad churl;
it's only a fir-tree with fissured bark.—
It is heavy labour this hewing timber;
but the devil and all when you hew and dream too.—
I'll have done with it all—with this dwelling in mist,
and, broad-awake, dreaming your senses away.—

You're an outlaw, lad !   You are banned to the woods.

(*Hews for a while rapidly.*)

Ay, an outlaw, ay.   You've no mother now
to spread your table and bring your food.
If you'd eat, my lad, you must help yourself,
fetch your rations raw from the wood and stream,
split your own fir-roots[1] and light your own fire,
bustle around, and arrange and prepare things.
Would you clothe yourself warmly, you must stalk your deer ;
would you found you a house, you must quarry the stones ;
would you build up its walls, you must fell the logs,
and shoulder them all to the building-place.—

(*His axe sinks down ; he gazes straight in front of
him.*)

Brave shall the building be.   Tower and vane
shall rise from the roof-tree, high and fair.
And then I will carve, for the knob on the gable,
a mermaid, shaped like a fish from the navel.
Brass shall there be on the vane and the door-locks.
Glass I must see and get hold of too.
Strangers, passing, shall ask amazed
what that is glittering far on the hillside.

(*Laughs angrily.*)

Devil's own lies !   There they come again.
You're an outlaw, lad !

(*Hewing vigorously.*)

A bark-thatched hovel
is shelter enough both in rain and frost.

(*Looks up at the tree.*)

Now he stands wavering.   There ; only a kick,

---

[1] "Tyri," resinous pine-wood which burns with a bright blaze.

and he topples and measures his length on the ground ;—
the thick-swarming undergrowth shudders around him !

> (*Begins lopping the branches from the trunk ;
> suddenly he listens, and stands motionless with
> his axe in the air.*)

There's some one after me !—Ay, are you that sort,
old Hegstad-churl ;—would you play me false ?

> (*Crouches behind the tree, and peeps over it.*)

A lad ! One only. He seems afraid.
He peers all round him. What's that he hides
'neath his jacket ? A sickle. He stops and looks round,—
now he lays his hand on a fence-rail flat.
What's this now ? Why does he lean like that——?
Ugh, ugh ! Why, he's chopped his finger off !
A whole finger off !—He bleeds like an ox.—
Now he takes to his heels with his fist in a clout.

> (*Rises.*)

What a devil of a lad ! An unmendable[1] finger !
Right off ! And with no one compelling him to it !
Ho, now I remember ! It's only thus
you can 'scape from having to serve the King.
That's it. They wanted to send him soldiering,
and of course the lad didn't want to go.—
But to chop off——? To sever for good and all——?
Ay, think of it—wish it done—*will* it to boot,—
but *do* it——! No, that's past my understanding !

> (*Shakes his head a little ; then goes on with his
> work.*)

---

[1] "Umistelig"—unlosable, indispensable, irreplaceable.

SCENE SECOND.

(*A room in* ÅSE'S *house. Everything in disorder; boxes
standing open; wearing apparel strewn around. A
cat is lying on the bed.*)
(ÅSE *and the* COTTAR'S WIFE *are hard at work packing
things together and putting them straight.*)

ÅSE
(*running to one side*).

Kari, come here!

KARI.

What now?

ÅSE
(*on the other side*).
                              Come here——!
Where is——? Where shall I find——? Tell me
where——?
What am I seeking? I'm out of my wits!
Where is the key of the chest?

KARI.
                              In the key-hole.

ÅSE.

What is that rumbling?

KARI.

                              The last cart-load
they're driving to Hegstad.

ÅSE

(*weeping*).

How glad I'd be
in the black chest myself to be driven away!
Oh, what must a mortal abide and live through!
God help me in mercy! The whole house is bare!
What the Hegstad-churl left now the Bailiff[1] has taken.
Not even the clothes on my back have they spared.
Fie! Shame on them all that have judged so hardly!

(*Seats herself on the edge of the bed.*)

Both the land and the farm-place are lost to our line;
the old man was hard, but the law was still harder;—
there was no one to help me, and none would show mercy;
Peer was away; not a soul to give counsel.

KARI.

But here, in this house, you may dwell till you die.

ÅSE.

Ay, the cat and I live on charity.

KARI.

God help you, mother; your Peer's cost you dear.

ÅSE.

Peer? Why, you're out of your senses, sure!
Ingrid came home none the worse in the end.
The right thing had been to hold Satan to reckoning;–
he was the sinner, ay, he and none other;
the ugly beast tempted my poor boy astray!

---

[1] "Lensmand," the lowest functionary in the Norwegian official
scale—a sort of parish officer.

KARI.

Had I not better send word to the parson?
Mayhap you're worse than you think you are.

ÅSE.

To the parson?   Truly I almost think so.
(*Starts up.*)
But, oh God, I can't!   I'm the boy's own mother;
and help him I must; it's no more than my duty;
I must do what I can when the rest forsake him.
They've left him this coat; I must patch it up.
I wish I dared snap up the fur-rug as well!
What's come of the hose?

KARI.

                   They are there, 'mid that rubbish.

ÅSE
(*rummaging about*).

Why, what have we here?   I declare it's an old
casting-ladle, Kari!   With this he would play
button-moulder, would melt, and then shape, and then
    stamp them.
One day—there was company—in the boy came,
and begged of his father a lump of tin.
"Not tin," says Jon, "but King Christian's coin;
silver; to show you're the son of Jon Gynt."
God pardon him, Jon; he was drunk, you see,
and then he cared neither for tin nor for gold.
Here are the hose.   Oh, they're nothing but holes;
they want darning, Kari!

KARI.

                   Indeed but they do.

ÅSE.

When that is done, I must get to bed;
I feel so broken, and frail, and ill——
(*Joyfully.*)
Two woollen-shirts, Kari;—they've passed them by!

KARI.

So they have indeed.

ÅSE.

It's a bit of luck.
One of the two you may put aside;
or rather, I think we'll e'en take them both;—
the one he has on is so worn and thin.

KARI.

But oh, Mother Åse, I fear it's a sin!

ÅSE.

Maybe; but remember, the priest holds out
pardon for this and our other sinnings.

SCENE THIRD.

(*In front of a settler's newly-built hut in the forest. A
reindeer's horns over the door. The snow is lying
deep around. It is dusk.*)
(PEER GYNT *is standing outside the door, fastening a large
wooden bar to it.*)

PEER
(*laughing betweenwhiles*).

Bars I must fix me; bars that can fasten
the door against troll-folk, and men, and women.

Bars I must fix me ; bars that can shut out
all the cantankerous little hobgoblins.—
  They come with the darkness, they knock and they rattle :
Open, Peer Gynt, we're as nimble as thoughts are !
  'Neath the bedstead we bustle, we rake in the ashes,
down the chimney we hustle like fiery-eyed dragons.
  Hee-hee ! Peer Gynt ; think you staples and planks
can shut out cantankerous hobgoblin-thoughts ?

    (SOLVEIG *comes on snow-shoes over the heath ; she
        has a shawl over her head, and a bundle in
        her hand.*)

SOLVEIG.

God prosper your labour.   You must not reject me.
You sent for me hither, and so you must take me.

PEER.

Solveig !   It cannot be——!   Ay, but it is !—
And you're not afraid to come near to me !

SOLVEIG.

One message you sent me by little Helga ;
others came after in storm and in stillness.
All that your mother told bore me a message,
that brought forth others when dreams sank upon me.
Nights full of heaviness, blank, empty days,
brought me the message that now I must come.
It seemed as though life had been quenched down there ;
I could nor laugh nor weep from the depths of my heart.
I knew not for sure how you might be minded ;
I knew but for sure what I should do and must do.

PEER.

But your father ?

SOLVEIG.

In all of God's wide earth
I have none I can call either father or mother.
I have loosed me from all of them.

PEER.

Solveig, you fair one—
and to come to me?

SOLVEIG.

Ay, to you alone ;
you must be all to me, friend and consoler.
(*In tears.*)
The worst was leaving my little sister ;—
but parting from father was worse, still worse ;
and worst to leave her at whose breast I was borne ;—
oh no, God forgive me, the worst I must call
the sorrow of leaving them all, ay all !

PEER.

And you know the doom that was passed in spring?
It forfeits my farm and my heritage.

SOLVEIG.

Think you for heritage, goods, and gear,
I forsook the paths all my dear ones tread?

PEER.

And know you the compact?　Outside the forest
whoever may meet me may seize me at will.

SOLVEIG.

I ran upon snow-shoes ; I asked my way on ;
they said " Whither go you ? " I answered, " I go home."

PEER.

Away, away then with nails and planks!
No need now for bars against hobgoblin-thoughts.
If you dare dwell with the hunter here,
I know the hut will be blessed from ill.
Solveig ! Let me look at you ! Not too near !
Only look at you ! Oh, but you are bright and pure !
Let me lift you ! Oh, but you are fine and light !
Let me carry you, Solveig, and I'll never be tired !
I will not soil you. With outstretched arms
I will hold you far out from me, lovely and warm one !
Oh, who would have thought I could draw you to me,—
ah, but I have longed for you, daylong and nightlong.
Here you may see I've been hewing and building ;—
it must down again, dear; it is ugly and mean——

SOLVEIG.

Be it mean or brave,—here is all to my mind.
One so lightly draws breath in the teeth of the wind.
Down below it was airless ; one felt as though choked ;
that was partly what drove me in fear from the dale.
But here, with the fir-branches soughing o'erhead,—
what a stillness and song !—I am here in my home.

PEER.

And know you that surely ? For all your days ?

SOLVEIG.

The path I have trodden leads back nevermore.

PEER.

You are mine then ! In ! In the room let me see you !
Go in ! I must go to fetch fir-roots[1] for fuel.

                    [1] See note, p. 96.

Warm shall the fire be and bright shall it shine,
you shall sit softly and never be a-cold.

> (*He opens the door;* SOLVEIG *goes in. He stands
> still for a while, then laughs aloud with joy
> and leaps into the air.*)

PEER.

My king's daughter!   Now I have found her and won her !
Hei !   Now the palace shall rise, deeply founded !

> (*He seizes his axe and moves away; at the same
> moment an* OLD-LOOKING WOMAN, *in a tattered
> green gown, comes out from the wood; an*
> UGLY BRAT, *with an ale-flagon in his hand,
> limps after, holding on to her skirt.*)

THE WOMAN.

Good evening, Peer Lightfoot !

PEER.

What is it ?   Who's there ?

THE WOMAN.

Old friends of yours, Peer Gynt !   My home is near by.
We are neighbours.

PEER.

Indeed ?   That is more than I know.

THE WOMAN.

Even as your hut was builded, mine built itself too.

PEER
(*going*).

I'm in haste——

THE WOMAN.

Yes, that you are always, my lad;
but I'll trudge behind you and catch you at last.

PEER.

You're mistaken, good woman!

THE WOMAN.

I was so before;
I was when you promised such mighty fine things.

PEER.

I promised——? What devil's own nonsense is this?

THE WOMAN.

You've forgotten the night when you drank with my sire?
You've forgot——?

PEER.

I've forgot what I never have known.
What's this that you prate of? When last did we meet?

THE WOMAN.

When last we met was when first we met.
(*To* THE BRAT.)
Give your father a drink; he is thirsty, I'm sure.

PEER.

Father? You're drunk, woman! Do you call him——?

THE WOMAN.

I should think you might well know the pig by its skin!
Why, where are your eyes? Can't you see that he's lame
in his shank, just as you too are lame in your soul?

PEER.

Would you have me believe——?

THE WOMAN.

Would you wriggle away——?

PEER.

This long-leggëd urchin——!

THE WOMAN.

He's shot up apace.

PEER.

Dare you, you troll-snout, father on me——?

THE WOMAN.

Come now, Peer Gynt, you're as rude as an ox!
(*Weeping.*)
Is it my fault if no longer I'm fair,
as I was when you lured me on hillside and lea?
Last fall, in my labour, the Fiend held my back,
and so 'twas no wonder I came out a fright.
But if you would see me as fair as before,
you have only to turn yonder girl out of doors,
drive her clean out of your sight and your mind;—
do but this, dear my love, and I'll soon lose my snout!

PEER.

Begone from me, troll-witch!

THE WOMAN.

Ay, see if I do!

PEER.

I'll split your skull open——!

THE WOMAN.

Just try if you dare!
Ho-ho, Peer Gynt, I've no fear of blows!
Be sure I'll return every day of the year.
I'll set the door ajar and peep in at you both.
When you're sitting with your girl on the fireside bench,—
when you're tender, Peer Gynt,—when you'd pet and caress
      her,—
I'll seat myself by you, and ask for my share.
She there and I—we will take you by turns.
Farewell, dear my lad, you can marry to-morrow!

PEER.

You nightmare of hell!

THE WOMAN.

By-the-bye, I forgot!
You must rear your own youngster, you light-footed scamp!
Little imp, will you go to your father?

THE BRAT
(*spits at him*).

Faugh!
I'll chop you with my hatchet; only wait, only wait!

THE WOMAN
(*kisses* THE BRAT).

What a head he has got on his shoulders, the dear!
You'll be father's living image when once you're a man!

PEER

(*stamping*).

Oh, would you were as far—— !

THE WOMAN.

As we now are near?

PEER

(*clenching his hands*).

And all this—— !

THE WOMAN.

For nothing but thoughts and desires !
It is hard on you, Peer !

PEER.

It is worst for another !—
Solveig, my fairest, my purest gold !

THE WOMAN.

Oh ay, 'tis the guiltless must smart, said the devil ;
his mother boxed his ears when his father was drunk !
(*She trudges off into the thicket with* THE BRAT, *who
throws the flagon at* PEER GYNT.)

PEER

(*after a long silence*).

The Boyg said, " Go roundabout ! "—so one must here.—
There fell my fine palace, with crash and clatter !
There's a wall around her whom I stood so near,
of a sudden all's ugly—my joy has grown old.—
Roundabout, lad ! There's no way to be found
right through all this from where you stand to her.
Right through ? Hm, surely there should be one.

There's a text on repentance, unless I mistake.
But what? What is it? I haven't the book,
I've forgotten it mostly, and here there is none
that can guide me aright in the pathless wood.—
  Repentance? And maybe 'twould take whole years,
ere I fought my way through. 'Twere a meagre life, that.
To shatter what's radiant, and lovely, and pure,
and clinch it together in fragments and shards?
You can do it with a fiddle, but not with a bell.
Where you'd have the sward green, you must mind not to
    trample.
  'Twas nought but a lie though, that witch-snout business!
Now all that foulness is well out of sight.—
Ay, out of sight maybe, not out of mind.
Thoughts will sneak stealthily in at my heel.
Ingrid! And the three, they that danced on the heights!
Will they too want to join us? With vixenish spite
will they claim to be folded, like her, to my breast,
to be tenderly lifted on outstretched arms?
Roundabout, lad; though my arms were as long
as the root of the fir, or the pine-tree's stem,—
I think even then I should hold her too near,
to set her down pure and untarnished again.—
  I must roundabout here, then, as best I may,
and see that it bring me nor gain nor loss.
One must put such things from one, and try to forget.—

(Goes a few steps towards the hut, but stops again.)

  Go in after this? So befouled and disgraced?
Go in with that troll-rabble after me still?
Speak, yet be silent; confess, yet conceal——?

(Throws away his axe.)

It's a holy-day evening. For me to keep tryst,
such as now I am, would be sacrilege.

SOLVEIG
(*in the doorway*).

Are you coming?

PEER
(*half aloud*).

Roundabout!

SOLVEIG.

What?

PEER.

You must wait.
It is dark, and I've got something heavy to fetch.

SOLVEIG.

Wait; I will help you; the burden we'll share.

PEER.

No, stay where you are! I must bear it alone.

SOLVEIG.

But don't go too far, dear!

PEER.

Be patient, my girl;
be my way long or short—you must wait.

SOLVEIG
(*nodding to him as he goes*).

Yes, I'll wait!

(PEER GYNT *goes down the wood-path.* SOLVEIG
remains standing in the open half-door.)

SCENE FOURTH.

(ÅSE's *room. Evening. The room is lighted by a wood
    fire on the open hearth. A cat is lying on a chair at
    the foot of the bed.*)
(ÅSE *lies in the bed, fumbling about restlessly with her
    hands on the coverlet.*)

ÅSE.

Oh, Lord my God, isn't he coming?
    The time drags so drearily on.
I have no one to send with a message;
    and I've much, oh so much, to say.
I haven't a moment to lose now!
    So quickly! Who could have foreseen!
Oh me, if I only were certain
    I'd not been too strict with him!

PEER GYNT
(*enters*).

Good evening!

ÅSE.

The Lord give you gladness!
You've come then, my boy, my dear!
But how dare you show face in the valley?
    You know your life's forfeit here.

PEER.

Oh, life must e'en go as it may go;
    I felt that I must look in.

ÅSE.

Ay, now Kari is put to silence,
　and I can depart in peace !

PEER.

Depart ?　Why, what are you saying ?
　Where is it you think to go ?

ÅSE.

Alas, Peer, the end is nearing ;
　I have but a short time left.

PEER
(*writhing, and walking towards the back of the room*).

See there now ! I'm fleeing from trouble ;
　I thought at least *here* I'd be free——!
Are your hands and your feet a-cold, then ?

ÅSE.

Ay, Peer ; all will soon be o'er.—
When you see that my eyes are glazing,
　you must close them carefully.
And then you must see to my coffin ;
　and be sure it's a fine one, dear.
Ah no, by-the-bye——

PEER.

Be quiet !
There's time yet to think of that.

ÅSE.

Ay, ay.
　　(*Looks restlessly around the room.*)
　　Here you see the little
they've left us !　It's like them, just.

8

PEER
(with a writhe).

Again !

(Harshly.)

    Well, I know it was my fault.
What's the use of reminding me?

ÅSE.

You !   No, that accursed liquor,
    from that all the mischief came !
Dear my boy, you know you'd been drinking ;
    and then no one knows what he does ;
and besides, you'd been riding the reindeer ;
    no wonder your head was turned !

PEER.

Ay, ay ; of that yarn enough now.
    Enough of the whole affair.
All that's heavy we'll let stand over
    till after—some other day.

(Sits on the edge of the bed.)

Now, mother, we'll chat together ;
    but only of this and that,—
forget what's awry and crooked,
    and all that is sharp and sore.—
Why see now, the same old pussy ;
    so she is alive then, still ?

ÅSE.

She makes such a noise o' nights now ;
    you know what that bodes, my boy !

PEER
(*changing the subject*).

What news is there here in the parish?

ÅSE
(*smiling*).

There's somewhere about, they say,
  a girl who would fain to the uplands——

PEER
(*hastily*).

Mads Moen, is he content?

ÅSE.

They say that she hears and heeds not
  the old people's prayers and tears.
You ought to look in and see them;——
  you, Peer, might perhaps bring help——

PEER.

The smith, what's become of him now?

ÅSE.

Don't talk of that filthy smith.
Her name I would rather tell you,
  the name of the girl, you know——

PEER.

No, now we will chat together,
  but only of this and that,—
forget what's awry and crooked,
  and all that is sharp and sore.

Are you thirsty ? I'll fetch you water.
  Can you stretch you ? The bed is short.
Let me see ;—if I don't believe, now,
  It's the bed that I had when a boy !
Do you mind, dear, how oft in the evenings
  you sat at my bedside here,
and spread the fur-coverlet o'er me,
  and sang many a lilt and lay?

ÂSE.

Ay, mind you ? And then we played sledges
  when your father was far abroad.
The coverlet served for sledge-apron,
  and the floor for an ice-bound fiord.

PEER.

Ah, but the best of all, though,—
  mother, you mind that too?—
the best was the fleet-foot horses——

ÂSE.

  Ay, think you that I've forgot?—
It was Kari's cat that we borrowed ;
  it sat on the log-scooped chair——

PEER.

To the castle west of the moon, and
  the castle east of the sun,
to Soria-Moria Castle
  the road ran both high and low.
A stick that we found in the closet,
  for a whip-shaft you made it serve.

ÂSE.

Right proudly I perked on the box-seat——

PEER.

Ay, ay ; you threw loose the reins,
and kept turning round as we travelled,
    and asked me if I was cold.
God bless you, ugly old mother,—
    you were ever a kindly soul—— !
What's hurting you now ?

ÂSE.

My back aches,
    because of the hard, bare boards.

PEER.

Stretch yourself; I'll support you.
    There now, you're lying soft.

ÂSE
(*uneasily*).

No, Peer, I'd be moving !

PEER.

Moving ?

ÂSE.

Ay, moving ; 'tis ever my wish.

PEER.

Oh, nonsense !   Spread o'er you the bed-fur.
    Let me sit at your bedside here.
There ; now we'll shorten the evening
    with many a lilt and lay.

ÅSE.

Best bring from the closet the prayer-book :
  I feel so uneasy of soul.

PEER.

In Soria-Moria Castle
  the King and the Prince give a feast.
On the sledge-cushions lie and rest you ;
  I'll drive you there over the heath——

ÅSE.

But, Peer dear, am I invited ?

PEER.

Ay, that we are, both of us.
    (*He throws a string round the back of the chair on
        which the cat is lying, takes up a stick, and
        seats himself at the foot of the bed.*)
Gee-up ! Will you stir yourself, Black-boy?
  Mother, you're not a-cold ?
Ay, ay ; by the pace one knows it,
  when Granë[1] begins to go !

ÅSE.

Why, Peer, what is it that's ringing——?

PEER.

  The glittering sledge-bells, dear !

[1] Granë (Grani) was the name of Sigurd Fafnir-bane's horse,
descended from Odin's Sleipnir. Sigurd's Granë was grey; Peer Gynt
calls his "Svarten," Black-boy, or Blackey.—See the "Volsunga
Saga," translated by Morris and Magnussen. Camelot edition, p. 43.

ÂSE.

Oh, mercy, how hollow it's rumbling!

PEER.

We're just driving over a fiord.

ÂSE.

I'm afraid!   What is that I hear rushing
    and sighing so strange and wild?

PEER.

It's the sough of the pine-trees, mother,
    on the heath.   Do you but sit still.

ÂSE.

There's a sparkling and gleaming afar now;
    whence comes all that blaze of light?

PEER.

From the castle's windows and doorways.
    Don't you hear, they are dancing?

ÂSE.

                         Yes.

PEER.

Outside the door stands Saint Peter,
    and prays you to enter in.

ÂSE.

Does he greet us?

PEER.

              He does, with honour,
    and pours out the sweetest wine.

ÅSE.

Wine! Has he cakes as well, Peer?

PEER.

Cakes? Ay, a heaped-up dish.
And the dean's wife[1] is getting ready
your coffee and your dessert.

ÅSE.

Oh, Christ; shall we two come together?

PEER.

As freely as ever you will.

ÅSE.

Oh, deary, Peer, what a frolic
you're driving me to, poor soul!

PEER
(*cracking his whip*).

Gee-up; will you stir yourself, Black-boy!

ÅSE.

Peer, dear, you're driving right?

PEER
(*cracking his whip again*).

Ay, broad is the way.

ÅSE.

This journey,
it makes me so weak and tired.

---

[1] "Salig provstinde," literally "the late Mrs. Provost."

PEER.

There's the castle rising before us;
　the drive will be over soon.

ASE.

I will lie back and close my eyes then,
　and trust me to you, my boy!

PEER.

Come up with you, Granë, my trotter!
　In the castle the throng is great;
they bustle and swarm to the gateway.
　Peer Gynt and his mother are here!
What say you, Master Saint Peter?
　Shall mother not enter in?
You may search a long time, I tell you,
　ere you find such an honest old soul.
Myself I don't want to speak of;
　I can turn at the castle gate.
If you'll treat me, I'll take it kindly;
　if not, I'll go off just as pleased.
I have made up as many flim-flams
　as the devil at the pulpit-desk,
and called my old mother a hen, too,
　because she would cackle and crow.
But her you shall honour and reverence,
　and make her at home indeed;
there comes not a soul to beat her
　from the parishes nowadays.—
Ho-ho; here comes God the Father!
　Saint Peter! you're in for it now!

　　　　　　　(*In a deep voice.*)

" Have done with these jack-in-office airs, sir ;
　　Mother Åse shall enter free ! "

　　　　　(*Laughs loudly, and turns towards his mother.*)

Ay, didn't I know what would happen?
　　Now they dance to another tune !

　　　　　　　　(*Uneasily.*)

Why, what makes your eyes so glassy?
　　Mother !　Have you gone out of your wits——?

　　　　　(*Goes to the head of the bed.*)

You mustn't lie there and stare so——!
　　Speak, mother ; it's I, your boy !

　　　　　(*Feels her forehead and hands cautiously; then
　　　　　　　throws the string on the chair, and says softly:*)

Ay, ay !—You can rest yourself, Granë ;
　　for even now the journey's done.

　　　　　(*Closes her eyes, and bends over her.*)

For all of your days I thank you,
　　for beatings and lullabys !—
But see, you must thank me back, now—

　　　　　(*Presses his cheek against her mouth.*)

There ; that was the driver's fare.[1]

　　　　　THE COTTAR'S WIFE
　　　　　　　(*entering*).

What?　Peer !　Ah, then we are over
　　the worst of the sorrow and need !
Dear Lord, but she's sleeping soundly—
　　or can she be——?

---

[1] *Tak for skyds*, literally " thanks for the drive."

PEER.

Hush ; she is dead.

(KARI *weeps beside the body ;* PEER GYNT *walks up and down the room for some time ; at last he stops beside the bed.*)

PEER.

See mother buried with honour.
　I must try to fare forth from here.

KARI.

Are you faring afar?

PEER.

To seaward.

KARI.

So far !

PEER.

Ay, and further still.
(*He goes.*)

ACT FOURTH.

SCENE FIRST.

*(On the south-west coast of Morocco. A palm-grove.
Under an awning, on ground covered with mat-
ting, a table spread for dinner. Further back in
the grove hammocks are slung. In the offing lies a
steam-yacht, flying the Norwegian and American
colours. A jolly-boat drawn up on the beach. It is
towards sunset.)*

*(PEER GYNT, a handsome middle-aged gentleman, in an
elegant travelling-dress, with a gold-rimmed double eyeglass hanging at his waistcoat, is doing the honours at
the head of the table. MR. COTTON,[1] MONSIEUR BALLON,
HERR VON EBERKOPF, and HERR TRUMPETERSTRÅLE,[2]
are seated at the table finishing dinner.)*

PEER GYNT.

Drink, gentlemen! If man is made
for pleasure, let him take his fill then.
You know 'tis written : Lost is lost,
and gone is gone——. What may I hand you?

TRUMPETERSTRÅLE.

As host you're princely, Brother Gynt!

---

[1] In the original, "Master Cotton."
[2] A Swede. The name means "trumpet-blast."

PEER.

I share the honour with my cash,
with cook and steward——

MR. COTTON.

Very well ;[1]
let's pledge a toast to all the four !

MONSIEUR BALLON.

Monsieur,[2] you have a *gout*,[2] a *ton*,[2]
that nowadays is seldom met with
among men living *en garçon*,—[2]
a certain—what's the word——?

VON EBERKOPF.

A dash,
a tinge of free soul-contemplation,
and cosmopolitanisation,[3]
an outlook through the cloudy rifts
by narrow prejudice unhemmed,
a stamp of high illumination,
an *Ur-Natur*,[2] with lore of life,
to crown the trilogy, united.
Nicht wahr, Monsieur, 'twas that you meant ?

MONSIEUR BALLON.

Yes, very possibly ; not quite
so loftily it sounds in French.

---

[1] In the original (early editions), " Werry well."
[2] So in original.
[3] This may not be a very lucid or even very precise rendering of *Verdensborgerdomsforpagtning* ; but this line, and indeed the whole speech, is pure burlesque ; and the exact sense of nonsense is naturally elusive.

VON EBERKOPF.

Ei was ![1]   That language is so stiff.—
But the phenomenon's final cause
if we would seek——

PEER.

                         It's found already.
The reason is that I'm unmarried.
Yes, gentlemen, completely clear
the matter is.   What should a man be?
Himself, is my concise reply.
He should regard *himself* and *his.*
But can he, as a sumpter-mule[2]
for others' woe and others' weal?

VON EBERKOPF.

But this same in-and-for-yourself-ness,
I'll answer for't, has cost you strife——

PEER.

Ah yes, indeed; in former days;
but always I came off with honour.
Yet one time I ran very near
to being trapped against my will.
I was a brisk and handsome lad,
and she to whom my heart was given,
she was of royal family——

MONSIEUR BALLON.

Of royal——?

----

[1] So in original.
[2] Literally, "pack-camel."

PEER
(*carelessly*).

One of those old stocks,
you know the kind——

TRUMPETERSTRÅLE
(*thumping the table*).

Those noble-trolls!

PEER
(*shrugging his shoulders*).

Old fossil Highnesses who make it
their pride to keep plebeian blots
excluded from their line's escutcheon.

MR. COTTON.

Then nothing came of the affair?

MONSIEUR BALLON.

The family opposed the marriage?

PEER.

Far from it !

MONSIEUR BALLON.

Ah!

PEER
(*with forbearance*).

You understand
that certain circumstances made for
their marrying us without delay.
But, truth to tell, the whole affair
was, first to last, distasteful to me.

I'm finical in certain ways,
and like to stand on my own feet.
And when my father-in-law came out
with delicately veiled demands
that I should change my name and station,
and undergo ennoblement,
with much else that was most distasteful,
not to say quite inacceptable,—
why then I gracefully withdrew,
point-blank declined his ultimatum—
and so renounced my youthful bride.

(*Drums on the table with a devout air.*)

Yes, yes; there is a ruling Fate !
On that we mortals may rely;
and 'tis a comfortable knowledge.

MONSIEUR BALLON.

And so the matter ended, eh ?

PEER.

Oh no, far otherwise I found it ;
for busy-bodies mixed themselves,
with furious outcries, in the business.
The juniors of the clan were worst ;
with seven of them I fought a duel.
That time I never shall forget,
though I came through it all in safety.
It cost me blood ; but that same blood
attests the value of my person,
and points encouragingly towards
the wise control of Fate aforesaid.

VON EBERKOPF.

Your outlook on the course of life
exalts you to the rank of thinker.

Whilst the mere commonplace empiric
sees separately the scattered scenes,
and to the last goes groping on,
you in one glance can focus all things.
One norm[1] to all things you apply.
You point each random rule of life,
till one and all diverge like rays
from one full-orbed philosophy.—
And you have never been to college?

PEER.

I am, as I've already said,
exclusively a self-taught man.
Methodically naught I've learned;
but I have thought and speculated,
and done much desultory reading.
I started somewhat late in life,
and then, you know, it's rather hard
to plough ahead through page on page,
and take in all of everything.
I've done my history piecemeal;
I never have had time for more.
And, as one needs in days of trial
some certainty to place one's trust in,
I took religion intermittently.
That way it goes more smoothly down.
One should not read to swallow all,
but rather see what one has use for.

MR. COTTON.

Ay, that is practical!

[1] So in original.

PEER
(*lights a cigar*).

Dear friends,
just think of my career in general.
In what case came I to the West?
A poor young fellow, empty-handed.
I had to battle sore for bread;
trust me, I often found it hard.
But life, my friends, ah, life is dear,
and, as the phrase goes, death is bitter.
Well! Luck, you see, was kind to me;
old Fate, too, was accommodating.
I prospered; and, by versatility,
I prospered better still and better.
In ten years' time I bore the name
of Crœsus 'mongst the Charleston shippers.
My fame flew wide from port to port,
and fortune sailed on board my vessels——

MR. COTTON.

What did you trade in?

PEER.

I did most
in negro slaves for Carolina,
and idol-images for China.

MONSIEUR BALLON.

Fi donc![1]

TRUMPETERSTRÅLE.

The devil, Uncle Gynt!

[1] So in original.

PEER.

You think, no doubt, the business hovered
on the outer verge of the allowable?
Myself I felt the same thing keenly.
It struck me even as odious.
But, trust me, when you've once begun,
it's hard to break away again.
At any rate it's no light thing,
in such a vast trade-enterprise,
that keeps whole thousands in employ,
to break off wholly, once for all.
That "once for all" I can't abide,
but own, upon the other side,
that I have always felt respect
for what are known as consequences;
and that to overstep the bounds
has ever somewhat daunted me.
Besides, I had begun to age,
was getting on towards the fifties;—
my hair was slowly growing grizzled;
and, though my health was excellent,
yet painfully the thought beset me:
Who knows how soon the hour may strike,
the jury-verdict be delivered
that parts the sheep and goats asunder?
　　　What could I do? To stop the trade
with China was impossible.
A plan I hit on—opened straightway
a new trade with the self-same land.
I shipped off idols every spring,
each autumn sent forth missionaries,
supplying them with all they needed,
as stockings, Bibles, rum, and rice——

MR. COTTON.

Yes, at a profit?

PEER.

Why, of course.
It prospered.   Dauntlessly they toiled.
For every idol that was sold
they got a coolie well baptised,
so that the effect was neutralised.
The mission-field lay never fallow,
for still the idol-propaganda
the missionaries held in check.

MR. COTTON.

Well, but the African commodities?

PEER.

There, too, my ethics won the day.
I saw the traffic was a wrong one
for people of a certain age.
One may drop off before one dreams of it.
And then there were the thousand pitfalls
laid by the philanthropic camp;
besides, of course, the hostile cruisers,
and all the wind-and-weather risks.
All this together won the day.
I thought: Now, Peter,[1] reef your sails;
see to it you amend your faults!
So in the South I bought some land,
and kept the last meat-importation,
which chanced to be a superfine one.
They throve so, grew so fat and sleek,
that 'twas a joy to me, and them too.

[1] So in original.

Yes, without boasting, I may say
I acted as a father to them,—
and found my profit in so doing.
I built them schools, too, so that virtue
might uniformly be maintained at
a certain general *niveau*,[1]
and kept strict watch that never its
thermometer should sink below it.
Now, furthermore, from all this business
I've beat a definite retreat ;—
I've sold the whole plantation, and
its tale of live-stock, hide and hair.
At parting, too, I served around,
to big and little, gratis grog,[1]
so men and women all got drunk,
and widows got their snuff as well.
So that is why I trust,—provided
the saying is not idle breath :
Whoso does not do ill, does good,—
my former errors are forgotten,
and I, much more than most, can hold
my misdeeds balanced by my virtues.

VON EBERKOPF
(*clinking glasses with him*).

How strengthening it is to hear
a principle thus acted out,
freed from the night of theory,
unshaken by the outward ferment !

PEER
(*who has been drinking freely during the preceding passages*).

We Northland men know how to carry
our battle through !   The key to the art

[1] So in original.

of life's affairs is simply this :
to keep one's ear close shut against
the ingress of one dangerous viper.

MR. COTTON.

What sort of viper, pray, dear friend?

PEER.

A little one that slyly wiles you
to tempt the irretrievable.
                    (*Drinking again.*)
The essence of the art of daring,
the art of bravery in act,
is this : To stand with choice-free foot
amid the treacherous snares of life,—
to know for sure that other days
remain beyond the day of battle,—
to know that ever in the rear
a bridge for your retreat stands open
This theory has borne me on,
has given my whole career its colour ;
and this same theory I inherit,
a race-gift, from my childhood's home.

MONSIEUR BALLON.
You are Norwegian ?

PEER.
                    Yes, by birth ;
but cosmopolitan in spirit.
For fortune such as I've enjoyed
I have to thank America.
My amply-furnished library
I owe to Germany's later schools.

From France, again, I get my waistcoats,
my manners, and my spice of wit,—
from England an industrious hand,
and keen sense for my own advantage.
The Jew has taught me how to wait.
Some taste for *dolce far niente*[1]
I have received from Italy,—
and one time, in a perilous pass,
to eke the measure of my days,
I had recourse to Swedish steel.

TRUMPETERSTRÅLE
(lifting up his glass).

Ay, Swedish steel—— ?

VON EBERKOPF.

The weapon's wielder
demands our homage first of all !
*(They clink glasses and drink with him.   The wine
begins to go to his head.)*

MR. COTTON.

All this is very good indeed ;—
but, sir,[1] I'm curious to know
what with your gold you think of doing.

PEER
(smiling).

Hm ; doing?   Eh ?

ALL FOUR
(coming closer).

Yes, let us hear !

[1] So in original.

PEER.

Well, first of all, I want to travel.
You see, that's why I shipped you four,
to keep me company, at Gibraltar.
I needed such a dancing-choir
of friends around my gold-calf-altar——

VON EBERKOPF.

Most witty!

MR. COTTON.

Well, but no one hoists
his sails for nothing but the sailing.
Beyond all doubt, you have a goal;
and that is——?

PEER.

To be Emperor.[1]

ALL FOUR.

What?

PEER
(*nodding*).

Emperor!

THE FOUR.

Where?

PEER.

O'er all the world.

MONSIEUR BALLON.

But how, friend——?

[1] In the original "kejser." We have elsewhere used the word
"Kaiser," but in this scene, and in Scenes 7 and 8 of this act, the
ordinary English form seemed preferable.

PEER.

By the might of gold!
That plan is not at all a new one;
it's been the soul of my career.
Even as a boy, I swept in dreams
far o'er the ocean on a cloud.
I soared with train and golden scabbard,—
and flopped down on all-fours again.
But still my goal, my friends, stood fast.—
There is a text, or else a saying,
somewhere, I don't remember where,
that if you gained the whole wide world,
but lost *yourself*, your gain were but
a garland on a cloven skull.
That is the text—or something like it;
and that remark is sober truth.

VON EBERKOPF.

But what then is the Gyntish Self?

PEER.

The world behind my forehead's arch,
in force of which I'm no one else
than I, no more than God's the Devil.

TRUMPETERSTRÅLE.

I understand now where you're aiming!

MONSIEUR BALLON.

Thinker sublime!

VON EBERKOPF.

Exalted poet!

PEER
(*more and more elevated*).

The Gyntish Self—it is the host
of wishes, appetites, desires,—
the Gyntish Self, it is the sea
of fancies, exigencies, claims,
all that, in short, makes *my* breast heave,
and whereby I, as I, exist.
But as our Lord requires the clay
to constitute him God o' the world,
so I, too, stand in need of gold,
if I as Emperor would figure.

MONSIEUR BALLON.

You have the gold, though !

PEER.

Not enough.
Ay, maybe for a nine-days' flourish,
as Emperor *à la*[1] Lippe-Detmold.
But I must be myself *en bloc*,[1]
must be the Gynt of all the planet,
Sir Gynt[1] throughout, from top to toe !

MONSIEUR BALLON
(*enraptured*).

Possess the earth's most exquisite beauty !

VON EBERKOPF.

All century-old Johannisberger !

TRUMPETERSTRÅLE.

And all the blades of Charles the Twelfth !

[1] So in original.

MR. COTTON.

But first a profitable opening
for business——

PEER.

That's already found ;
our anchoring here supplied me with it.
To-night we set off northward ho !
The papers I received on board
have brought me tidings of importance——!
(*Rises with uplifted glass.*)
It seems that Fortune ceaselessly
aids him who has the pluck to seize it——

THE GUESTS.

Well ?   Tell us——!

PEER.

Greece is in revolt.

ALL FOUR
(*springing up*).

What ! Greece——?

PEER.

The Greeks have risen in Hellas.

THE FOUR.

Hurrah !

PEER.

And Turkey's in a fix !
(*Empties his glass.*)

MONSIEUR BALLON.

To Hellas !   Glory's gate stands open !
I'll help them with the sword of France !

VON EBERKOPF.

And I with war-whoops—from a distance

MR. COTTON.

And I as well—by taking contracts !

TRUMPETERSTRÅLE.

Lead on !   I'll find again in Bender
the world-renownèd spur-strap-buckles !¹

MONSIEUR BALLON
(*falling on* PEER GYNT'S *neck*).

Forgive me, friend, that I at first
misjudged you quite !

VON EBERKOPF
(*pressing his hands*).

I, stupid hound,
took you for next door to a scoundrel !

MR. COTTON.

Too strong that ; only for a fool——

TRUMPETERSTRÅLE
(*trying to kiss him*).

I, Uncle, for a specimen
of Yankee riff-raff's meanest spawn—— !
Forgive me—— !

---

¹ An allusion to the spurs with which Charles XII. is said to have
torn the caftan of the Turkish Vizier who announced to him that the
Sultan had concluded a truce with Russia. The boots and spurs, it
would appear, have been preserved, but with the buckles missing.

VON EBERKOPF.

We've been in the dark——

PEER.

What stuff is this?

VON EBERKOPF.

We now see gathered
in glory all the Gyntish host
of wishes, appetites, and desires——!

MONSIEUR BALLON
(*admiringly*).

So *this* is being Monsieur[1] Gynt!

VON EBERKOPF
(*in the same tone*).

This I call being Gynt with honour!

PEER.

But tell me——?

MONSIEUR BALLON.

Don't you understand?

PEER.

May I be hanged if I begin to!

MONSIEUR BALLON.

What?   Are you not upon your way
to join the Greeks, with ship and money——?

———
[1] So in original.

PEER

(*contemptuously*).

No, many thanks! I side with strength,
and lend my money to the Turks.

MONSIEUR BALLON.

Impossible!

VON EBERKOPF.

Witty, but a jest!

PEER

(*after a short silence, leaning on a chair and assuming
a dignified mien*).

Come, gentlemen, I think it best
we part before the last remains
of friendship melt away like smoke.
Who nothing owns will lightly risk it.
When in the world one scarce commands
the strip of earth one's shadow covers,
one's born to serve as food for powder.
But when a man stands safely landed,
as I do, then his stake is greater.
Go you to Hellas. I will put you
ashore, and arm you gratis too.
The more you eke the flames of strife,
the better will it serve my purpose.
Strike home for freedom and for right!
Fight! storm! make hell hot for the Turks;—
and gloriously end your days
upon the Janissaries lances.—
But I—excuse me——

(*Slaps his pocket.*)

I have cash,
and am myself, Sir Peter Gynt.[1]

(*Puts up his sunshade, and goes into the grove, where the hammocks are partly visible.*)

TRUMPETERSTRÅLE.

The swinish cur!

MONSIEUR BALLON.

No taste for glory—— !

MR. COTTON.

Oh, glory's neither here nor there ;
but think of the enormous profits
we'd reap if Greece should free herself.

MONSIEUR BALLON.

I saw myself a conqueror,
by lovely Grecian maids encircled.

TRUMPETERSTRÅLE.

Grasped in my Swedish hands, I saw
the great, heroic spur-strap-buckles !

VON EBERKOPF.

I my gigantic Fatherland's
culture saw spread o'er earth and sea—— !

MR. COTTON.

The worst's the loss in solid cash.
God dam![1]   I scarce can keep from weeping!
I saw me owner of Olympus.

[1] So in original.

If to its fame the mountain answers,
there must be veins of copper in it,
that could be opened up again.
And furthermore, that stream Castalia,[1]
which people talk so much about,
with fall on fall, at lowest reckoning,
must mean a thousand horse-power good——!

TRUMPETERSTRÅLE.

Still I will go!   My Swedish sword
is worth far more than Yankee gold!

MR. COTTON.

Perhaps; but, jammed into the ranks,
amid the press we'd all be drowned;
and then where would the profit be?

MONSIEUR BALLON.

Accurst!   So near to fortune's summit,
and now stopped short beside its grave!

MR. COTTON
(shakes his fist towards the yacht).

That long black chest holds coffered up
the nabob's golden nigger-sweat——!

VON EBERKOPF.

A royal notion!   Quick!   Away!
It's all up with his empire now!
Hurrah!

MONSIEUR BALLON.

What would you?

---

[1] Mr. Cotton seems to have confounded Olympus with Parnassus.

VON EBERKOPF.

Seize the power !
The crew can easily be bought.
On board then !　I annex the yacht !

MR. COTTON.

You—what——?

VON EBERKOPF.

I grab the whole concern !
(*Goes down to the jolly-boat.*)

MR. COTTON.

Why then self-interest commands me
to grab my share.

(*Goes after him.*)

TRUMPETERSTRÅLE.

What scoundrelism !

MONSIEUR BALLON.

A scurvy business—but—*enfin !* [1]

(*Follows the others.*)

TRUMPETERSTRÅLE.

I'll have to follow, I suppose,—
but I protest to all the world—— ! [2]

(*Follows.*)

[1] So in original.

[2] An allusion to the attitude of Sweden during the Danish War of
1863-64, with special reference to the diplomatic notes of the Minister
for Foreign Affairs, Grev Manderström. He is also aimed at in the
character of Hussein in the last scene of this act. See Introduction,
page xiii.

SCENE SECOND.

(Another part of the coast.   Moonlight with drifting clouds.
The yacht is seen far out, under full steam.)
(PEER GYNT comes running along the beach ; now pinching
his arms, now gazing out to sea.)

PEER.

A nightmare !—Delusion !—I'll soon be awake !
She's standing to sea !   And at furious speed !—
Mere delusion !   I'm sleeping !   I'm dizzy and drunk !
(Clenches his hands.)
It's not possible I should be going to die !
(Tearing his hair.)
A dream !   I'm determined it shall be a dream !
Oh, horror !   It's only too real, worse luck !
My brute-beasts of friends——!   Do but hear me, oh Lord !
Since thou art so wise and so righteous——!   Oh judge——!
(With upstretched arms.)

It is *I,* Peter[1] Gynt !   Oh, our Lord, give but heed !
Hold thy hand o'er me, Father ; or else I must perish !
Make them back the machine !   Make them lower the gig !
Stop the robbers !   Make something go wrong with the
     rigging !
Hear me !   Let other folks' business lie over !
The world can take care of itself for the time !—
I'm blessed if he hears me !   He's deaf as his wont is !
Here's a nice thing !   A God that is bankrupt of help !
(Beckons upwards.)

---

[1] So in original.

Hist ! I've abandoned the nigger-plantation !
And missionaries I've exported to Asia !
Surely one good turn should be worth another !
Oh, help me on board——!

> (*A jet of fire shoots into the air from the yacht,
> followed by thick clouds of smoke ; a hollow
> report is heard.* PEER GYNT *utters a shriek,
> and sinks down on the sands. Gradually the
> smoke clears away ; the ship has disappeared.*)

PEER

(*softly, with a pale face*).

That's the sword of wrath !
In a crack to the bottom, every soul, man and mouse !
Oh, for ever blest be the lucky chance——

(*With emotion.*)

A chance ? No, no, it was more than chance.
I was to be rescued and they to perish.
Oh, thanks and praise for that thou hast kept me,
hast cared for me, spite of all my sins !—

(*Draws a deep breath.*)

What a marvellous feeling of safety and peace
it gives one to know oneself specially shielded !
But the desert ! What about food and drink ?
Oh, something I'm sure to find. *He'll* see to that.
There's no cause for alarm ;—

(*Loud and insinuatingly.*)

He would never allow
a poor little sparrow like me to perish !
Be but lowly of spirit. And give him time.
Leave it all in the Lord's hands ; and don't be cast down.—

(*With a start of terror.*)

Can that be a lion that growled in the reeds——?
                (*His teeth chattering.*)
No, it wasn't a lion.
                (*Mustering up courage.*)
                A lion, forsooth !
Those beasts, they'll take care to keep out of the way.
They know it's no joke to fall foul of their betters.
They have instinct to guide them ;—they feel, what's a fact,
that it's dangerous playing with elephants.—
        But all the same——.   I must find a tree.
There's a grove of acacias and palms over there ;
if I once can climb up, I'll be sheltered and safe,—
most of all if I knew but a psalm or two.

                (*Clambers up.*)
Morning and evening are not alike ;
that text has been oft enough weighed and pondered.

                (*Seats himself comfortably.*)
How blissful to feel so uplifted in spirit.
To think nobly is more than to know oneself rich.
Only trust in Him.   He knows well what share
of the chalice of need I can bear to drain.
He takes fatherly thought for my personal weal ;—

        (*Casts a glance over the sea, and whispers with
        a sigh :*)

but economical—no, that he isn't !

SCENE THIRD.

(*Night. An encampment of Moroccan troops on the edge of the desert. Watch-fires, with* SOLDIERS *resting by them.*)

A SLAVE
(*enters, tearing his hair*).

Gone is the Emperor's milk-white charger!

ANOTHER SLAVE
(*enters, rending his garments*).

The Emperor's sacred robes are stolen!

AN OFFICER
(*enters*).

A hundred stripes upon the foot-soles
for all who fail to catch the robber!
　　　(*The troopers mount their horses, and gallop away
　　　in every direction.*)

SCENE FOURTH.

(*Daybreak. The grove of acacias and palms.*)
(PEER GYNT *in his tree with a broken branch in his hand,
trying to beat off a swarm of monkeys.*)

PEER.

Confound it! A most disagreeable night.
　　　(*Laying about him.*)

Are you there again ?   This is most accursëd !
Now they're throwing fruit.   No, it's something else.
A loathsome beast is your Barbary ape !
The Scripture says : Thou shalt watch and fight.
But I'm blest if I can ; I am heavy and tired.

(Is again attacked ; impatiently :)

I must put a stopper upon this nuisance !
I must see and get hold of one of these scamps,
get him hung and skinned, and then dress myself up,
as best I may, in his shaggy hide,
that the others may take me for one of themselves.—
What are we mortals ?   Motes, no more ;
and it's wisest to follow the fashion a bit.—
Again a rabble !   They throng and swarm.
Off with you !   Shoo !   They go on as though crazy.
If only I had a false tail to put on now,—
only something to make me a bit like a beast.—
What now ?   There's a pattering over my head——— !

(Looks up.)

It's the grandfather ape,—with his fists full of filth——— !

*(Huddles together apprehensively, and keeps still
for a while.   The ape makes a motion ;* PEER
GYNT *begins coaxing and wheedling him, as he
might a dog.)*

Ay,—are you there, my good old Bus !
He's a good beast, he is !   He will listen to reason !
He wouldn't throw ;—I should think not, indeed !
It is me ! Pip-pip !   We are first-rate friends !
Ai–ai !   Don't you hear, I can talk your language ?
Bus and I, we are kinsfolk, you see ;—
Bus shall have sugar to-morrow——— !   The beast !
The whole cargo on top of me !   Ugh, how disgusting !—
Or perhaps it was food ?   'Twas in taste—indefinable ;

and taste's for the most part a matter of habit.
What thinker is it who somewhere says :
You must spit and trust to the force of habit?—
Now here come the small-fry !
   (Hits and slashes around him.)
       It's really too bad
that man, who by rights is the lord of creation,
should find himself forced to—— ! O murder ! murder !
the old one was bad, but the youngsters are worse !

SCENE FIFTH.

*(Early morning. A stony region, with a view out over the
 desert. On one side a cleft in the hill, and a cave.)*
(A THIEF *and a* RECEIVER *hidden in the cleft, with the
 Emperor's horse and robes. The horse, richly capar-
 isoned, is tied to a stone. Horsemen are seen afar
 off.)*

THE THIEF.

The tongues of the lances
all flickering and flashing,—
see, see !

THE RECEIVER.

Already my head seems
to roll on the sand-plain !
Woe, woe !

THE THIEF
(folds his arms over his breast).

My father he thieved ;
so his son must be thieving.

THE RECEIVER.

My father received ;
so his son keeps receiving.[1]

THE THIEF.

Thy lot shalt thou bear still ;
thyself shalt thou be still.

THE RECEIVER
(*listening*).

Steps in the brushwood !
Flee, flee ! But where ?

THE THIEF.

The cavern is deep,
and the Prophet great !

> (*They make off, leaving the booty behind them. The
> horsemen gradually disappear in the distance.*)

PEER GYNT
(*enters, cutting a reed whistle*).

What a delectable morning-tide !—
The dung-beetle's rolling his ball in the dust ;
the snail creeps out of his dwelling-house.
The morning ; ay, it has gold in its mouth.—
It's a wonderful power, when you think of it,
that Nature has given to the light of day.
One feels so secure, and so much more courageous,—
one would gladly, at need, take a bull by the horns.—
What a stillness all round ! Ah, the joys of Nature,—
strange enough I should never have prized them before.

---

[1] This is not to be taken as a burlesque instance of the poet's
supposed preoccupation with questions of heredity, but simply as an
allusion to the fact that, in the East, thieving and receiving are regular
and hereditary professions.

Why go and imprison oneself in a city,
for no end but just to be bored by the mob.—
Just look how the lizards are whisking about,
snapping, and thinking of nothing at all.
What innocence ev'n in the life of the beasts !
Each fulfils the Creator's behest unimpeachably,
preserving its own special stamp undefaced ;
is itself, is itself, both in sport and in strife,
itself, as it was at his primal : Be.!

(*Puts on his eye-glasses.*)

A toad. In the middle of a sandstone block.
Petrifaction all round him. His head alone peering.
There he's sitting and gazing as though through a window
at the world, and is—to himself enough.—

(*Reflectively.*)

Enough ? To himself——? Where is it that's written ?
I've read it, in youth, in some so-called classic.
In the family prayer-book ? Or Solomon's Proverbs ?
Alas, I notice that, year by year,
my memory for dates and for places is fading.

(*Seats himself in the shade.*)

Here's a cool spot to rest and to stretch out one's feet.
Why, look, here are ferns growing—edible roots.

(*Eats a little.*)

'Twould be fitter food for an animal ;—
but the text says : Bridle the natural man !
Furthermore it is written : The proud shall be humbled,
and whoso abaseth himself, exalted.

(*Uneasily.*)

Exalted ? Yes, that's what will happen with me ;—
no other result can so much as be thought of.
Fate will assist me away from this place,

and arrange matters so that I get a fresh start.
This is only a trial ; deliverance will follow,—
if only the Lord lets me keep my health.

   (*Dismisses his misgivings, lights a cigar, stretches
    himself, and gazes out over the desert.*)

What an enormous, limitless waste !—
Far in the distance an ostrich is striding.—
What can one fancy was really God's
meaning in all of this voidness and deadness?
This desert, bereft of all sources of life ;
this burnt-up cinder, that profits no one ;
this patch of the world, that for ever lies fallow ;
this corpse, that never, since earth's creation,
has brought its Maker so much as thanks,—
why was it created ?—How spendthrift is Nature !—
Is that sea in the east there, that dazzling expanse
all gleaming ? It can't be ; 'tis but a mirage.
The sea's to the west ; it lies piled up behind me,
dammed out from the desert by a sloping ridge.

   (*A thought flashes through his mind.*)

Dammed out? Then I could——? The ridge is narrow.
Dammed out ? It wants but a gap, a canal,—
like a flood of life would the waters rush
in through the channel, and fill the desert ![1]
Soon would the whole of yon red-hot grave
spread forth, a breezy and rippling sea.
The oases would rise in the midst, like islands ;
Atlas would tower in green cliffs on the north ;
sailing-ships would, like stray birds on the wing,
skim to the south, on the caravans' track.

  [1] This proposal was seriously mooted about ten years after the
appearance of *Peer Gynt*.

Life-giving breezes would scatter the choking
vapours, and dew would distil from the clouds.
People would build themselves town on town,
and grass would grow green round the swaying palm-trees.
The southland, behind the Sahara's wall,
would make a new seaboard for civilisation.
Steam would set Timbuctoo's factories spinning;
Bornu would be colonised apace;
the naturalist would pass safely through Habes
in his railway-car to the Upper Nile.
In the midst of my sea, on a fat oasis,
I will replant the Norwegian race;
the Dalesman's blood is next door to royal;
Arabic crossing will do the rest.
Skirting a bay, on a shelving strand,
I'll build the chief city, Pecropolis.
The world is decrepit!   Now comes the turn
of Gyntiana, my virgin land!

(Springs up.)

Had I but capital, soon 'twould be done.—
A gold key to open the gate of the sea!
A crusade against Death!   The close-fisted old churl
shall open the sack he lies brooding upon.
Men rave about freedom in every land;—
like the ass in the ark, I will send out a cry
o'er the world, and will baptise to liberty
the beautiful, thrall-bounden coasts that shall be.
I must on!   To find capital, eastward or west!
My kingdom—well, half of it, say—for a horse!

(The horse in the cleft neighs.)

A horse!   Ay, and robes!—Jewels too,—and a sword!

(Goes closer.)

It can't be!   It is though——!   But how?   I have read,

I don't quite know where, that the will can move
    mountains ;—
but how about moving a horse as well—— ?
Pooh ! Here stands the horse, that's a matter of fact ;—
for the rest, why, *ab esse ad posse*, et cetera.

       (*Puts on the dress and looks down at it.*)

Sir Peter—a Turk, too, from top to toe !
Well, one never knows what may happen to one.—
Gee-up, now, Granë, my trusty steed !

         (*Mounts the horse.*)

Gold-slipper stirrups beneath my feet !—
You may know the great by their riding-gear !

      (*Gallops off into the desert.*)

SCENE SIXTH.

(*The tent of an Arab chief, standing alone on an oasis.*)
(PEER GYNT, *in his eastern dress, resting on cushions. He
   is drinking coffee, and smoking a long pipe.* ANITRA,
   and a bevy of GIRLS, *dancing and singing before him.*)

CHORUS OF GIRLS.

The Prophet is come !
The Prophet, the Lord, the All-Knowing One,
to us, to us is he come,
o'er the sand-ocean riding !
The Prophet, the Lord, the Unerring One,
to us, to us is he come,
o'er the sand-ocean sailing !
    Wake the flute and the drum !
The Prophet, the Prophet is come !

ANITRA.

His courser is white as the milk is
that streams in the rivers of Paradise.
Bend every knee !　Bow every head !
His eyes are as bright-gleaming, mild-beaming stars.
Yet none earth-born endureth
the rays of those stars in their blinding splendour !
　　　Through the desert he came.
Gold and pearl-drops sprang forth on his breast.
Where he rode there was light.
Behind him was darkness ;
behind him raged drought and the simoom.
He, the glorious one, came !
Through the desert he came,
like a mortal apparelled.
Kaaba, Kaaba stands void ;—
he himself hath proclaimed it !

THE CHORUS OF GIRLS.

Wake the flute and the drum !
The Prophet, the Prophet is come !
　　　(*They continue the dance, to soft music.*)

PEER.

I have read it in print—and the saying is true —
that no one's a prophet in his native land.—
This position is very much more to my mind
than my life over there 'mong the Charleston merchants.
There was something hollow in the whole affair,
something foreign at the bottom, something dubious behind
　　　it ;—
I was never at home in their company,
nor felt myself really one of the guild.
What tempted me into that galley at all ?

To grub and grub in the bins of trade—
as I think it all over, I can't understand it ;—
it *happened* so ; that's the whole affair.—
     To be oneself on a basis of gold
is no better than founding one's house on the sand.
For your watch, and your ring, and the rest of your
          trappings
the good people fawn on you, grovelling to earth ;
they lift their hats to your jewelled breast-pin ;
but your ring and your breast-pin are not your person.—[1]
A prophet; ay, that is a clearer position.
At least one knows on what footing one stands.
If you make a success, it's *yourself* that receives
the ovation, and not your pounds-sterling and shillings.[2]
One is what one is, and no nonsense about it ;
one owes nothing to chance or to accident,
and needs neither licence nor patent to lean on.—
A prophet ; ay, that is the thing for me.
And I slipped so utterly unawares into it,—
just by coming galloping over the desert,
and meeting these children of nature *en route.*
The Prophet had come to them ; so much was clear.
It was really not my intent to deceive—— ;
there's a difference 'twixt lies and oracular answers ;
and then I can always withdraw again.
I'm in no way bound ; it's a simple matter— ;
the whole thing is private, so to speak ;
I can go as I came ; there's my horse ready saddled ;
I am master, in short, of the situation.

ANITRA
(*approaching from the tent-door*).

Prophet and Master !

---

[1] Or "ego."   [2] In original, "Pundsterling og shilling."

PEER.

What would my slave?

ANITRA.

The sons of the desert await at thy tent-door;
they pray for the light of thy countenance——

PEER.

Stop!

Say in the distance I'd have them assemble;
say from the distance I hear all their prayers.
Add that I suffer no menfolk in here!
    Men, my child, are a worthless crew,—
inveterate rascals you well may call them!
Anitra, you can't think how shamelessly
they have swind—— I mean they have sinned, my child!—[1]
Well, enough now of that; you may dance for me, damsels!
The Prophet would banish the memories that gall him.

THE GIRLS
(*dancing*).

The Prophet is good! The Prophet is grieving
for the ill that the sons of the dust have wrought!
The Prophet is mild; to his mildness be praises;
he opens to sinners his Paradise!

PEER
(*his eyes following* ANITRA *during the dance*).

Legs as nimble as drumsticks flitting.
She's a dainty morsel indeed, that wench!
It's true she has somewhat extravagant contours,—
not quite in accord with the norms of beauty.

---

[1] In the original, "De har snydt—— hm; jeg mener syndet, mit
barn!"

But what is beauty?   A mere convention,—
a coin made current by time and place.
And just the extravagant seems most attractive
when one of the normal has drunk one's fill.
In the law-bound one misses all intoxication.
Either plump to excess or excessively lean;
either parlously young or portentously old ;—
the medium is mawkish.—
Her feet—they are not altogether clean ;
no more are her arms ; in especial one of them.
But that is at bottom no drawback at all.
I should rather call it a qualification—
Anitra, come listen !

ANITRA
(*approaching*).

Thy handmaiden hears !

PEER.

You are tempting, my daughter ! The Prophet is touched.
If you don't believe me, then hear the proof ;—
I'll make you a Houri in Paradise !

ANITRA.

Impossible, Lord !

PEER.

What ?   You think I am jesting?
I'm in sober earnest, as true as I live !

ANITRA.

But I haven't a soul.

PEER.

Then of course you must get one !

ANITRA.

How, Lord?

PEER.

Just leave *me* alone for that ;—
I shall look after your education.
No soul? Why, truly you're not over bright,
as the saying goes. I've observed it with pain.
But pooh! for a soul you can always find room.
Come here! let me measure your brain-pan, child.—
There is room, there is room, I was sure there was.
It's true you never will penetrate
very deep; to a *large* soul you'll scarcely attain ;—
but never you mind; it won't matter a bit ;—
you'll have plenty to carry you through with credit——

ANITRA.

The Prophet is gracious——

PEER.

You hesitate? Speak!

ANITRA.

But I'd rather——

PEER.

Say on; don't waste time about it!

ANITRA.

I don't care so much about having a soul ;—
give me rather——

PEER.

What, child?

11

ANITRA

(*pointing to his turban*).

That lovely opal!

PEER

(*enchanted, handing her the jewel*).

Anitra! Anitra! true daughter of Eve!
I feel thee magnetic; for I am a man.
And, as a much-esteemed author has phrased it:
"Das Ewig-Weibliche zieht uns hinan!"[1]

SCENE SEVENTH.

(*A moonlight night.   The palm-grove outside* ANITRA'S
tent.)
(PEER GYNT *is sitting beneath a tree, with an Arabian lute
in his hands.   His beard and hair are clipped; he
looks considerably younger.*)

PEER GYNT

(*plays and sings*).

I double-locked my Paradise,
    and took its key with me.
The north-wind bore me seaward ho!
while lovely women all forlorn
    wept on the ocean strand.

Still southward, southward clove my keel
    the salt sea-currents through.

[1] Ibsen writes "Ziehet uns an."   We have ventured to restore the
exact wording of Goethe's lines.

Where palms were swaying proud and fair,
a garland round the ocean-bight,
    I set my ship afire.

I climbed aboard the desert ship,
    a ship on four stout legs.
It foamed beneath the lashing whip ;—
oh, catch me ; I'm a flitting bird ;—
    I'm twittering on a bough !

Anitra, thou'rt the palm-tree's must ;
    that know I now full well !
Ay, even the Angora goat-milk cheese
is scarcely half such dainty fare,
    Anitra, ah, as thou !
        (*He hangs the lute over his shoulder, and comes forward.*)
Stillness !   Is the fair one listening ?
Has she heard my little song ?
Peeps she from behind the curtain,
veil and so forth cast aside ?—
Hush !   A sound as though a cork
from a bottle burst amain !
Now once more !   And yet again !
Love-sighs can it be ? or songs ?—
No, it is distinctly snoring.—
Dulcet strain !   Anitra sleepeth !
Nightingale, thy warbling stay !
Every sort of woe betide thee,
if with gurgling trill thou darest -
but, as says the text : Let be !
Nightingale, thou art a singer ;
ah, even such an one am I.
He, like me, ensnares with music
tender, shrinking little hearts.

Balmy night is made for music;
music is our common sphere;
in the act of singing, we are
we, Peer Gynt and nightingale.
And the maiden's very sleeping
is my passion's crowning bliss;—
for the lips protruded o'er the
beaker yet untasted quite——
but she's coming, I declare !
After all, it's best she should.

ANITRA
(*from the tent*).

Master, call'st thou in the night ?

PEER.

Yes indeed, the Prophet calls.
I was wakened by the cat
with a furious hunting-hubbub——

ANITRA.

Ah, not hunting-noises, Master;
it was something much, much worse.

PEER.

What, then, was't ?

ANITRA.

Oh, spare me !

PEER.

Speak !

ANITRA.

Oh, I blush to——

PEER
(*approaching*).

Was it, mayhap,
that which filled me so completely
when I let you have my opal?

ANITRA
(*horrified*).

Liken thee, O earth's great treasure,
to a horrible old cat!

PEER.

Child, from passion's standpoint viewed,
may a tom-cat and a prophet
come to very much the same.

ANITRA.

Master, jest like honey floweth
from thy lips.

PEER.

My little friend,
you, like other maidens, judge
great men by their outsides only.
I am full of jest at bottom,
most of all when we're alone.
I am forced by my position
to assume a solemn mask.
Duties of the day constrain me;
all the reckonings and worry
that I have with one and all,
make me oft a cross-grained prophet;
but it's only from the tongue out.—

Fudge, avaunt! *En tête-à-tête*
I'm Peer—well, the man I am.
Hei, away now with the prophet;
me, myself, you have me here!

> (*Seats himself under a tree, and draws her to him.*)

Come, Anitra, we will rest us
underneath the palm's green fan-shade!
I'll lie whispering, you'll lie smiling;
afterwards our rôles exchange we;
then shall your lips, fresh and balmy,
to my smiling, passion whisper!

ANITRA

(lies down at his feet).

All thy words are sweet as singing,
though I understand but little.
Master, tell me, can thy daughter
catch a soul by listening?

PEER.

Soul, and spirit's light and knowledge,
all in good time you shall have them.
When in east, on rosy streamers
golden types print: Here is day,—
then, my child, I'll give you lessons;
you'll be well brought-up, no fear.
But, 'mid night's delicious stillness,
it were stupid if I should,
with a threadbare wisdom's remnants,
play the part of pedagogue.—
And the soul, moreover, is not,
looked at properly, the main thing.
It's the heart that really matters.

ANITRA.

Speak, O Master! When thou speakest,
I see gleams, as though of opals!

PEER.

Wisdom in extremes is folly;
coward blossoms into tyrant;
truth, when carried to excess,
ends in wisdom written backwards.
Ay, my daughter, I'm forsworn
as a dog if there are not
folk with o'erfed souls on earth
who shall scarce attain to clearness.
Once I met with such a fellow,
of the flock the very flower;
and even he mistook his goal,
losing sense in blatant sound.—
See the waste round this oasis.
Were I but to swing my turban,
I could force the ocean-flood
to fill up the whole concern.
But I were a blockhead, truly,
seas and lands to go creating.
Know you what it is to live?

ANITRA.

Teach me!

PEER.

It is to be wafted
dry-shod down the stream of time,
wholly, solely as oneself.
Only in full manhood can I
be the man I am, dear child!

Aged eagle moults his plumage,
aged fogey lags declining,
aged dame has ne'er a tooth left,
aged churl gets withered hands,—
one and all get withered souls.
Youth! Ah, youth! I mean to reign,
as a sultan, whole and fiery,—
not on Gyntiana's shores,
under trellised vines and palm-leaves,—
but enthronëd[1] in the freshness
of a woman's virgin thoughts.—

    See you now, my little maiden,
why I've graciously bewitched you,—
why I have your heart selected,
and established, so to speak,
there my being's Caliphate?
All your longings shall be mine.
I'm an autocrat in passion!
You shall live for me alone.
I'll be he who shall enthrall
you like gold and precious stones.
Should we part, then life is over,—
that is, *your* life, *nota bene!*
Every inch and fibre of you,
will-less, without yea or nay,
I must know filled full of me.
Midnight beauties of your tresses,
all that's lovely to be named,
shall, like Babylonian gardens,
tempt your Sultan to his tryst.

    After all, I don't complain, then,
of your empty forehead-vault.
With a soul, one's oft absorbed in

---

[1] Literally, "on the basis of."

contemplation of oneself.
Listen, while we're on the subject,---
if you like it, faith, you shall
have a ring about your ankle :—
'twill be best for both of us.
I will be your soul by proxy ;
for the rest—why, *status quo.*

               (ANITRA *snores.*)

What ! She sleeps ! Then has it glided
bootless past her, all I've said ?—
No ; it marks my influence o'er her
that she floats away in dreams
on my love-talk as it flows.

          (*Rises, and lays trinkets in her lap.*)

Here are jewels ! Here are more !
Sleep, Anitra ! Dream of Peer——.
Sleep ! In sleeping, you the crown have
placed upon your Emperor's brow !
Victory on his Person's basis
has Peer Gynt this night achieved.

SCENE EIGHTH.

(*A caravan route. The oasis is seen far off in the back-
    ground.*)
(PEER GYNT *comes galloping across the desert on his white
    horse, with* ANITRA *before him on his saddle-bow.*)

ANITRA.

Let be, or I'll bite you !

PEER.

          You little rogue !

ANITRA.

What would you?

PEER.

What would I?   Play hawk and dove!
Run away with you!   Frolic and frisk a bit!

ANITRA.

For shame!   An old prophet like you——!

PEER.

Oh, stuff!

The prophet's not old at all, you goose!
Do you think all this is a sign of age?

ANITRA.

Let me go!   I want to go home!

PEER.

Coquette!
What, home!   To father-in-law!   That would be fine!
We madcap birds that have flown from the cage
must never come into his sight again.
Besides, my child, in the self-same place
it's wisest never to stay too long;
for familiarity lessens respect;——
most of all when one comes as a prophet or such.
One should show oneself glimpse-wise, and pass like a
    dream.
Faith, 'twas time that the visit should come to an end.
They're unstable of soul, are these sons of the desert;——
both incense and prayers dwindled off towards the end.

ANITRA.

Yes, but *are* you a prophet?

PEER.

Your Emperor I am !

(*Tries to kiss her.*)

Why just see now how coy the wee woodpecker is !

ANITRA.

Give me that ring that you have on your finger.

PEER.

Take, sweet Anitra, the whole of the trash !

ANITRA.

Thy words are as songs !　Oh, how dulcet their sound !

PEER.

How blessëd to know oneself loved to this pitch !
I'll dismount !　Like your slave, I will lead your palfrey !

(*Hands her his riding-whip, and dismounts.*)

There now, my rosebud, my exquisite flower !
Here I'll go trudging my way through the sand,
till a sunstroke o'ertakes me and finishes me.
I'm young, Anitra ; bear that in mind !
You mustn't be shocked at my escapades.
Frolics and high-jinks are youth's sole criterion !
And so, if your intellect weren't so dense,
you would see at a glance, oh my fair oleander,—
your lover is frolicsome—*ergo*, he's young !

ANITRA.

Yes, you are young.　Have you any more rings ?

PEER.

Am I not?   There, grab!   I can leap like a buck!
Were there vine-leaves around, I would garland my brow.
To be sure I am young!   Hei, I'm going to dance!
(Dances and sings.)

I am a blissful game-cock!
Peck me, my little pullet!
Hop-sa-sa!   Let me trip it;—
I am a blissful game-cock!

ANITRA.

You are sweating, my prophet; I fear you will melt;—
hand me that heavy bag hung at your belt.

PEER.

Tender solicitude!   Bear the purse ever;—
hearts that can love are content without gold!
(Dances and sings again.)

Young Peer Gynt is the maddest wag;—
he knows not what foot he shall stand upon.
Pooh, says Peer;—pooh, never mind!
Young Peer Gynt is the maddest wag!

ANITRA.

What joy when the Prophet steps forth in the dance!

PEER.

Oh, bother the Prophet!—Suppose we change clothes!
Heisa!   Strip off!

ANITRA.

Your caftan were too long,
your girdle too wide, and your stockings too tight——

PEER.

Eh bien! [1]

(*Kneels down.*)

But vouchsafe me a vehement sorrow;—
to a heart full of love, it is sweet to suffer!
Listen; as soon as we're home at my castle——

ANITRA.

In your Paradise;—have we far to ride?

PEER.

Oh, a thousand miles or——

ANITRA.

Too far!

PEER.

Oh, listen;—
you shall have the soul that I promised you once——

ANITRA.

Oh, thank you; I'll get on without the soul.
But you asked for a sorrow——

PEER

(*rising*).

Ay, curse me, I did!
A keen one, but short,—to last two or three days!

_____
[1] So in original.

ANITRA.

Anitra obeyeth the Prophet!—Farewell!

> (*Gives him a smart cut across the fingers, and
> dashes off, at a tearing gallop, back across the
> desert.*)

PEER
(*stands for a long time thunderstruck*).

Well now, may I be——!

SCENE NINTH.

(*The same place, an hour later.*)
(PEER GYNT *is stripping off his Turkish costume, soberly
and thoughtfully, bit by bit. Last of all, he takes his
little travelling-cap out of his coat-pocket, puts it on,
and stands once more in European dress.*)

PEER GYNT
(*throwing the turban far away from him*).

There lies the Turk, then, and here stand I!—
These heathenish doings are no sort of good.
It's lucky 'twas only a matter of clothes,
and not, as the saying goes, bred in the bone.—
What tempted me into that galley at all?
It's best, in the long run, to live as a Christian,
to put away peacock-like ostentation,
to base all one's dealings on law and morality,
to be ever oneself, and to earn at the last a
speech at one's grave-side, and wreaths on one's coffin.
> (*Walks a few steps.*)

The hussy;—she was on the very verge
of turning my head clean topsy-turvy.
May I be a troll if I understand
what it was that dazed and bemused me so.
Well; it's well that's done: had the joke been carried
but one step on, I'd have looked absurd.—
I have erred;——but at least it's a consolation
that my error was due to the false situation.
It wasn't my personal self that fell.
'Twas in fact this prophetical way of life,
so utterly lacking the salt of activity,
that took its revenge in these qualms of bad taste.
It's a sorry business this prophetising!
One's office compels one to walk in a mist;
in playing the prophet, you throw up the game[1]
the moment you act like a rational being.[2]
In *so* far I've done what the occasion demanded,
in the mere fact of paying my court to that goose.
But, nevertheless——

　　　　　(*Bursts out laughing.*)

　　　　　　　Hm, to think of it now!
To try to make time stop by jigging and dancing,
and to cope with the current by capering and prancing!
To thrum on the lute-strings, to fondle and sigh,
and end, like a rooster,—by getting well plucked!
Such conduct is truly prophetic frenzy.—
Yes, plucked!—Phew! I'm plucked clean enough indeed.
Well, well, I've a trifle still left in reserve;
I've a little in America, a little in my pocket;
so I won't be quite driven to beg my bread.—
And at bottom this middle condition is best.

[1] Literally, "you're looed" or "euchred."
[2] Literally, "behave as though sober and wakeful."

I'm no longer a slave to my coachman and horses;
I haven't to fret about postchaise or baggage;
I am master, in short, of the situation.—
What path should I choose?   Many paths lie before me;
and a wise man is known from a fool by his choice.
My business life is a finished chapter;
my love-sports, too, are a cast-off garment.
I feel no desire to live back like a crab.
"Forward or back, and it's just as far;
out or in, and it's just as strait,"—
so I seem to have read in some luminous[1] work.—
I'll try something new, then; ennoble my course;
find a goal worth the labour and money it costs.
Shall I write my life without dissimulation,—
a book for guidance and imitation?
Or stay——!   I have plenty of time at command;—
what if, as a travelling scientist,
I should study past ages and time's voracity?
Ay, sure enough; *that* is the thing for me!
Legends I read e'en in childhood's days,
and since then I've kept up that branch of learning.—
I will follow the path of the human race!
Like a feather I'll float on the stream of history,
make it all live again, as in a dream,—
see the heroes battling for truth and right,
as an onlooker only, in safety ensconced,—
see thinkers perish and martyrs bleed,
see empires founded and vanish away,—
see world-epochs grow from their trifling seeds;
in short, I will skim off the cream of history.—
I must try to get hold of a volume of Becker,
and travel as far as I can by chronology.—
It's true—my grounding's by no means thorough,

---

[1] Literally, "*spirituel*."

and history's wheels within wheels are deceptive ;—
but pooh ; the wilder the starting-point,
the result will oft be the more original.—
How exalting it is, now, to choose a goal,
and drive straight for it, like flint and steel !
                    (*With quiet emotion.*)
To break off all round one, on every side,
the bonds that bind one to home and friends,—
to blow into atoms one's hoarded wealth,—
to bid one's love and its joys good-night,—
all simply to find the arcana of truth,—
                    (*Wiping a tear from his eye.*)
that is the test of the true man of science !—
I feel myself happy beyond all measure.
Now I have fathomed my destiny's riddle.
Now 'tis but persevering through thick and thin !
It's excusable, sure, if I hold up my head,
and feel my worth, as the man, Peer Gynt,
also called Human-life's Emperor.—
I will own the sum-total of bygone days ;
I'll nevermore tread in the paths of the living.
The present is not worth so much as a shoe-sole ;
all faithless and marrowless the doings of men ;
their soul has no wings and their deeds no weight ;——
                    (*Shrugs his shoulders.*)
and women,—ah, they are a worthless crew !
                    (*Goes off.*)

SCENE TENTH.

*(A summer day. Far up in the North. A hut in the
forest. The door, with a large wooden bar, stands
open. Reindeer-horns over it. A flock of goats by
the wall of the hut.)*

(A MIDDLE-AGED WOMAN, *fair-haired and comely, sits
spinning outside in the sunshine.)*

THE WOMAN
(glances down the path, and sings).

Maybe both the winter and spring will pass by,
and the next summer too, and the whole of the year;—
but thou wilt come one day, that know I full well;
and I will await thee, as I promised of old.[1]

(Calls the goats, spins, and sings again.)

God strengthen thee, whereso thou goest in the world!
God gladden thee, if at his footstool thou stand!
Here will I await thee till thou comest again;
and if thou wait up yonder, then there we'll meet, my
    friend!

SCENE ELEVENTH.

(In Egypt. Daybreak. MEMNON'S STATUE *amid the
sands.)*

*(*PEER GYNT *enters on foot, and looks around him for a
while.)*

PEER GYNT.

Here I might fittingly start on my wanderings.—
So now, for a change, I've become an Egyptian;
but Egyptian on the basis of the Gyntish I.

---

[1] *Sidst*—literally, "when last we met."

To Assyria next I will bend my steps.
To begin right back at the world's creation
would lead to nought but bewilderment.
I will go round about[1] all the Bible history;
its secular traces I'll always be coming on;
and to look, as the saying goes, into its seams,
lies entirely outside both my plan and my powers.

(Sits upon a stone.)

Now I will rest me, and patiently wait
till the statue has sung its habitual dawn-song.
When breakfast is over, I'll climb up the pyramid;
if I've time, I'll look through its interior afterwards.
Then I'll go round the head of the Red Sea by land;
perhaps I may hit on King Potiphar's grave.—
Next I'll turn Asiatic.   In Babylon I'll seek for
the far-renowned harlots and hanging gardens,—
that's to say, the chief traces of civilisation.
Then at one bound to the ramparts of Troy.
From Troy there's a fareway by sea direct
across to the glorious ancient Athens;—
there on the spot will I, stone by stone,
survey the Pass that Leonidas guarded.
I will get up the works of the better philosophers,
find the prison where Socrates suffered, a martyr—— ;
oh no, by-the-bye—there's a war there at present——!
Well then, my Hellenism must even stand over.

(Looks at his watch.)

It's really too bad, such an age as it takes
for the sun to rise.   I am pressed for time.
Well then, from Troy—it was there I left off——

(Rises and listens.)

What is that strange sort of murmur that's rushing——?

(Sunrise.)

---

[1] "Gå udenom," the phrase used by the Boyg, Act ii., Sc. 7.

MEMNON'S STATUE
(*sings*).

From the demigod's ashes there soar, youth-renewing,
    birds ever singing.
    Zeus the Omniscient
    shaped them contending
    Owls of wisdom,
my birds, where do they slumber?
Thou must die if thou rede not
    the song's enigma!

PEER.

How strange now,—I really fancied there came
from the statue a sound.   Music, this, of the Past.
I heard the stone-accents now rising, now sinking.—
I will register it, for the learned to ponder.

(*Notes in his pocket-book.*)

"The statue did sing.   I heard the sound plainly,
but didn't quite follow the text of the song.
The whole thing, of course, was hallucination.—
Nothing else of importance observed to-day."

(*Proceeds on his way.*)

———————

SCENE TWELFTH.

(Near the village of Gizeh.　The great SPHINX *carved out of the rock.　In the distance the spires and minarets of Cairo.)*

*(*PEER GYNT *enters; he examines the* SPHINX *attentively, now through his eyeglass, now through his hollowed hand.)*

PEER GYNT.

Now, where in the world have I met before
something half forgotten that's like this hobgoblin?
For met it I have, in the north or the south.
Was it a person?　And, if so, who?
That Memnon, it afterwards crossed my mind,
was like the Old Men of the Dovrë, so called,
just as he sat there, stiff and stark,
planted on end on the stumps of pillars.—
But this most curious mongrel here,
this changeling, a lion and woman in one,—
does he come to me, too, from a fairy-tale,
or from a remembrance of something real?
From a fairy-tale?　Ho, I remember the fellow!
Why, of course it's the Boyg, that I smote on the skull,—
that is, I dreamt it,—I lay in fever.—
　　　　　　(Going closer.)
The self-same eyes, and the self-same lips;—
not quite so lumpish; a little more cunning;
but the same, for the rest, in all essentials.—
Ay, so that's it, Boyg; so you're like a lion
when one sees you from behind and meets you in the day-
　　　time!

Are you still good at riddling? Come, let us try.
Now we shall see if you answer as last time !
(*Calls out towards the* SPHINX.)
Hei, Boyg, who are you?

A VOICE
(*behind the* SPHINX).

Ach, Sphinx, wer bist du?

PEER.

What! Echo answers in German ! How strange !

THE VOICE.

Wer bist du?

PEER.

It speaks it quite fluently too !
That observation is new, and my own.
(*Notes in his book.*)
"Echo in German. Dialect, Berlin."
(BEGRIFFENFELDT *comes out from behind the*
SPHINX.)

BEGRIFFENFELDT.

A man !

PEER.

Oh, then it was *he* that was chattering.
(*Notes again.*)
"Arrived in the sequel at other results."

BEGRIFFENFELDT
(*with all sorts of restless antics*).

Excuse me, mein Herr[1]—— ! Eine Lebensfrage—— ![1]
What brings you to this place precisely to-day?

[1] So in original.

PEER.

A visit.   I'm greeting a friend of my youth.

BEGRIFFENFELDT.

What?   The Sphinx——?

PEER
(*nods*).

Yes, I knew him in days gone by.

BEGRIFFENFELDT.

Famos![1]—And that after such a night !
My temples are hammering as though they would burst !
You know him, man ! Answer ! Say on ! Can you tell
what he is?

PEER.

What he is ? Yes, that's easy enough.
He's *himself.*

BEGRIFFENFELDT
(*with a bound*).

Ha, the riddle of life lightened forth
in a flash to my vision !—It's certain he is
himself?

PEER.

Yes, he says so, at any rate.

BEGRIFFENFELDT.

Himself ! Revolution ! thine hour is at hand !
(*Takes off his hat.*)
Your name, pray, mein Herr?[1]

PEER.

I was christened Peer Gynt.

_____
[1] So in original.

BEGRIFFENFELDT
(*in rapt admiration*).

Peer Gynt!   Allegoric!   I might have foreseen it.—
Peer Gynt?   That must clearly imply : The Unknown,—
the Comer whose coming was foretold to me——

PEER.

What, really?   And now you are here to meet——?

BEGRIFFENFELDT.

Peer Gynt!   Profound!   Enigmatic!   Incisive!
Each word, as it were, an abysmal lesson!
What are you?

PEER
(*modestly*).

I've always endeavoured to be
myself.   For the rest, here's my passport, you see.

BEGRIFFENFELDT.

Again that mysterious word at the bottom.
(*Seizes him by the wrist.*)
To Cairo!   The Interpreters' Kaiser is found!

PEER.

Kaiser?

BEGRIFFENFELDT.

Come on!

PEER.

Am I really known——?

BEGRIFFENFELDT
(*dragging him away*).

The Interpreters' Kaiser—on the basis of Self!

SCENE THIRTEENTH.

(*In Cairo.   A large courtyard, surrounded by high walls
and buildings.   Barred windows; iron cages.*)
(THREE KEEPERS *in the courtyard.*   A FOURTH *comes in.*)

THE NEW-COMER.

Schafmann, say, where's the director gone?

A KEEPER.

He drove out this morning some time before dawn.

THE FIRST.

I think something must have occurred to annoy him;
for last night——

ANOTHER.

Hush, be quiet; he's there at the door!

(BEGRIFFENFELDT *leads* PEER GYNT *in, locks the
gate, and puts the key in his pocket.*)

PEER
(*to himself*).

Indeed an exceedingly gifted man;
almost all that he says is beyond comprehension.

(*Looks around.*)

So this is the Club of the Savants, eh?

BEGRIFFENFELDT.

Here you will find them, every man jack of them;—
the group of Interpreters threescore and ten;[1]

---

[1] This is understood to refer to the authors of the Greek version
of the Old Testament, known as the Septuagint.   We are unable to
account for the hundred and sixty recruits to their company.

it's been lately increased by a hundred and sixty——
(*Shouts to the* KEEPERS.)
Mikkel, Schlingelberg, Schafmann, Fuchs,—
into the cages with you at once !

THE KEEPERS.
We !

BEGRIFFENFELDT.
Who else, pray ?   Get in, get in !
When the world twirls around, we must twirl with it too.
(*Forces them into a cage.*)
He's arrived this morning, the mighty Peer ;—
the rest you can guess,—I need say no more.
(*Locks the cage door, and throws the key into a well.*)

PEER.
But, my dear Herr Doctor and Director, pray——?

BEGRIFFENFELDT.
Neither one nor the other !   I was before——
Herr Peer, are you secret ?   I must ease my heart——

PEER
(with increasing uneasiness).
What is it ?

BEGRIFFENFELDT.
Promise you will not tremble.

PEER.
I will do my best, but——

BEGRIFFENFELDT
(*draws him into a corner, and whispers*).
The Absolute Reason
departed this life at eleven last night.

PEER.

God help me——!

BEGRIFFENFELDT.

　　　　　Why, yes, it's extremely deplorable.
And as *I'm* placed, you see, it is doubly unpleasant;
for this institution has passed up to now
for what's called a madhouse.

PEER.

A madhouse, ha !

BEGRIFFENFELDT.

Not *now*, understand !

PEER
(*softly, pale with fear*).

　　　　　Now I see what the place is !
And the man is mad ;—and there's none that knows it !
(*Tries to steal away.*)

BEGRIFFENFELDT
(*following him*).

However, I hope you don't misunderstand me?
When I said he was dead, I was talking stuff.
He's beside himself.　Started clean out of his skin,—
just like my compatriot Münchausen's fox.

PEER.

Excuse me a moment——

BEGRIFFENFELDT
(*holding him back*).

　　　　　I meant like an eel ;—
it was not like a fox.　A needle through his eye ;—
and he writhed on the wall——

PEER.

Where can rescue be found!

BEGRIFFENFELDT.

A snick round his neck, and whip! out of his skin!

PEER.

He's raving!   He's utterly out of his wits!

BEGRIFFENFELDT.

Now it's patent, and can't be dissimulated,
that this from-himself-going must have for result
a complete revolution by sea and land.
The persons one hitherto reckoned as mad,
you see, became normal last night at eleven,
accordant with Reason in its newest phase.
And more, if the matter be rightly regarded,
it's patent that, at the aforementioned hour,
the sane folks, so called, began forthwith to rave.

PEER.

You mentioned the hour, sir; my time is but scant——

BEGRIFFENFELDT.

Your time, did you say?   There you jog my remembrance!
          (*Opens a door and calls out.*)
Come forth all!   The time that shall be is proclaimed!
Reason is dead and gone; long live Peer Gynt!

PEER.

Now, my dear good fellow——!
          (*The* LUNATICS *come one by one, and at intervals,
          into the courtyard.*)

BEGRIFFENFELDT.

Good morning ! Come forth,
and hail the dawn of emancipation !
Your Kaiser has come to you !

PEER.

Kaiser ?

BEGRIFFENFELDT.

Of course !

PEER.

But the honour's so great, so entirely excessive——

BEGRIFFENFELDT.

Oh, do not let any false modesty sway you
at an hour such as this.

PEER.

But at least give me time——!
No, indeed, I'm not fit; I'm completely dumfounded !

BEGRIFFENFELDT.

A man who has fathomed the Sphinx's meaning !
A man who's himself !

PEER.

Ay, but that's just the rub.
It's true that in everything I am myself;
but here the point is, if I follow your meaning,
to be, so to phrase it, outside oneself.

BEGRIFFENFELDT.

Outside ? No, there you are strangely mistaken !
It's here, sir, that one is oneself with a vengeance ;
oneself, and nothing whatever besides.

We go, full sail, as our very selves.
Each one shuts himself up in the barrel of self,
in the self-fermentation he dives to the bottom,—
with the self-bung he seals it hermetically,
and seasons the staves in the well of self.
No one has tears for the other's woes;
no one has mind for the other's ideas.
We're our very selves, both in thought and tone,
ourselves to the spring-board's uttermost verge,—
and so, if a Kaiser's to fill the throne,
it is clear that you are the very man.

PEER.

O would that the devil——!

BEGRIFFENFELDT.

                    Come, don't be cast down;
almost all things in nature are new at the first.
"Oneself;"—come, here you shall see an example;
I'll choose you at random the first man that comes——

(*To a gloomy figure.*)

Good-day, Huhu! Well, my boy, wandering round
for ever with misery's impress upon you?

HUHU. [1]

Can I help it, when the people,
race[2] by race, dies untranslated?[3]

(*To* PEER GYNT.)

You're a stranger; will you listen?

PEER
(*bowing*).

Oh, by all means!

---

[1] See Introduction, p. xiii.   [2] Literally, "generation."
[3] Literally, "uninterpreted."

HUHU.

Lend your ear then. —
Eastward far, like brow-borne garlands,
lie the Malabarish seaboards.
Hollanders and Portugueses
compass all the land with culture.
There, moreover, swarms are dwelling
of the pure-bred Malabaris.
These have muddled up the language,
they now lord it in the country.—
But in long-departed ages
there the orang-outang was ruler.
He, the forest's lord and master,
freely fought and snarled in freedom.
As the hand of nature shaped him,
just so grinned he, just so gaped he.
He could shriek unreprehended;
he was ruler in his kingdom.—
Ah, but then the foreign yoke came,
marred the forest-tongue primeval.
Twice two hundred years of darkness[1]
brooded o'er the race of monkeys;
and, you know, nights *so* protracted
bring a people to a standstill.—
Mute are now the wood-notes primal;
grunts and growls are heard no longer;—
if we'd utter our ideas,
it must be by means of language.
What constraint on all and sundry!
Hollanders and Portugueses,
half-caste race and Malabaris,
all alike must suffer by it.—

[1] An allusion to the long period of stagnation in the history of
Norway under the Danish rule—say, from 1400 to 1800.

I have tried to fight the battle
of our real, primal wood-speech,—
tried to bring to life its carcass,—
proved the people's right of shrieking,—
shrieked myself, and shown the need of
shrieks in poems for the people.—
Scantly, though, my work is valued.—
Now I think you grasp my sorrow.
Thanks for lending me a hearing;—
have you counsel, let me hear it!

PEER
(*softly*).

It is written : Best be howling
with the wolves that are about you.

(*Aloud.*)

Friend, if I remember rightly,
there are bushes in Morocco,
where orang-outangs in plenty
live with neither bard nor spokesman;—
their speech sounded Malabarish;—
it was classical and pleasing.
Why don't you, like other worthies,
emigrate to serve your country?

HUHU.

Thanks for lending me a hearing;—
I will do as you advise me.

(*With a large gesture.*)

East! thou hast disowned thy singer!
West! thou hast orang-outangs still!

(*Goes.*)

BEGRIFFENFELDT.

Well, was he himself?   I should rather think so.
He's filled with his own affairs, simply and solely.
He's himself in all that comes out of him,—
himself, just because he's beside himself.
Come here!   Now I'll show you another one,
who's no less, since last evening, accordant with Reason.

(*To a* FELLAH, *with a mummy on his back.*)

King Apis, how goes it, my mighty lord?

THE FELLAH
(*wildly, to* PEER GYNT).

Am I King Apis?

PEER
(*getting behind the* DOCTOR).

I'm sorry to say
I'm not quite at home in the situation;
but I certainly gather, to judge by your tone——

THE FELLAH.

Now you too are lying.

BEGRIFFENFELDT.

Your Highness should state
how the whole matter stands.

THE FELLAH.

Yes, I'll tell him my tale.
(*Turns to* PEER GYNT.)

Do you see whom I bear on my shoulders?
His name was King Apis of old.
Now he goes by the title of mummy,
and withal he's completely dead.

13

All the pyramids yonder he builded,
and hewed out the mighty Sphinx,
and fought, as the Doctor puts it,
with the Turks, both to rechts and links.
      And therefore the whole of Egypt
exalted him as a god,
and set up his image in temples,
in the outward shape of a bull.—
      But *I* am this very King Apis,
I see that as clear as day;
and if you don't understand it,
you shall understand it soon.
      King Apis, you see, was out hunting,
and got off his horse awhile,
and withdrew himself unattended
to a part of my ancestor's land.
      But the field that King Apis manured
has nourished *me* with its corn;
and if further proofs are demanded,
know, I have invisible horns.
      Now, isn't it most accursëd
that no one will own my might!
By birth I am Apis of Egypt,
but a fellah in other men's sight.
      Can you tell me what course to follow?—
then counsel me honestly.—
The problem is how to make me
resemble King Apis the Great.

PEER.

Build pyramids then, your highness,
and carve out a greater Sphinx,
and fight, as the Doctor puts it,
with the Turks, both to rechts and links.

THE FELLAH.

Ay, that is all mighty fine talking !
A fellah !   A hungry louse !
I, who scarcely can keep my hovel
clear even of rats and mice.
        Quick, man,—think of something better,
that'll make me both great and safe,
and further, exactly like to
King Apis that's on my back !

PEER.

What if your highness hanged you,
and then, in the lap of earth,
'twixt the coffin's natural frontiers,
kept still and completely dead.

THE FELLAH.

I'll do it !   My life for a halter !
To the gallows with hide and hair !—
At first there will be some difference,
but that time will smooth away.
        (*Goes off and prepares to hang himself.*)

BEGRIFFENFELDT.

There's a personality for you, Herr Peer,—
a man of method——

PEER.

                    Yes, yes ; I see——;
but he'll really hang himself !   God grant us grace !
I'll be ill ;—I can scarcely command my thoughts !

BEGRIFFENFELDT.

A state of transition ; it won't last long.

PEER.

Transition?   To what?   With your leave—I must go——

BEGRIFFENFELDT
(*holding him*).

Are you crazy?

PEER.

Not yet——.   Crazy?   Heaven forbid !
(*A commotion.   The Minister* HUSSEIN[1] *forces his
way through the crowd.*)

HUSSEIN.

They tell me a Kaiser has come to-day.
(*To* PEER GYNT.)

It is you?

PEER
(*in desperation*).

Yes, that is a settled thing !

HUSSEIN.

Good.—Then no doubt there are notes to be answered?

PEER
(*tearing his hair*).

Come on !   Right you are, sir ;—the madder the better !

HUSSEIN.

Will you do me the honour of taking a dip ?
(*Bowing deeply.*)

I am a pen.

PEER
(*bowing still deeper*).

Why then I am quite clearly
a rubbishy piece of imperial parchment.

[1] See note, p. 145.

HUSSEIN.

My story, my lord, is concisely this :
they take me for a sand-box,[1] and I am a pen.

PEER.

My story, Sir Pen, is, to put it briefly :
I'm a blank sheet of paper that no one will write on.

HUSSEIN.

No man understands in the least what I'm good for;
they all want to use me for scattering sand with !

PEER.

I was in a woman's keeping a silver-clasped book ;—
it's one and the same misprint to be either mad or sane !

HUSSEIN.

Just fancy, what an exhausting life:
to be a pen and never taste the edge of a knife !

PEER
(with a high leap).

Just fancy, for a reindeer to leap from on high —
to fall and fall—and never feel the ground beneath your
　　hoofs !

HUSSEIN.

A knife ! I am blunt ;—quick, mend me and slit me !
The world will go to ruin if they don't mend my point for me !

PEER.

A pity for the world which, like other self-made things,
was reckoned by the Lord to be so excellently good.

---

[1] The sand-box has not yet been quite superseded by blotting-paper
in Norway.

BEGRIFFENFELDT.

Here's a knife!

HUSSEIN

(*seizing it*).

Ah, how I shall lick up the ink now!
Oh, what rapture to cut oneself!

(*Cuts his throat.*)

BEGRIFFENFELDT

(*stepping aside*).

Pray do not sputter.

PEER

(*in increasing terror*).

Hold him!

HUSSEIN.

Ay, hold me! That is the word!
Hold! Hold the pen! On the desk with the paper——!

(*Falls.*)

I'm outworn. The postscript—remember it, pray:
He lived and he died as a fate-guided pen![1]

PEER

(*dizzily*).

What shall I——! What am I? Thou mighty——, hold
    fast!
I am all that thou wilt,—I'm a Turk, I'm a sinner——
a hill-troll——; but help;—there was something that
    burst——!

(*Shrieks.*)

I cannot just hit on thy name at the moment;—
oh, come to my aid, thou—all madmen's protector!

(*Sinks down insensible.*)

---

[1] "En påholden pen." "Underskrive med påholden pen"—to sign
by touching a pen which is guided by another.

BEGRIFFENFELDT

(with a wreath of straw in his hand, gives a bound and sits astride of him).

Ha! See him in the mire enthronëd ;—
beside himself——! To crown him now!

(Presses the wreath on PEER GYNT'S *head, and shouts :)*

Long life, long life to Self-hood's Kaiser!

SCHAFMANN
(in the cage).

Es lebe hoch der grosse Peer!

ACT FIFTH.

SCENE FIRST.

(*On board a ship on the North Sea, off the Norwegian
coast. Sunset. Stormy weather.*)

(PEER GYNT, *a vigorous old man, with grizzled hair and
beard, is standing aft on the poop. He is dressed half
sailor-fashion, with a pea-jacket and long boots. His
clothing is rather the worse for wear; he himself is
weather-beaten, and has a somewhat harder expression.
The* CAPTAIN *is standing beside the steersman at the
wheel. The crew are forward.*)

PEER GYNT

(*leans with his arms on the bulwark, and gazes
towards the land*).

Look at Hallingskarv [1] in his winter furs ;—
he's ruffling it, old one, in the evening glow.
The Jökel,[1] his brother, stands behind him askew ;
he's got his green ice-mantle still on his back.
The Folgefånn,[1] now, she is mighty fine,—
lying there like a maiden in spotless white.
Don't you be madcaps, old boys that you are !
Stand where you stand ; you're but granite knobs.

[1] Mountains and glaciers.

THE CAPTAIN
(*shouts forward*).

Two hands to the wheel, and the lantern aloft !

PEER.

It's blowing up stiff——

THE CAPTAIN.

——for a gale to-night.

PEER.

Can one see the Rondë Hills from the sea ?

THE CAPTAIN.

No, how should you ?   They lie at the back of the snow-
fields.

PEER.

Or Blåhö ?[1]

THE CAPTAIN.

No ; but from up in the rigging,
you've a glimpse, in clear weather, of Galdhöpiggen.[1]

PEER.

Where does Hårteig[1] lie ?

THE CAPTAIN
(*pointing*).

About over there.

PEER.

I thought so.

THE CAPTAIN.

You know where you are, it appears.

[1] Mountains and glaciers.

PEER.

When I left the country, I sailed by here ;
And the dregs, says the proverb, hang in to the last.

(*Spits, and gazes at the coast.*)

In there, where the scaurs and the clefts lie blue, —
where the valleys, like trenches, gloom narrow and black, —
and underneath, skirting the open fiords, —
it's in places like *these* human beings abide.

(*Looks at the* CAPTAIN.)

They build far apart in this country.

THE CAPTAIN.

Ay ;
few are the dwellings and far between.

PEER.

Shall we get in by day-break ?

THE CAPTAIN.

Thereabouts ;
if we don't have too dirty a night altogether.

PEER.

It grows thick in the west.

THE CAPTAIN.

It does so.

PEER.

Stop a bit !
You might put me in mind when we make up accounts—

I'm inclined, as the phrase goes, to do a good turn
to the crew——

THE CAPTAIN.

I thank you.

PEER.

It won't be much.
I have dug for gold, and lost what I found ;—
we are quite at loggerheads, Fate and I.
You know what I've got in safe keeping on board—
that's all I have left ;—the rest's gone to the devil.

THE CAPTAIN.

It's more than enough, though, to make you of weight
among people at home here.

PEER.

I've no relations.
There's no one awaiting the rich old curmudgeon.—
Well; that saves you, at least, any scenes on the pier !

THE CAPTAIN.

Here comes the storm.

PEER.

Well, remember then—
If any of your crew are in real need,
I won't look too closely after the money——

THE CAPTAIN.

That's kind.　They are most of them ill enough off;
they have all got their wives and their children at home.
With their wages alone they can scarce make ends meet ;
but if they come home with some cash to the good,
it will be a return not forgot in a hurry.

PEER.

What do you say?   Have they wives and children?
Are they married?

THE CAPTAIN.

                    Married?   Ay, every man of them.
But the one that is worst off of all is the cook;
black famine is ever at home in his house.

PEER.

Married?   They've folks that await them at home?
Folks to be glad when they come?   Eh?

THE CAPTAIN.

                                        Of course,
in poor people's fashion.

PEER.

                    And come they one evening,
what then?

THE CAPTAIN.

          Why, I daresay the goodwife will fetch
something good for a treat——

PEER.

                    And a light in the sconce?

THE CAPTAIN.

Ay, ay, may be two; and a dram to their supper.

PEER.

And there they sit snug!   There's a fire on the hearth!
They've their children about them!   The room's full of
     chatter;

not one hears another right out to an end,
for the joy that is on them——!

THE CAPTAIN.

It's likely enough.
So it's really kind, as you promised just now,
to help eke things out.

PEER
(*thumping the bulwark*).

I'll be damned if I do!
Do you think I am mad? Would you have me fork out
for the sake of a parcel of other folks' brats?
I've slaved much too sorely in earning my cash!
There's nobody waiting for old Peer Gynt.

THE CAPTAIN.

Well well; as you please then; your money's your own.

PEER.

Right! Mine it is, and no one else's.
We'll reckon as soon as your anchor is down!
Take my fare, in the cabin, from Panama here.
Then brandy all round to the crew. Nothing more.
If I give a doit more, slap my jaw for me, Captain.

THE CAPTAIN.

I owe you a quittance, and not a thrashing;—
but excuse me, the wind's blowing up to a gale.

(*He goes forward. It has fallen dark; lights are
lit in the cabin. The sea increases. Fog and
thick clouds.*)

PEER.

To have a whole bevy of youngsters at home ;—
still to dwell in their minds as a coming delight ;—
to have others' thoughts follow you still on your path !—
There's never a soul gives a thought to me.—
Lights in the sconces !   I'll put out those lights.
I will hit upon something !—I'll make them all drunk ;—
not one of the devils shall go sober ashore.
They shall all come home drunk to their children and wives !
They shall curse; bang the table till it rings again,—
they shall scare those that wait for them out of their wits !
The goodwife shall scream and rush forth from the house,—
clutch her children along !   All their joy gone to ruin !

(*The ship gives a heavy lurch; he staggers and
keeps his balance with difficulty.*)

Why, that was a buffet and no mistake.
The sea's hard at labour, as though it were paid for it ;—
it's still itself here on the coasts of the north ;—
a cross-sea, as wry and wrong-headed as ever——

(*Listens.*)

Why, what can those screams be ?

THE LOOK-OUT
(*forward*).

A wreck a-lee !

THE CAPTAIN
(*on the main deck, shouts*).

Helm hard a-starboard !   Bring her up to the wind !

THE MATE.

Are there men on the wreck ?

THE LOOK-OUT.

I can just see three !

PEER,

Quick ! lower the stern boat——

THE CAPTAIN.

She'd fill ere she floated.

(*Goes forward.*)

PEER.

Who can think of that now ?

(*To some of the crew.*)

If you're men, to the rescue !
What the devil, if you should get a bit of a ducking !

THE BOATSWAIN.

It's out of the question in such a sea.

PEER,

They are screaming again ! There's a lull in the wind.—
Cook, will you risk it ? Quick ! I will pay——

THE COOK.

No, not if you offered me twenty pounds-sterling[1]——

PEER.

You hounds ! You chicken-hearts ! Can you forget
these are men that have goodwives and children at home?
There they're sitting and waiting——

[1] So in original.

THE BOATSWAIN.

Well, patience is wholesome.

THE CAPTAIN.

Bear away from that sea !

THE MATE.

There the wreck turned over !

PEER.

All is silent of a sudden——— !

THE BOATSWAIN.

Were they married, as you think,
there are three new-baked widows even now in the world.

(*The storm increases.*   PEER GYNT *moves away aft.*)

PEER.

There is no faith left among men any more,—
no Christianity,—well may they say it and write it ;—
their good deeds are few and their prayers are still fewer,
and they pay no respect to the Powers above them.—
In a storm like to-night's, he's a terror, the Lord is.
These beasts should be careful, and think, what's the truth,
that it's dangerous playing with elephants ;—
and yet they must openly brave his displeasure !
I am no whit to blame; for the sacrifice
I can prove I stood ready, my money in hand.
But how does it profit me ?—What says the proverb ?
A conscience at ease is a pillow of down.
Oh ay, that is all very well on dry land,
but I'm blest if it matters a snuff on board ship,
when a decent man's out on the seas with such riff-raff.

At sea one never can be one's self;
one must go with the others from deck to keel;
if for boatswain and cook the hour of vengeance should
　　strike,
I shall no doubt be swept to the deuce with the rest;—
one's personal welfare is clean set aside;—
one counts but as a sausage in slaughtering-time.—
　　My mistake is this : I have been too meek;
and I've had no thanks for it after all.
Were I younger, I think I would shift the saddle,
and try how it answered to lord it awhile.
There is time enough yet ! They shall know in the parish
that Peer has come sailing aloft o'er the seas !
I'll get back the farmstead by fair means or foul;—
I will build it anew; it shall shine like a palace.
But none shall be suffered to enter the hall !
They shall stand at the gateway, all twirling their caps;—
they shall beg and beseech—*that* they freely may do;
but none gets so much as a farthing of mine.
If *I've* had to howl 'neath the lashes of fate,
trust me to find folks I can lash in my turn——

THE STRANGE PASSENGER

(*stands in the darkness at* PEER GYNT'S *side, and salutes
him in friendly fashion*).

Good evening !

PEER.

Good evening ! What——? Who are you ?

THE PASSENGER.

Your fellow-passenger, at your service.

PEER.

Indeed ? I thought I was the only one.

THE PASSENGER.

A mistaken impression, which now is set right.

PEER.

But it's singular that, for the first time to-night,
I should see you——

THE PASSENGER.

I never come out in the day-time.

PEER.

Perhaps you are ill? You're as white as a sheet——

THE PASSENGER.

No, thank you—my health is uncommonly good.

PEER.

What a raging storm!

THE PASSENGER.

Ay, a blessëd one, man!

PEER.

A blessëd one?

THE PASSENGER.

The sea's running high as houses.
Ah, one can feel one's mouth watering!
Just think of the wrecks that to-night will be shattered;—
and think, too, what corpses will drive ashore!

PEER.

Lord save us!

THE PASSENGER.

Have ever you seen a man strangled,
or hanged,—or drowned?

PEER.

This is going too far——!

THE PASSENGER.

The corpses all laugh.   But their laughter is forced ;
and the most part are found to have bitten their tongues.

PEER.

Hold off from me——!

THE PASSENGER.

Only one question pray !
If we, for example, should strike on a rock,
and sink in the darkness——

PEER.

You think there is danger ?

THE PASSENGER.

I really don't know what I ought to say.
But suppose, now, I float and you go to the bottom——

PEER.

Oh, rubbish——

THE PASSENGER.

It's just a hypothesis.
But when one is placed with one foot in the grave,
one grows soft-hearted and open-handed——

PEER
(*puts his hand in his pocket*).

Ho, money !

THE PASSENGER.

No, no ; but perhaps you would kindly
make me a gift of your much-esteemed carcass——?

PEER.

This is *too* much!

THE PASSENGER.

No more than your body, you know!
To help my researches in science——

PEER.

Begone!

THE PASSENGER.

But think, my dear sir—the advantage is yours!
I'll have you laid open and brought to the light.
What I specially seek is the centre of dreams,—
and with critical care I'll look into your seams——

PEER.

Away with you!

THE PASSENGER.

Why, my dear sir—a drowned corpse——!

PEER.

Blasphemer! You're goading the rage of the storm!
I call it too bad! Here it's raining and blowing,
a terrible sea on, and all sorts of signs
of something that's likely to shorten our days;—
And you carry on so as to make it come quicker!

THE PASSENGER.

You're in no mood, I see, to negotiate further;
but time, you know, brings with it many a change——
(*Nods in a friendly fashion.*)
We'll meet when you're sinking, if not before;
perhaps I may then find you more in the humour.
(*Goes into the cabin.*)

PEER.

Unpleasant companions these scientists are !
With their freethinking ways——

(*To the* BOATSWAIN, *who is passing.*)

Hark, a word with you, friend !
That passenger?   What crazy creature is he ?

THE BOATSWAIN.

I know of no passenger here but yourself.

PEER.

No others?   This thing's getting worse and worse.

(*To the* SHIP'S BOY, *who comes out of the cabin.*)

Who went down the companion just now ?

THE BOY.

The ship's dog, sir !

(*Passes on.*)

THE LOOK-OUT
(*shouts*).

Land close ahead !

PEER.

Where's my box?   Where's my trunk?
All the baggage on deck !

THE BOATSWAIN.

We have more to attend to !

PEER.

It was nonsense, captain !   'Twas only my joke ;—
as sure as I'm here I will help the cook——

THE CAPTAIN.

The jib's blown away!

THE MATE.

And there went the foresail!

THE BOATSWAIN
(*shrieks from forward*).

Breakers under the bow!

THE CAPTAIN.

She will go to shivers!
(*The ship strikes.   Noise and confusion.*)

SCENE SECOND.

(*Close under the land, among sunken rocks and surf.   The
ship sinks.   The jolly-boat, with two men in her, is
seen for a moment through the scud.   A sea strikes
her; she fills and upsets.   A shriek is heard; then
all is silent for a while.   Shortly afterwards the boat
appears floating bottom upwards.*)
(PEER GYNT *comes to the surface near the boat.*)

PEER.

Help! Help!   A boat!   Help!   I'll be drowned!
Save me, oh Lord—as saith the text!
(*Clutches hold of the boat's keel.*)

THE COOK

(*comes up on the other side*).

Oh, Lord God—for my children's sake,
have mercy !   Let me reach the land !

(*Seizes hold of the keel.*)

PEER.

Let go !

THE COOK.

Let go !

PEER.

I'll strike !

THE COOK.

So'll I !

PEER.

I'll crush you down with kicks and blows !
Let go your hold !   She won't float two !

THE COOK.

I know it !   Yield !

PEER.

Yield you !

THE COOK.

Oh yes !

(*They fight; one of the* COOK'S *hands is disabled; he
clings on with the other.*)

PEER.

Off with that hand !

THE COOK.

Oh, kind sir—spare !
Think of my little ones at home !

PEER.

I need my life far more than you,
for I am lone and childless still.

THE COOK.

Let go !   You've lived, and I am young !

PEER.

Quick ; haste you ; sink ;—you drag us down.

THE COOK.

Have mercy !   Yield in heaven's name !
There's none to miss and mourn for you—
          (*His hand slips; he screams:*)
I'm drowning !

PEER
(*seizing him*).

By this wisp of hair
I'll hold you ; say your Lord's Prayer, quick !

THE COOK.

I can't remember ; all turns black——

PEER.

Come, the essentials in a word——!

THE COOK.

Give us this day——!

PEER.

Skip that part, Cook;
you'll get all *you* need, safe enough.

THE COOK.

Give us this day——

PEER.

The same old song!
One sees you were a cook in life——
(*The* COOK *slips from his grasp.*)

THE COOK
(*sinking*).

Give us this day our——
(*Disappears.*)

PEER.

Amen, lad!
to the last gasp you were yourself.—
(*Draws himself up on to the bottom of the boat.*)
So long as there is life there's hope——

THE STRANGE PASSENGER
(*catches hold of the boat*).

Good morning!

PEER.

Hoy!

THE PASSENGER.

I heard you shout.—
It's pleasant finding you again.
Well? So my prophecy came true!

PEER.

Let go!   Let go!   'Twill scarce float *one* /

THE PASSENGER.

I'm striking out with my left leg.
I'll float, if only with their tips
my fingers rest upon this ledge.
But apropos : your body——

PEER.

Hush !

THE PASSENGER.

The rest, of course, is done for, clean——

PEER.

No more !

THE PASSENGER.

Exactly as you please.
(*Silence.*)

PEER.

Well?

THE PASSENGER.

I am silent.

PEER.

Satan's tricks !—
What now ?

THE PASSENGER.

I'm waiting.

PEER

(*tearing his hair*).

I'll go mad !—

What are you ?

THE PASSENGER

(*nods*).

Friendly.

PEER.

What else ? Speak !

THE PASSENGER.

What think you ? Do you know none other
that's like me ?

PEER.

Do I know the devil——?

THE PASSENGER

(*in a low voice*).

Is it his way to light a lantern
for life's night-pilgrimage through fear ?

PEER.

Ah, come ! When once the thing's cleared up,
you'd seem a messenger of light ?

THE PASSENGER.

Friend,—have you *once* in each half-year
felt all the earnestness of dread ?[1]

---

[1] "Angst"—literally, "dread" or "terror"—probably means here
something like "conviction of sin." The influence of the Danish
theologian, Sören Kierkegård, may be traced in this passage.

PEER.

Why, one's afraid when danger threatens ;—
but all your words have double meanings.[1]

THE PASSENGER.

Ay, have you gained but *once* in life
the victory that is given in dread?

PEER

(*looks at him*).

Came you to ope for me a door,
'twas stupid not to come before.
What sort of sense is there in choosing
your time when seas gape to devour one?

THE PASSENGER.

Were, then, the victory more likely
beside your hearth-stone, snug and quiet?

PEER.

Perhaps not ; but your talk befooled me.
How could you fancy it awakening?

THE PASSENGER.

Where I come from, there smiles are prized
as highly as pathetic style.

PEER.

All has its time ; what fits the taxman,[2]
so says the text, would damn the bishop.

---

[1] Literally, "Are set on screws."
[2] "Tolder," the biblical "publican."

THE PASSENGER.

The host whose dust inurned has slumbered
treads not on week-days the cothurnus.

PEER.

Avaunt thee, bugbear! Man, begone!
I will not die! I *must* ashore!

THE PASSENGER.

Oh, as for that, be reassured;—
one dies not midmost of Act Five.

(*Glides away.*)

PEER.

Ah, there he let it out at last;—
he was a sorry moralist.

SCENE THIRD.

(*Churchyard in a high-lying mountain parish.*)
(*A funeral is going on.   By the grave, the* PRIEST *and a
gathering of people.   The last verse of the psalm is
being sung.*   PEER GYNT *passes by on the road.*)

PEER
(*at the gate*).

Here's a countryman going the way of all flesh.
God be thanked that it isn't me.

(*Enters the churchyard.*)

THE PRIEST
(speaking beside the grave).

Now, when the soul has gone to meet its doom,
and here the dust lies, like an empty pod,—
now, my dear friends, we'll speak a word or two
about this dead man's pilgrimage on earth.

He was not wealthy, neither was he wise,
his voice was weak, his bearing was unmanly,
he spoke his mind abashed and faltering,
he scarce was master at his own fireside ;
he sidled into church, as though appealing
for leave, like other men, to take his place.

It was from Gudbrandsdale, you know, he came.
When here he settled he was but a lad ;—
and you remember how, to the very last,
he kept his right hand hidden in his pocket.

That right hand in the pocket was the feature
that chiefly stamped his image on the mind, —
and therewithal his writhing, his abashed
shrinking from notice wheresoe'er he went.

But, though he still pursued a path aloof,
and ever seemed a stranger in our midst,
you all know what he strove so hard to hide,—
the hand he muffled had four fingers only.—

I well remember, many years ago,
one morning ; there were sessions held at Lundë.
'Twas war-time, and the talk in every mouth
turned on the country's sufferings and its fate.

I stood there watching. At the table sat
the Captain, 'twixt the Bailiff[1] and the sergeants ;
lad after lad was measured up and down,
passed, and enrolled, and taken for a soldier.

---

[1] See footnote, p. 99.

The room was full, and from the green outside,
where thronged the young folks, loud the laughter rang.
   A name was called, and forth another stepped,
one pale as snow upon the glacier's edge.
They bade the youth advance; he reached the table;
we saw his right hand swaddled in a clout;—
he gasped, he swallowed, battling after words,—
but, though the Captain urged him, found no voice.
Ah yes, at last!   Then with his cheek aflame,
his tongue now failing him, now stammering fast,
he mumbled something of a scythe that slipped
by chance, and shore his finger to the skin.
   Straightway a silence fell upon the room.
Men bandied meaning glances; they made mouths;
they stoned the boy with looks of silent scorn.
He felt the hail-storm, but he saw it not.
Then up the Captain stood, the grey old man;
he spat, and pointed forth, and thundered "Go!"
   And the lad went.   On both sides men fell back,
till through their midst he had to run the gauntlet.
He reached the door; from there he took to flight;—
up, up he went,—through wood and over hillside,
up through the stone-slips, rough, precipitous.
He had his home up there among the mountains.—
   It was some six months later he came here,
with mother, and betrothed, and little child.
He leased some ground upon the high hillside,
there where the waste lands trend away towards Lomb.
He married the first moment that he could;
he built a house; he broke the stubborn soil;
he throve, as many a cultivated patch
bore witness, bravely clad in waving gold.
At church he kept his right hand in his pocket,—
but sure I am at home his fingers nine

toiled every bit as hard as others' ten.—
One spring the torrent washed it all away.

Their lives were spared.   Ruined and stripped of all,
he set to work to make another clearing;
and, ere the autumn, smoke again arose
from a new, better-sheltered, mountain farm-house.
Sheltered? From torrent—not from avalanche;
two years, and all beneath the snow lay buried.

But still the avalanche could not daunt his spirit.
He dug, and raked, and carted—cleared the ground —
and the next winter, ere the snow-blasts came,
a third time was his little homestead reared.

Three sons he had, three bright and stirring boys;
they must to school, and school was far away;—
and they must clamber where the hill-track failed,
by narrow ledges through the headlong scaur.
What did he do?   The eldest had to manage
as best he might, and, where the path was worst,
his father cast a rope round him to stay him;—
the others on his back and arms he bore.

Thus he toiled, year by year, till they were men.
Now might he well have looked for some return.
In the New World, three prosperous gentlemen
their school-going and their father have forgotten.

He was short-sighted.   Out beyond the circle
of those most near to him he nothing saw.
To him seemed meaningless as cymbals' tinkling
those words that to the heart should ring like steel.
His race, his fatherland, all things high and shining,
stood ever, to his vision, veiled in mist.

But he was humble, humble, was this man;
and since that sessions-day his doom oppressed him,
as surely as his cheeks were flushed with shame,
and his four fingers hidden in his pocket.—

Offender 'gainst his country's laws? Ay, true!
But there is one thing that the law outshineth
sure as the snow-white tent of Glittertind[1]
has clouds, like higher rows of peaks, above it.
No patriot was he. Both for church and state
a fruitless tree. But there, on the upland ridge,
in the small circle where he saw his calling,
there he was great, because he was himself.
His inborn note rang true unto the end.
His days were as a lute with muted strings.
And therefore, peace be with thee, silent warrior,
that fought the peasant's little fight, and fell!

   It is not ours to search the heart and reins;—
that is no task for dust, but for its ruler;—
yet dare I freely, firmly, speak my hope:
he scarce stands crippled now before his God!

      (*The gathering disperses.*   PEER GYNT *remains
      behind, alone.*)

           PEER.

   Now *that* is what I call Christianity!
Nothing to seize on one's mind unpleasantly.—
And the topic—immovably being oneself,—
that the pastor's homily turned upon,—
is full, in its essence, of edification.

        (*Looks down upon the grave.*)

Was it he, I wonder, that hacked through his knuckle
that day I was out hewing logs in the forest?
Who knows? If I weren't standing here with my staff
by the side of the grave of this kinsman in spirit,
I could almost believe it was I that slept,
and heard in a vision my panegyric.—

---

[1] A mountain in the Jotunheim. The name means "glittering
peak."

It's a seemly and Christianlike custom indeed
this casting a so-called memorial glance
in charity over the life that is ended.
I shouldn't at all mind accepting my verdict
at the hands of this excellent parish priest.
Ah well, I dare say I have some time left
ere the gravedigger comes to invite me to stay with him ;—
and as Scripture has it : What's best is best,—
and : Enough for the day is the evil thereof,—[1]
and further : Discount not thy funeral.—
Ah, the church, after all, is the true consoler.
I've hitherto scarcely appreciated it ;—
but now I feel clearly how blessëd it is
to be well assured upon sound authority :
Even as thou sowest thou shalt one day reap.—
One must be oneself; for oneself and one's own
one must do one's best, both in great and in small things.
If the luck goes against you, at least you've the honour
of a life carried through in accordance with principle.—
Now homewards !   Though narrow and steep the path,
though Fate to the end may be never so biting—
still old Peer Gynt will pursue his own way,
and remain what he is : poor, but virtuous ever.

(*Goes out.*)

---

[1] "Den tid den sorg"—literally, "That time that sorrow," or
"care."

SCENE FOURTH.

(*A hillside seamed by the dry bed of a torrent. A ruined mill-house beside the stream. The ground is torn up, and the whole place waste. Further up the hill, a large farm-house.*)

(*An auction is going on in front of the farm-house. There is a great gathering of people, who are drinking, with much noise.* PEER GYNT *is sitting on a rubbish-heap beside the mill.*)

PEER.

Forward and back, and it's just as far ;
out and in, and it's just as strait.—
Time wears away and the river gnaws on.
Go roundabout, the Boyg said ;—and here one must.

A MAN DRESSED IN MOURNING.

Now there is only rubbish left over.
(*Catches sight of* PEER GYNT.)
Are there strangers here too? God be with you, good
friend !

PEER.

Well met ! You have lively times here to-day.
Is't a christening junket or a wedding feast ?

THE MAN IN MOURNING.

I'd rather call it a house-warming treat ;—
the bride is laid in a wormy bed.

PEER.

And the worms are squabbling for rags and clouts.

THE MAN IN MOURNING.

That's the end of the ditty ; it's over and done.

PEER.

All the ditties end just alike ;
and they're all old together ; I knew 'em as a boy.

A LAD OF TWENTY
(*with a casting-ladle*).

Just look what a rare thing I've been buying !
In this Peer Gynt cast his silver buttons.

ANOTHER.

Look at mine, though !   The money-bag[1] bought for a halfpenny.

A THIRD.

No more, eh?   Twopence for the pedlar's pack !

PEER.

Peer Gynt?   Who was he?

THE MAN IN MOURNING.

All I know is this :
he was kinsman to Death and to Aslak the Smith.

A MAN IN GREY.

You're forgetting me, man !   Are you mad or drunk?

THE MAN IN MOURNING.

You forget that at Hegstad was a storehouse door.

[1] Literally, "the bushel." See note, p. 9.

THE MAN IN GREY.

Ay, true; but we know you were never dainty.

THE MAN IN MOURNING.

If only she doesn't give Death the slip——

THE MAN IN GREY.

Come, kinsman! A dram, for our kinship's sake!

THE MAN IN MOURNING.

To the deuce with your kinship! You're maundering in
    drink——

THE MAN IN GREY.

Oh, rubbish; blood's never so thin as all that;
one cannot but feel one's akin to Peer Gynt.
        (Goes off with him.)

PEER
(to himself).

One meets with acquaintances.

A LAD
(calls after the MAN IN MOURNING).

                Mother that's dead
will be after you, Aslak, if you wet your whistle.

PEER
(rises).

The agriculturists' saying seems scarce to hold here:
The deeper one harrows the better it smells.

A LAD
(*with a bear's skin*).

Look, the cat of the Dovrë![1]   Well, only his fell.
It was he chased the trolls out on Christmas Eve.

ANOTHER
(*with a reindeer-skull*).

Here is the wonderful reindeer that bore,
at Gendin, Peer Gynt over edge and scaur.

A THIRD
(*with a hammer*, *calls out to the* MAN IN MOURNING).

Hei, Aslak, this sledge-hammer, say, do you know it?
Was it this that you used when the devil clove the wall?

A FOURTH
(*empty-handed*).

Mads Moen, here's the invisible cloak
Peer Gynt and Ingrid flew off through the air with.

PEER.

Brandy here, boys!   I feel I'm grown old;—
I must put up to auction my rubbish and lumber!

A LAD.

What have you to sell, then?

PEER.

            A palace I have;—
it lies in the Rondë; it's solidly built.

<hr>

[1] See Appendix, p. 286.

THE LAD.

A button is bid!

PEER.

You must run to a dram.
'Twere a sin and a shame to bid anything less.

ANOTHER.

He's a jolly old boy this!
(*The bystanders crowd round him.*)

PEER

(*shouts*).

Granë,[1] my steed;

who bids?

ONE OF THE CROWD.

Where's he running?

PEER.

Why, far in the west!
Near the sunset, my lads! Ah, that courser can fly
as fast, ay, as fast as Peer Gynt could lie.

VOICES.

What more have you got?

PEER.

I've both rubbish and gold
I bought it with ruin; I'll sell it at a loss.

A LAD.

Put it up!

[1] See footnote, p. 118.

PEER.

A dream of a silver-clasped book!
That you can have for an old hook and eye.

THE LAD.

To the devil with dreams!

PEER.

Here's my Kaiserdom!
I throw it in the midst of you; scramble for it!

THE LAD.

Is the crown given in?

PEER.

Of the loveliest straw.
It will fit whoever first puts it on.
Hei, there is more yet!   An addled egg!
A madman's grey hair!   And the Prophet's beard!
All these shall be his that will show on the hillside
a post that has writ on it: Here lies your path!

THE BAILIFF[1]
(*who has come up*).

You're carrying on, my good man, so that almost
I think that your path will lead straight to the lock-up.

PEER
(*hat in hand*).

Quite likely.   But, tell me, who was Peer Gynt?

THE BAILIFF.

Oh, nonsense——

[1] See footnote, p. 99.

PEER.

Your pardon !　Most humbly I beg——!

THE BAILIFF.

Oh, he's said to have been an abominable liar——[1]

PEER.

A liar——?

THE BAILIFF.

Yes—all that was strong and great
he made believe always that *he* had done it.
But, excuse me, friend—I have other duties——
(*Goes.*)

PEER.

And where is he now, this remarkable man?

AN ELDERLY MAN.

He fared over seas to a foreign land;
it went ill with him there, as one well might foresee ;—
it's many a year now since he was hanged.

PEER.

Hanged ?　Ay, ay !　Why, I thought as much ;
our lamented Peer Gynt was himself to the last.
(*Bows.*)
Good-bye,—and best thanks for to-day's merry meeting.
(*Goes a few steps, but stops again.*)
You joyous youngsters, you comely lasses,—
shall I pay my shot with a traveller's tale ?

---

[1] "Digter"; means also "poet."

SEVERAL VOICES.

Yes; do you know any?

PEER.

Nothing more easy.—
(*He comes nearer; a look of strangeness com·s over
him.*)

I was gold-digging once in San Francisco.
There were mountebanks swarming all over the town.
One with his toes could perform on the fiddle;
another could dance a Spanish halling[1] on his knees;
a third, I was told, kept on making verses
while his brain-pan was having a hole bored right through it.
To the mountebank-meeting came also the devil;—
thought he'd try his luck with the rest of them.
His talent was this: in a manner convincing,
he was able to grunt like a flesh-and-blood pig.
He was not recognised, yet his manners[2] attracted.
The house was well filled; expectation ran high.
He stepped forth in a cloak with an ample cape to it;
man muss sich ärappiren, as the Germans say.
But under the mantle—what none suspected—
he'd managed to smuggle a real live pig.
And now he opened the representation;
the devil he pinched, and the pig gave voice.
The whole thing purported to be a fantasia
on the porcine existence, both free and in bonds;
and all ended up with a slaughter-house squeal—
whereupon the performer bowed low and retired.—
The critics discussed and appraised the affair;
the tone of the whole was attacked and defended.

---

[1] See footnote, p. 29.
In the original, "Personlighed"—personality.

Some fancied the vocal expression too thin,
while some thought the death-shriek too carefully studied ;
but all were agreed as to one thing : *qua* grunt,
the performance was grossly exaggerated.—
Now *that*, you see, came of the devil's stupidity
in not taking the measure of his public first.

> (*He bows and goes off. A puzzled silence comes
> over the crowd.*)

SCENE FIFTH.

> (*Whitsun Eve.—In the depths of the forest. To the back,
> in a clearing, is a hut with a pair of reindeer horns
> over the porch-gable.*)
> (PEER GYNT *is creeping among the undergrowth, gathering
> wild onions.*)

PEER.

Well, this is one standpoint. Where is the next ?
One should try all things and choose the best.
Well, I have done so,—beginning from Cæsar,
and downwards as far as to Nebuchadnezzar.
So I had, after all, to go through Bible history ;—
the old boy's had to take to his mother again.
After all it is written : Of the earth art thou come.—
The main thing in life is to fill one's belly.
Fill it with onions ? That's not much good ;—
I must take to cunning, and set out snares.
There's water in the beck here ; I shan't suffer thirst ;
and I count as the first 'mong the beasts after all.
When my time comes to die—as most likely it will,—
I shall crawl in under a wind-fallen tree ;

like the bear, I will heap up a leaf-mound above me,
and I'll scratch in big print on the bark of the tree :
Here rests Peer Gynt, that decent soul,
Kaiser o'er all of the other beasts.—
Kaiser ?

(*Laughs inwardly.*)

Why, you old soothsayer-humbug !
no Kaiser are you ; you are nought but an onion.
I'm going to peel you now, my good Peer !
You won't escape either by begging or howling.

(*Takes an onion and pulls off layer after layer.*)

There lies the outermost layer, all torn ;
that's the shipwrecked man on the jolly-boat's keel.
Here's the passenger layer, scanty and thin ;—
and yet in its taste there's a tang of Peer Gynt.
Next underneath is the gold-digger ego ;
the juice is all gone—if it ever had any.
This coarse-grained layer with the hardened skin
is the peltry-hunter by Hudson's Bay.
The next one looks like a crown ;—oh, thanks !
we'll throw it away without more ado.
Here's the archæologist, short but sturdy ;
and here is the Prophet, juicy and fresh.
He stinks, as the Scripture has it, of lies,
enough to bring the water to an honest man's eyes.
This layer that rolls itself softly together
is the gentleman, living in ease and good cheer.
The next one seems sick.   There are black streaks upon it ;—
black symbolises both parsons and niggers.

(*Pulls off several layers at once.*)

What an enormous number of swathings !
Isn't the kernel soon coming to light ?

(*Pulls the whole onion to pieces.*)   ˙

I'm blest if it is! To the innermost centre,
it's nothing but swathings—each smaller and smaller.—
Nature is witty!

(*Throws the fragments away.*)
The devil take brooding!
If one goes about thinking, one's apt to stumble.
Well, *I* can at any rate laugh at that danger;—
for here on all fours I am firmly planted.

(*Scratches his head.*)
A queer enough business, the whole concern!
Life, as they say, plays with cards up its sleeve;[1]
but when one snatches at them, they've disappeared,
and one grips something else,—or else nothing at all.

(*He has come near to the hut; he catches sight of it
and starts.*)

This hut? On the heath——! Ha!

(*Rubs his eyes.*)
It seems exactly
as though I had known this same building before.—
The reindeer-horns jutting above the gable!—
A mermaid, shaped like a fish from the navel!—
Lies! there's no mermaid! But nails—and planks,—
bars too, to shut out hobgoblin thoughts!—

SOLVEIG

(*singing in the hut*).

Now all is ready for Whitsun Eve.
Dearest boy of mine, far away,
comest thou soon?

---

[1] This and the following line, literally translated, run thus: "Life,
as it's called, has a fox behind its ear. But when one grasps at him,
Reynard takes to his heels." "To have a fox behind the ear" is a
proverbial expression for insincerity, double-dealing.

Is thy burden heavy,
　　take time, take time;—
I will await thee;
I promised of old.[1]

PEER

(*rises, quiet and deadly pale*).

One that's remembered,—and one that's forgot.
One that has squandered,—and one that has saved.—
Oh, earnest!—and never can the game be played o'er!
Oh, dread![2]—*here* was my Kaiserdom!

　　(*Hurries off along the wood path.*)

SCENE SIXTH.

(*Night.　A heath, with fir-trees.　A forest fire has been raging; charred tree-trunks are seen stretching for miles.　White mists here and there clinging to the earth.*)
(PEER GYNT *comes running over the heath.*)

PEER.

Ashes, fog-scuds, dust wind-driven,—
here's enough for building with!
Stench and rottenness within it;
all a whited sepulchre.
Figments, dreams, and still-born knowledge
lay the pyramid's foundation;
o'er them shall the work mount upwards,
with its step on step of falsehood.

----

[1] See footnote, p. 178.　　　　　　[2] See footnote, p. 219.

Earnest shunned, repentance dreaded,
flaunt at the apex like a scutcheon,
fill the trump of judgment with their:
Petrus Gyntus Cæsar fecit!

(*Listens.*)

What is this, like children's weeping?
Weeping, but half-way to song.—
Thread-balls [1] at my feet are rolling!—

(*Kicking at them.*)

Off with you! You block my path!

THE THREAD-BALLS
(*on the ground*).

We are thoughts;
thou shouldst have thought us;—
feet to run on
thou shouldst have given us!

PEER
(*going round about*).

I have given life to *one;*—
'twas a bungled, crook-legged thing!

THE THREAD-BALLS.

We should have soared up
like clangorous voices,—
and here we must trundle
as grey-yarn thread-balls.

PEER
(*stumbling*).

Thread-clue! You accursed scamp!
Would you trip your father's heels?

(*Flees.*)

---

[1] See Introduction, p. vi.

WITHERED LEAVES
(*flying before the wind*).

We are a watchword ;
thou shouldst have proclaimed us !
See how thy dozing
has wofully riddled us.
The worm has gnawed us
in every crevice ;
we have never twined us
like wreaths round fruitage.

PEER.

Not in vain your birth, however ;—
lie but still and serve as manure.

A SIGHING IN THE AIR.

We are songs ;
thou shouldst have sung us !—
a thousand times over
hast thou cowed us and smothered us.
Down in thy heart's pit
we have lain and waited ;—
we were never called forth.
In thy gorge be poison !

PEER.

Poison *thee*, thou foolish stave !
Had I time for verse and stuff?

(*Attempts a short cut.*)

DEWDROPS
(*dripping from the branches*).

We are tears
unshed for ever.

Ice-spears, sharp-wounding,
we could have melted.
Now the barb rankles
in the shaggy bosom ;—
the wound is closed over ;
our power is ended.

PEER.

Thanks ;—I wept in Rondë-cloisters,—
none the less they tied the tail on !

BROKEN STRAWS.

We are deeds ;
thou shouldst have achieved us !
Doubt, the throttler,
has crippled and riven us.
On the Day of Judgment
we'll come a-flock,
and tell the story,—
then woe to you !

PEER.

Rascal-tricks !   How dare you debit
what is *negative* against me ?

(*Hastens away.*)

ÅSE'S VOICE
(*far away*).

Fie, what a post-boy !
Hu, you've upset me !
Snow's newly fallen here ;—
sadly it's smirched me.—
You've driven me the wrong way.
Peer, where's the castle ?
The Fiend has misled you
with the switch from the cupboard !

PEER.

Better haste away, poor fellow !
With the devil's sins upon you,
soon you'll faint upon the hillside ;—
hard enough to bear one's own sins.

(*Runs off.*)

SCENE SEVENTH.

(*Another part of the heath.*)

PEER GYNT
(*sings*).

A sexton ! A sexton ! where are you, hounds ?
A song from braying precentor-mouths ;
around your hat-brim a mourning band ;—
my dead are many ; I must follow their biers !

(THE BUTTON-MOULDER, *with a box of tools, and a
large casting-ladle, comes from a side path.*)

THE BUTTON-MOULDER.

Well met, old gaffer !

PEER.

Good evening, friend.

THE BUTTON-MOULDER.

The man's in a hurry.   Why, where is he going ?

PEER.

To a grave-feast.

THE BUTTON-MOULDER.

Indeed?   My sight's not very good ;—
excuse me,—your name doesn't chance to be Peer?

PEER.

Peer Gynt, as the saying is.

THE BUTTON-MOULDER.

That I call luck !
It's precisely Peer Gynt I am sent for to-night.

PEER.

You're sent for?   What do you want?

THE BUTTON-MOULDER.

Why, see here ;
I'm a button-moulder.   You're to go into my ladle.

PEER.

And what to do there?

THE BUTTON-MOULDER.

To be melted up.

PEER.

To be melted?

THE BUTTON-MOULDER.

Here it is, empty and scoured.
Your grave is dug ready, your coffin bespoke.
The worms in your body will live at their ease ;—
but I have orders, without delay,
on Master's behalf to fetch in your soul.

PEER.

It can't be!   Like this, without any warning——!

THE BUTTON-MOULDER.

It's an old tradition at burials and births
to appoint in secret the day of the feast,
with no warning at all to the guest of honour.

PEER.

Ay, ay, that's true.   All my brain's awhirl.
You are—— ?

THE BUTTON-MOULDER.

Why, I told you—a button-moulder.

PEER.

I see!   A pet child has many nicknames.
So that's it, Peer; it is *there* you're to harbour!
But these, my good man, are most unfair proceedings!
I'm sure I deserve better treatment than this;—
I'm not nearly so bad as perhaps you think,—
I've done a good deal of good in the world;—
at worst you may call me a sort of a bungler,—
but certainly not an exceptional sinner.

THE BUTTON-MOULDER.

Why that is precisely the rub, my man;
you're no sinner at all in the higher sense;
that's why you're excused all the torture-pangs,
and land, like others, in the casting-ladle.

PEER.

Give it what name you please—call it ladle or pool;[1]
spruce ale and swipes, they are both of them beer.
Avaunt from me, Satan!

       [1] " Pöl," otherwise " Svovlpöl "—the sulphur pool of hell.

THE BUTTON-MOULDER.

You can't be so rude
as to take my foot for a horse's hoof?

PEER.

On horse's hoof or on fox's claws[1]—
be off; and be careful what you're about!

THE BUTTON-MOULDER.

My friend, you're making a great mistake.
We're both in a hurry, and so, to save time,
I'll explain the reason of the whole affair.
You are, with your own lips you told me so,
no sinner on the so-called heroic scale,—
scarce middling even——

PEER.

Ah, now you're beginning
to talk common sense——

THE BUTTON-MOULDER.

Just have patience a bit—
but to call you virtuous would be going too far.—

PEER.

Well, you know I have never laid claim to that.

THE BUTTON-MOULDER.

You're nor one thing nor t'other then, only so-so.
A sinner of really grandiose style
is nowadays not to be met on the highways.
It wants much more than merely to wallow in mire;
for both vigour and earnestness go to a sin.

[1] See footnote, p. 237.

PEER.

Ay, it's very true, that remark of yours;
one has to lay on, like the old Berserkers.

THE BUTTON-MOULDER.

You, friend, on the other hand, took your sin lightly.

PEER.

Only outwardly, friend, like a splash of mud.

THE BUTTON-MOULDER.

Ah, we'll soon be at one now.   The sulphur pool
is no place for you, who but plashed in the mire.

PEER.

And in consequence, friend, I can go as I came?

THE BUTTON-MOULDER.

No, in consequence, friend, I must melt you up.

PEER.

What tricks are these that you've hit upon
at home here, while I've been in foreign parts?

THE BUTTON-MOULDER.

The custom's as old as the Snake's creation;
it's designed to prevent loss of good material.
You've worked at the craft—you must know that often
a casting turns out, to speak plainly, mere dross;
the buttons, for instance, have sometimes no loop to them.
What did *you* do, then?

PEER.

Flung the rubbish away.

THE BUTTON-MOULDER.

Ah, yes; Jon Gynt was well known for a waster,
so long as he'd aught left in wallet or purse.
But Master, you see, he is thrifty, he is;
and that is why he's so well-to-do.
He flings nothing away as entirely worthless
that can be made use of as raw material.
Now, *you* were designed for a shining button
on the vest of the world; but your loop gave way;
so into the waste-box you needs must go,
and then, as they phrase it, be merged in the mass.

PEER.

You're surely not meaning to melt me up,
with Dick, Tom, and Harry,[1] into something new?

THE BUTTON-MOULDER.

That's just what I do mean, and nothing else.
We've done it already to plenty of folks.
At Kongsberg[2] they do just the same with money
that's been current so long that its stamp's worn away.

PEER.

But this is the wretchedest miserliness!
My dear good friend, let me get off free;—
a loopless button, a worn out farthing,—
what is *that* to a man in your Master's position?

THE BUTTON-MOULDER.

Oh, so long, and inasmuch as, the spirit's in one,
one always has value as so much metal.

---

[1] Literally, " With Peter and Paul."
[2] The Royal Mint is at Kongsberg, a town in southern Norway.

PEER.

No, I say! No! With both teeth and claws
I'll fight against this! Sooner anything else!

THE BUTTON-MOULDER.

But what else? Come now, be reasonable.
You know you're not airy enough for heaven——

PEER.

I'm not hard to content; I don't aim so high;—
but I won't be deprived of one doit of my Self.
Have me judged by the law in the old-fashioned way!
For a certain time place me with Him of the Hoof;—
say a hundred years, come the worst to the worst;
that, now, is a thing that one surely can bear;
for they say the torment is only moral,
so it can't after all be so pyramidal.
It is, as 'tis written, a mere transition;
and as the fox said: One waits; there comes
an hour of deliverance; one lives in seclusion,
and hopes in the meantime for happier days.—
But this other notion—to have to be merged,
like a mote, in the carcass of some outsider,—
this casting-ladle business, this Gynt-cessation,—
it stirs up my innermost soul in revolt!

THE BUTTON-MOULDER.

Bless me, my dear Peer, there is surely no need
to get so wrought up about trifles like this.
Yourself you never have been at all;—
then what does it matter, your dying right out?

PEER.

Have *I* not been——? I could almost laugh!
Peer Gynt, then, has been something else, I suppose!

No, Button-moulder, you judge in the dark.
If you could but look into my very reins,
you'd find only Peer there, and Peer all through,—
nothing else in the world, no, nor anything more.

THE BUTTON-MOULDER.

It's impossible.   Here I have got my orders.
Look, here it is written : Peer Gynt shalt thou summon.
He has set at defiance his life's design ;
clap him into the ladle with other spoilt goods.

PEER.

What nonsense !   They must mean some other person.
Is it really Peer ?   It's not Rasmus, or Jon ?

THE BUTTON-MOULDER.

It is many a day since I melted them.
So come quietly now, and don't waste my time.

PEER.

I'll be damned if I do !   Ay, 'twould be a fine thing
if it turned out to-morrow some one else was meant.
You'd better take care what you're at, my good man !
think of the onus you're taking upon you——

THE BUTTON-MOULDER.

I have it in writing——

PEER.

At least give me time !

THE BUTTON-MOULDER.

What good would that do you ?

PEER.

I'll use it to prove
that I've been myself all the days of my life ;
and that's the question that's in dispute.

THE BUTTON-MOULDER.

You'll prove it ?   And how ?

PEER.

Why, by vouchers and witnesses.

THE BUTTON-MOULDER.

I'm sadly afraid Master will not accept them.

PEER.

Impossible !   However, enough for the day[1]—!
My dear man, allow me a loan of myself;
I'll be back again shortly.   One is born only once,
and one's self, as created, one fain would stick to.
Come, are we agreed ?

THE BUTTON-MOULDER.

Very well then, so be it.
But remember, we meet at the next cross-roads.

(PEER GYNT *runs off.*)

[1] See footnote, p. 226.

SCENE EIGHTH.

(A further point on the heath.)

PEER
(running hard).

Time is money, as the scripture says.
If I only knew where the cross-roads are;—
they may be near and they may be far.
The earth burns beneath me like red-hot iron.
A witness! A witness! Oh, where shall I find one?
It's almost unthinkable here in the forest.
The world is a bungle! A wretched arrangement,
when a man must prove a right that's as patent as day!

　　(An OLD MAN, *bent with age, with a staff in his hand*
　　　and a bag on his back, is trudging in front of him.)

THE OLD MAN
(stops).

Dear, kind sir—a trifle to a houseless soul!

PEER.

Excuse me; I've got no small change in my pocket——

THE OLD MAN.

Prince Peer! Oh, to think we should meet again——!

PEER

Who are you?

THE OLD MAN.

You forget the Old Man in the Rondë?

PEER.

Why, you're never——?

THE OLD MAN.

The King of the Dovrë, my boy!

PEER.

The Dovrë-King? Really? The Dovrë-King? Speak!

THE OLD MAN.

Oh, I've come terribly down in the world——!

PEER.

Ruined?

THE OLD MAN.

Ay, plundered of every stiver.
Here am I tramping it, starved as a wolf.

PEER.

Hurrah! Such a witness doesn't grow on the trees!

THE OLD MAN.

My Lord Prince, too, has grizzled a bit since we met.

PEER.

My dear father-in-law, the years gnaw and wear one.—
Well well, a truce to all private affairs,—
and pray, above all things, no family jars.
I was then a sad madcap——

THE OLD MAN.

Oh yes; oh yes;—
His Highness was young; and what won't one do then?

But his Highness was wise in rejecting his bride ;
he saved himself thereby both worry and shame ;
for since then she's utterly gone to the bad——

PEER.

Indeed !

THE OLD MAN.

She has led a deplorable life ;[1]
and, just think,—she and Trond are now living together.

PEER.

Which Trond ?

THE OLD MAN.

Of the Valfjeld.

PEER.

It's he ?   Aha ;
it was he I cut out with the sæter-girls.

THE OLD MAN.

But my grandson has flourished—grown both stout and
    great,
and has strapping children all over the country——

PEER.

Now, my dear man, spare us this flow of words ;—
I've something quite different troubling my mind.—
I've got into rather a ticklish position,
and am greatly in need of a witness or voucher ;—
that's how you could help me best, father-in-law,
and I'll find you a trifle to drink my health with.

---

[1] " Hun gik nu for koldt vand og lud "—literally, " to live on cold
water and lye "—to live wretchedly and be badly treated.

THE OLD MAN.

You don't say so ; can I be of use to his Highness ?
You'll give me a character, then, in return ?

PEER.

Most gladly.   I'm somewhat hard pressed for cash,
and must cut down expenses in every direction.
Now hear what's the matter.   No doubt you remember
that night when I came to the Rondë a-wooing——

THE OLD MAN.

Why, of course, my Lord Prince !

PEER.

Oh, no more of the Prince !
But no matter.   You wanted, by sheer brute force,
to bias my sight, with a slit in the lens,
and to change me about from Peer Gynt to a troll.
What did *I* do then ?   I stood out against it,—
swore I would stand on no feet but my own ;
love, power, and glory at once I renounced,
and all for the sake of remaining myself.
Now this fact, you see, you must swear to in Court——

THE OLD MAN.

No, I'm blest if I can.

PEER.

Why, what nonsense is this ?

THE OLD MAN.

You surely don't want to compel me to lie?
You pulled on the troll-breeches, don't you remember,
and tasted the mead——

PEER.

Ay, you lured me seductively ;—
but I flatly declined the decisive test,
and *that* is the thing you must judge your man by.
It's the end of the ditty that all depends on.

THE OLD MAN.

But it ended, Peer, just in the opposite way.

PEER.

What rubbish is this?

THE OLD MAN.

When you left the Rondë,
you inscribed my motto upon your 'scutcheon.[1]

PEER.

What motto?

THE OLD MAN.

The potent and sundering word.

PEER.

The word?

THE OLD MAN.

That which severs the whole race of men
from the troll-folk. *Troll!   To thyself be enough!*

PEER
(*falls back a step*).

Enough!

THE OLD MAN.

And with every nerve in your body,
you've being living up to it ever since.

---

[1] Literally, " Wrote my motto behind your ear."

PEER.

What, I?   Peer Gynt?

THE OLD MAN
(*weeps*).

It's ungrateful of you!
You've lived as a troll, but have still kept it secret.
The word I taught you has shown you the way
to swing yourself up as a man of substance ;—
and now you must needs come and turn up your nose
at me and the word you've to thank for it all.

PEER.

Enough!   A hill-troll!   An egoist!
This must be all rubbish ; that's perfectly certain !

THE OLD MAN
(*pulls out a bundle of old newspapers*).

I daresay you think that we've no newspapers?
Wait; here I'll show you in red and black,[1]
how the *Bloksberg Post* eulogises you;
and the *Heklefjeld Journal* has done the same
ever since the winter you left the country.—
Do you care to read them?   You're welcome, Peer.
Here's an article, look you, signed "Stallionhoof."
And here too is one : "On Troll-Nationalism."
The writer points out and lays stress on the truth
that horns and a tail are of little importance,
so long as one has but a strip of the hide.
"Our *enough*," he concludes, "gives the hall-mark of trolldom
to man,"—and proceeds to cite you as an instance.

---

[1] Clearly the troll-substitute for "in black and white."

PEER.

A hill-troll?   I?

THE OLD MAN.

Yes, that's perfectly clear.

PEER.

Might as well have stayed quietly where I was?
Might have stopped in the Rondë in comfort and peace
Saved my trouble and toil and no end of shoe-leather?
Peer Gynt—a troll?   Why it's rubbish!   It's stuff!
Good-bye!   There's a halfpenny to buy you tobacco.

THE OLD MAN.

Nay, my good Prince Peer!

PEER.

Let me go!   You're mad,
or else doting.   Off to the hospital with you!

THE OLD MAN.

Oh, that is exactly what I'm in search of.
But, as I told you, my grandson's offspring
have become overwhelmingly strong in the land,
and they say that I only exist in books.
The saw says : One's kin are unkindest of all ;
I've found to my cost that that saying is true.
It's cruel to count as mere figment and fable——

PEER.

My dear man, there are others who share the same fate.

THE OLD MAN.

And ourselves we've no Mutual Aid Society,
no alms-box or Penny Savings Bank ;—
in the Rondë, of course, they'd be out of place.

PEER.

No, that cursed : *To thyself be enough* was the word there !

THE OLD MAN.

Oh, come now, the Prince can't complain of the word.
And if he could manage by hook or by crook——

PEER.

My man, you have got on the wrong scent entirely ;
I'm myself, as the saying goes, fairly cleaned out[1]——

THE OLD MAN.

You surely can't mean it ?   His Highness a beggar ?

PEER.

Completely.   His Highness's ego's in pawn.
And it's all your fault, you accursëd trolls !
That's what comes of keeping bad company.

THE OLD MAN.

So there came my hope toppling down from its perch again !
Good-bye !   I had best struggle on to the town——

PEER.

What would you do there ?

THE OLD MAN.

                              I will go to the theatre.
The papers are clamouring for national talents——

PEER.

Good luck on your journey ; and greet them from me.
If I can but get free, I will go the same way.

[1] Literally, "On a naked hill."

A farce I will write them, a mad and profound one ;
its name shall be : " Sic transit gloria mundi."

> (*He runs off along the road; the* OLD MAN *shouts after him.*)

SCENE NINTH.

(*At a cross-road.*)

PEER GYNT.

Now comes the pinch, Peer, as never before !
This Dovrish *Enough* has passed judgment upon you.
The vessel's a wreck ; one must float with the spars.
All else ; only not to the spoilt-goods heap !

THE BUTTON-MOULDER
(*at the cross-road*).

Well now, Peer Gynt, have you found your voucher ?

PEER.

Have we reached the cross-road ?   Well, that's short work !

THE BUTTON-MOULDER.

I can see on your face, as it were on a signboard,
the gist of the paper before I've read it.

PEER.

I got tired of the hunt ;—one might lose one's way——

THE BUTTON-MOULDER.

Yes ; and what does it lead to, after all ?

PEER.

True enough ; in the wood, and by night as well——

THE BUTTON-MOULDER.

There's an old man, though, trudging. Shall we call him
here?

PEER.

No, let him go. He is drunk, my dear fellow !

THE BUTTON-MOULDER.

But perhaps he might——

PEER.

Hush ; no—let him be !

THE BUTTON-MOULDER.

Well, shall we turn to then ?

PEER.

One question only :
What is it, at bottom, this " being oneself"?

THE BUTTON-MOULDER.

A singular question, most odd in the mouth
of a man who just now——

PEER.

Come, a straightforward answer.

THE BUTTON-MOULDER.

To be oneself is : to slay oneself.
But on you that answer is doubtless lost ;

and therefore we'll say : to stand forth everywhere
with Master's intention displayed like a signboard.

PEER.

But suppose a man never has come to know
what Master meant with him ?

THE BUTTON-MOULDER.

He must divine it.

PEER.

But how oft are divinings beside the mark,—
then one's carried *ad undas*[1] in middle career.

THE BUTTON-MOULDER.

That is certain, Peer Gynt ; in default of divining
the cloven-hoofed gentleman finds his best hook.

PEER.

This matter's excessively complicated.—
See here !   I no longer plead being myself ;—
it might not be easy to get it proven.
That part of my case I must look on as lost.
But just now, as I wandered alone o'er the heath,
I felt my conscience-shoe pinching me ;
I said to myself : After all, you're a sinner——

THE BUTTON-MOULDER.

You seem bent on beginning all over again——

PEER.

No, very far from it ; a *great* one I mean ;
not only in deeds, but in words and desires.
I've lived a most damnable life abroad——

1 So in original.

THE BUTTON-MOULDER.

Perhaps; I must ask you to show me the schedule!

PEER.

Well well, give me time; I will find out a parson,
confess with all speed, and then bring you his voucher.

THE BUTTON-MOULDER.

Ay, if you can bring me that, then it is clear
you escape this business of the casting-ladle.
But Peer, I'd my orders——

PEER.

                    The paper is old;
it dates no doubt from a long past period;—
at one time I lived with disgusting slackness,
went playing the prophet, and trusted in Fate.
Well, may I try?

THE BUTTON-MOULDER.

          But——!

PEER.

                    My dear fellow,
I'm sure you can't have so much to do.
Here, in this district, the air is so bracing,
it adds an ell to the people's ages.
Recollect what the Justedal parson wrote:
"It's seldom that any one dies in this valley."

THE BUTTON-MOULDER.

To the next cross-roads then; but not a step further.

PEER.

A priest I must catch, if it be with the tongs.
(*He starts running.*)

SCENE TENTH.

(*A heather-clad hillside with a path following the windings
of the ridge.*)

PEER.

This may come in useful in many ways,
said Esben as he picked up a magpie's wing.
Who could have thought one's account of sins
would come to one's aid on the last night of all?
Well, whether or no, it's a ticklish business;
a move from the frying-pan[1] into the fire;—
but then there's a proverb of well-tried validity
which says that as long as there's life there's hope.

(A LEAN PERSON, *in a priest's cassock, kilted-up
high, and with a birding-net over his shoulder,
comes hurrying along the ridge.*)

PEER.

Who goes there? A priest with a fowling-net!
Hei, hop! I'm the spoilt child of fortune indeed!
Good evening, Herr Pastor! the path is bad——

THE LEAN ONE.

Ah yes; but what wouldn't one do for a soul?

[1] Literally, "the ashes."

PEER.

Aha! then there's some one bound heavenwards?

THE LEAN ONE.

No;
I hope he is taking a different road.

PEER.

May I walk with Herr Pastor a bit of the way?

THE LEAN ONE.

With pleasure; I'm partial to company.

PEER.

I should like to consult you——

THE LEAN ONE.

Heraus![1] Go ahead!

PEER.

You see here before you a good sort of man.
The laws of the state I have strictly observed,
have made no acquaintance with fetters or bolts;—
but it happens at times that one misses one's footing
and stumbles——

THE LEAN ONE.

Ah yes; that occurs to the best of us.

PEER.

Now these trifles you see——

[1] So in original.

THE LEAN ONE.

Only trifles?

PEER.

Yes ;
from sinning *en gros* [1] I have ever refrained.

THE LEAN ONE.

Oh then, my dear fellow, pray leave me in peace ;—
I'm not the person you seem to think me.—
You look at my fingers?   What see you in them?

PEER.

A nail-system somewhat extremely developed.

THE LEAN ONE.

And now?   You are casting a glance at my feet?

PEER

(*pointing*).

That's a natural hoof?

THE LEAN ONE.

So I flatter myself.

PEER

(*raises his hat*).

I'd have taken my oath you were simply a parson ;
and I find I've the honour——.   Well, best is best ;--
when the hall door stands wide,—shun the kitchen way;
when the king's to be met with,—avoid the lackey.

[1] So in original.

THE LEAN ONE.

Your hand! You appear to be free from prejudice.
Say on then, my friend; in what way can I serve you?
Now you mustn't ask me for wealth or power;
I couldn't supply them although I should hang for it.
You can't think how slack the whole business is;—
transactions have dwindled most pitiably.
Nothing doing in souls; only now and again
a stray one——

PEER.

The race has improved so remarkably?

THE LEAN ONE.

No, just the reverse; it's sunk shamefully low;—
the majority end in a casting-ladle.

PEER.

Ah yes—I have heard that ladle mentioned;
in fact, 'twas the cause of my coming to you.

THE LEAN ONE.

Speak out!

PEER.

If it were not too much to ask,
I should like——

THE LEAN ONE.

A harbour of refuge? eh?

PEER.

You've guessed my petition before I have asked.
You tell me the business is going awry;
so I daresay you will not be over-particular.

THE LEAN ONE.

But, my dear——

PEER.

My demands are in no way excessive.
I shouldn't insist on a salary;
but treatment as friendly as things will permit.

THE LEAN ONE.

A fire in your room?

PEER.

Not too much fire;—and chiefly
the power of departing in safety and peace,—
the right, as the phrase goes, of freely withdrawing
should an opening offer for happier days.

THE LEAN ONE.

My dear friend, I vow I'm sincerely distressed;
but you cannot imagine how many petitions
of similar purport good people send in
when they're quitting the scene of their earthly activity.

PEER.

But now that I think of my past career,
I feel I've an absolute claim to admission——

THE LEAN ONE.

'Twas but trifles, you said——

PEER.

In a certain sense;—
but, now I remember, I've trafficked in slaves—- -

THE LEAN ONE.

There are men that have trafficked in wills and souls,
but who bungled it so that they failed to get in.

PEER.

I've shipped Bramah-figures in plenty to China.

THE LEAN ONE.

Mere fustian again !   Why, we laugh at such things.
There are people that ship off far gruesomer figures
in sermons, in art, and in literature—
yet have to stay out in the cold——

PEER.

Ah, but then,
do you know—I once went and set up as prophet !

THE LEAN ONE.

In foreign parts ?   Humbug !   Why, most people's *sehen
ins Blaue*[1] ends in the casting-ladle.
If you've no more than that to rely upon,
with the best of goodwill, I can't possibly house you.

PEER.

But hear this :   In a shipwreck—I clung to a boat's keel,—
and it's written : A drowning man grasps at a straw,—
furthermore it is written : You're nearest yourself,—
so I half-way divested a cook of his life.

THE LEAN ONE.

It were all one to me if a kitchen-maid
you had half-way divested of something else.

_____

[1] So in original.

What sort of stuff is this half-way jargon,
saving your presence?　Who, think you, would care
to throw away dearly-bought fuel in times
like these on such spiritless rubbish as this?
There now, don't be enraged; 'twas your sins that I
　　scoffed at;
and excuse my speaking my mind so bluntly.—
Come, my dearest friend, banish this stuff from your head,[1]
and get used to the thought of the casting-ladle.
What would you gain if I lodged you and boarded you?
Consider; I know you're a sensible man.
Well, you'd keep your memory; that's so far true;—
but the retrospect o'er recollection's domain
would be, both for heart and for intellect,
what the Swedes call "Mighty poor sport"[2] indeed.
You have nothing either to howl or to smile about,
no cause for rejoicing nor yet for despair,
nothing to make you feel hot or cold;
only a sort of a something to fret over.

PEER.

It is written: It's never so easy to know
where the shoe is tight that one isn't wearing.

THE LEAN ONE.

Very true; I have—praise be to so-and-so!—
no occasion for more than a single odd shoe.
But it's lucky we happened to speak of shoes;
it reminds me that I must be hurrying on;—
I'm after a roast that I hope will prove fat;
so I really mustn't stand gossiping here.—

---

[1] Literally, "knock out that tooth."
[2] "Bra litet rolig."

PEER.

And may one inquire, then, what sort of sin-diet
the man has been fattened on?

THE LEAN ONE.

           I understand
he has been himself both by night and by day,
and that, after all, is the principal point.

PEER.

Himself? Then do such folks belong to your parish?

THE LEAN ONE.

That depends; the door, at least, stands ajar for them.
Remember, in two ways a man can be
himself—there's a right and wrong side to the jacket.
You know they have lately discovered in Paris
a way to take portraits by help of the sun.
One can either produce a straightforward picture,
or else what is known as a negative one.
In the latter the lights and the shades are reversed,
and they're apt to seem ugly to commonplace eyes;
but for all that the likeness is latent in them,
and all you require is to bring it out.
If, then, a soul shall have pictured itself
in the course of its life by the negative method,
the plate is not therefore entirely cashiered,—
but without more ado they consign it to me.
I take it in hand, then, for further treatment,
and by suitable methods effect its development.
I steam it, I dip it, I burn it, I scour it,
with sulphur and other ingredients like that,
till the image appears which the plate was designed for,—

that, namely, which people call positive.
But if one, like you, has smudged himself out,
neither sulphur nor potash avails in the least.

PEER.

I see; one must come to you black as a raven
to turn out a white ptarmigan?   Pray what's the name
inscribed 'neath the negative counterfeit
that you're now to transfer to the positive side?

THE LEAN ONE.

The name's Peter[1] Gynt.

PEER.

Peter Gynt?   Indeed?
Is Herr Gynt himself?

THE LEAN ONE.

Yes, he vows he is.

PEER.

Well, he's one to be trusted, that same Herr Peter.

THE LEAN ONE.

You know him, perhaps?

PEER.

Oh yes, after a fashion;—
one knows all sorts of people.

THE LEAN ONE.

I'm pressed for time;
where saw you him last?

[1] So in original.

PEER.

It was down at the Cape.

THE LEAN ONE.

Di Buona Speranza?

PEER.

Just so; but he sails
very shortly again, if I'm not mistaken.

THE LEAN ONE.

I must hurry off then without delay.
I only hope I may catch him in time!
That Cape of Good Hope—I could never abide it;—
it's ruined by missionaries from Stavanger.

(*He rushes off southwards.*)

PEER.

The stupid hound!   There he takes to his heels
with his tongue lolling out.   He'll be finely sold.
It delights me to humbug an ass like that.
He to give himself airs, and to lord it forsooth!
He's a mighty lot, truly, to swagger about!
He'll scarcely grow fat at his present trade;—
he'll soon drop from his perch with his whole apparatus.—
Hm, *I'm* not over-safe in the saddle either;
I'm expelled, one may say, from self-owning nobility.[1]

(*A shooting star is seen; he nods after it.*)

[1] "*Selvejer*-Adlen."   "Selvejer" (literally, "self-owner") means a
freeholder, as opposed to a "husmand" or tenant.   There is of course
a play upon words in the original.

Bear all hail from Peer Gynt, Brother Starry-Flash !
To flash forth, to go out, and be naught at a gulp—

> (*Pulls himself together as though in terror, and*
> *goes deeper in among the mists; stillness for*
> *awhile; then he cries:*)

Is there no one, no one in all the turmoil,—
in the void no one, no one in heaven—!

> (*He comes forward again further down, throws his*
> *hat upon the ground, and tears at his hair.*
> *By degrees a stillness comes over him.*)

So unspeakably poor, then, a soul can go
back to nothingness, into the grey of the mist.
Thou beautiful earth, be not angry with me
that I trampled thy grasses to no avail.
Thou beautiful sun, thou hast squandered away
thy glory of light in an empty hut.
There was no one within it to hearten and warm ;—
the owner, they tell me, was never at home.
Beautiful sun and beautiful earth,
you were foolish to bear and give light to my mother.
The spirit is niggard and nature lavish ;
and dearly one pays for one's birth with one's life.—
I will clamber up high, to the dizziest peak ;
I will look once more on the rising sun,
gaze till I'm tired o'er the promised land ;
then try to get snowdrifts piled up over me.
They can write above them : " Here *No One* lies buried ; "
and afterwards,—then——!   Let things go as they can.

CHURCH-GOERS

(*singing on the forest path*).

Oh, morning thrice blessèd,
when the tongues of God's kingdom

struck the earth like to flaming steel !
from the earth to His dwelling
now the heirs' song ascendeth
in the tongue of the kingdom of God.

PEER

(*crouches as in terror*).

Never look there ! *there* all's desert and waste.—
I fear I was dead long before I died.

(*Tries to slink in among the bushes, but comes upon
the cross-roads.*)

THE BUTTON-MOULDER.

Good morning, Peer Gynt !   Where's the list of your sins ?

PEER.

Do you think that I haven't been whistling and shouting
as hard as I could ?

THE BUTTON-MOULDER.

And met no one at all ?

PEER.

Not a soul but a tramping photographer.

THE BUTTON-MOULDER.

Well, the respite is over.

PEER.

Ay, everything's over.
The owl smells the daylight.   Just list to the hooting !

THE BUTTON-MOULDER.

It's the matin-bell ringing——

PEER
(*pointing*).

What's that shining yonder ?

THE BUTTON-MOULDER.

Only light from a hut.

PEER.

And that wailing sound——?

THE BUTTON-MOULDER.

But a woman singing.

PEER.

Ay, there—there I'll find
the list of my sins——

THE BUTTON-MOULDER
(*seizing him*).

Set your house in order !
(*They have come out of the underwood, and are standing
near the hut. Day is dawning.*)

PEER.

Set my house in order? It's there ! Away !
Get you gone ! Though your ladle were huge as a coffin,
it were too small, I tell you, for me and my sins !

THE BUTTON-MOULDER.

Well, to the third cross-road, Peer ; but then——!
(*Turns aside and goes.*)

PEER
(*approaches the hut*).

Forward and back, and it's just as far.
Out and in, and it's just as strait.
(*Stops.*)

No !—like a wild, an unending lament,
is the thought: to come back, to go in, to go home.
     (Takes a few steps on, but stops again.)
Round about, said the Boyg !
     (Hears singing in the hut.)
          Ah no; this time at least
right through, though the path may be never so strait !

     (He runs towards the hut; at the same moment
     SOLVEIG *appears in the doorway, dressed for*
     church, with a psalm-book wrapped in a kerchief,
     and a staff in her hand. She stands there erect
     and mild.)

PEER
(flings himself down on the threshold).

Hast thou doom for a sinner, then speak it forth !

SOLVEIG.

He is here ! He is here ! Oh, to God be the praise !
     (Stretches out her arms as though groping for him.)

PEER.

Cry out all my sins and my trespasses !

SOLVEIG.

In nought hast thou sinned, oh my own only boy.
     (Gropes for him again, and finds him.)

THE BUTTON-MOULDER
(behind the house).

The sin-list, Peer Gynt?

PEER.

Cry aloud my crime !

SOLVEIG

(*sits down beside him*).

Thou hast made all my life as a beautiful song.
Blessëd be thou that at last thou hast come !
Blessëd, thrice blessëd our Whitsun-morn meeting !

PEER.

Then I am lost !

SOLVEIG.

There is one that rules all things.

PEER

(*laughs*).

Lost !   Unless thou canst answer riddles.

SOLVEIG.

Tell me them.

PEER.

Tell them !   Come on !   To be sure !
Canst thou tell where Peer Gynt has been since we parted ?

SOLVEIG.

Been?

PEER.

With his destiny's seal on his brow ;
been, as in God's thought he first sprang forth !
Canst thou tell me ?   If not, I must get me home,—
go down to the mist-shrouded regions.

SOLVEIG

(*smiling*).

Oh, that riddle is easy.

PEER.

Then tell what thou knowest!
Where was I, as myself, as the whole man, the true man?
where was I, with God's sigil upon my brow?

SOLVEIG.

In my faith, in my hope, and in my love.[1]

PEER

(*starts back*).

What sayest thou——? Peace! These are juggling words.
Thou art mother thyself to the man that's there.

SOLVEIG.

Ay, that I am; but who is his father?
Surely he that forgives at the mother's prayer.

PEER

(*a light shines in his face; he cries:*)

My mother; my wife; oh, thou innocent woman!—
in thy love—oh, there hide me, hide me!

(*Clings to her and hides his face in her lap. A long silence. The sun rises.*)

---

[1] "I min Tro, i mit Haab og i min Kjærlighed."

We have entirely sacrificed the metre of the line, feeling it impossible to mar its simplicity by any padding. "Kjærlighed" also means "charity," in the biblical sense.

SOLVEIG

(*sings softly*).

Sleep thou, dearest boy of mine!
I will cradle thee, I will watch thee——

The boy has been sitting on his mother's lap.
They two have been playing all the life-day long.

The boy has been resting at his mother's breast
all the life-day long.   God's blessing on my joy!

The boy has been lying close in to my heart
all the life-day long.   He is weary now.

Sleep thou, dearest boy of mine!
I will cradle thee, I will watch thee.

THE BUTTON-MOULDER'S VOICE

(*behind the house*).

We'll meet at the last cross-road again, Peer;
and *then* we'll see whether——; I say no more.

SOLVEIG

(*sings louder in the full daylight*).

I will cradle thee, I will watch thee;
Sleep and dream thou, dear my boy!

ERRATA.

Page 22, line 6 from top, *for* " I must be down " *read* "I must down."

Page 61, line 2 from bottom, *for* "elling" *read* " telling."

Page 255, last line, *for* " being " *read* " been."

APPENDIX.

———•◉•———

[THE stories of Peer Gynt and Gudbrand Glesnë both occur in Asbjörnsen's " Reindeer-hunting in the Rondë Hills " (*Norske Huldre-Eventyr og Folkesagn*, Christiania, 1848). They are told by the peasant guides or gillies who accompany a shooting party into the mountains—the first by Peer Fugleskjelle, the second by Thor Ulvsvolden. Our translation of " Peer Gynt " is based on Mr. H. L. Brækstad's version, published in *Round the Yule Log*, London, 1881.]

PEER GYNT.

IN the old days there lived in Kvam a hunter, whose name was Peer Gynt. He was always up in the mountains shooting bears and elks ; for in those days there were more forests on the mountains to harbour such wild beasts. One time, late in the autumn, long after the cattle had been driven home, Peer set out for the hills. Every one had left the uplands except three sæter-girls. When Peer came up towards Hövring, where he was to pass the night in a sæter, it was so dark that he could not see his fist before him, and the dogs fell to barking and baying so that it was quite uncanny. All of a sudden he ran against something, and when he put his hand out he felt it was cold and slippery and big. Yet he did not seem to have got off the road, so he couldn't think what this could be ; but unpleasant it was at any rate.

"Who is it ?" asked Peer, for he felt it moving.

18*

"Oh, it's the Boyg,"[1] was the answer.

Peer was no wiser for this, but skirted along it for a bit, thinking that somewhere he must be able to pass. Suddenly he ran against something again, and when he put out his hand, it too was big, and cold, and slippery.

"Who is it?" asked Peer Gynt.

"Oh, it's the Boyg," was the answer again.

"Well, straight or crooked, you'll have to let me pass," said Peer; for he understood that he was walking in a ring, and that the Boyg had curled itself round the sæter. Thereupon it shifted a little, so that Peer got past. When he came inside the sæter, it was no lighter there than outside. He was feeling along the wall for a place to hang up his gun and his bag; but as he was groping his way forward he again felt something cold, and big, and slippery.

"Who is it?" shouted Peer.

"Oh, it's the great Boyg," was the answer. Wherever he put his hands out or tried to get past, he felt the Boyg encircling him.

"It's not very pleasant to be here," thought Peer, "since this Boyg is both out and in; but I think I can make short work of the nuisance."

So he took his gun and went out again, groping his way till he found the creature's head.

"What are you?" asked Peer.

"Oh, I am the big Boyg from Etnedale," said the Troll-Monster. Peer did not lose a moment, but fired three shots right into its head.

"Fire another," said the Boyg. But Peer knew better; if he had fired another shot, the bullet would have rebounded against himself.

Thereupon Peer and his dogs took hold of the Troll-Monster and dragged him out, so that they could get into the sæter. Meanwhile there was jeering and laughing in all the hills around.

"Peer Gynt dragged hard, but the dogs dragged harder," said a voice.

[1] See footnote, p. xiv.

Next morning he went out stalking. When he came out on the uplands he saw a girl, who was calling some sheep up a hillside. But when he came to the place the girl was gone and the sheep too, and he saw nothing but a great flock of bears.

"Well, I never saw bears in a flock before," thought Peer to himself. When he came nearer, they had all disappeared except one.

> "Look after your pig :
> Peer Gynt is out
> with his gun so big,"[1]

shouted a voice over in a hillock.

"Oh, it'll be a bad business for Peer, but not for my pig ; for he hasn't washed himself to-day," said another voice in the hill. Peer washed his hands with the water he had, and shot the bear. There was more laughter and jeering in the hill.

"You should have looked after your pig !" cried a voice.

"I didn't remember he had a water-jug between his legs," answered the other.

Peer skinned the bear and buried the carcass among the stones, but the head and the hide he took with him. On his way home he met a fox.

"Look at my lamb, how fat it is," said a voice in a hill.

"Look at that gun[2] of Peer's, how high it is," said a voice in another hill, just as Peer took aim and shot the fox. He skinned the fox and took the skin with him, and when he came to the sæter he put the heads on the wall outside, with their jaws gaping. Then he lighted a fire and put a pot on to boil some soup, but the chimney smoked so terribly that he could scarcely keep his eyes open, and so he had to set wide a small window. Suddenly a Troll came and poked his nose in through the window; it was so long that it reached across the room to the fireplace.

---

[1] Literally, "with his tail." A gun loosely slung over the shoulder bears a certain resemblance to a tail sticking up in the air.

[2] Literally, "tail."

" Here's a proper snout for you to see," said the Troll.

"And here's proper soup for you to taste," said Peer Gynt; and he poured the whole potful of soup over the Troll's nose. The Troll ran away howling; but in all the hills around there was jeering and laughing and voices shouting—

" Soup-snout Gyri! Soup-snout Gyri!"

All was quiet now for a while; but before long there was a great noise and hubbub outside again. Peer looked out and saw that there was a cart there, drawn by bears. They hoisted up the Troll-Monster, and carted him away into the mountain. Just then a bucket of water came down the chimney and put out the fire, so that Peer was left in the dark. Then a jeering and laughing began in all the corners of the room, and a voice said—

" It'll go no better with Peer now than with the sæter-girls at Vala."

Peer made up the fire again, took his dogs with him, shut up the house, and set off northward to the Vala sæter, where the three girls were. When he had gone some distance he saw such a glare of light that it seemed to him the sæter must be on fire. Just then he came across a pack of wolves; some of them he shot, and some he knocked on the head. When he came to the Vala sæter he found it pitch dark; there was no sign of any fire; but there were four strangers in the house carrying on with the sæter-girls. They were four Hill-Trolls, and their names were Gust of Værö, Tron of the Valfjeld, Tjöstöl Aabakken, and Rolf Eldförpungen. Gust of Værö was standing at the door to keep watch, while the others were in with the girls courting. Peer fired at Gust, but missed him, and Gust ran away. When Peer came inside he found the Trolls carrying on desperately with the girls. Two of the girls were terribly frightened and were saying their prayers, but the third, who was called Mad Kari, wasn't afraid; she said they might come there for all she cared; she would like to see what stuff there was in such fellows. But when the Trolls found that Peer was in the room they began to howl, and told Eldförpungen to make up the fire. At that instant the dogs set upon Tjöstöl and pulled him over on his back into the fireplace, so that the ashes and sparks flew up all round him.

"Did you see my snakes, Peer?" asked Tron of the Valfjeld
—that was what he called the wolves.

"You shall go the same way as your snakes," said Peer, and
shot him ; and then he killed Aabakken with the butt-end of his
rifle. Eldförpungen had escaped up the chimney. After this
Peer took the girls back to their homes, for they didn't dare to
stay any longer up at the sæter.

Shortly before Christmas-time Peer set out again. He had
heard of a farm on the Dovrefjeld which was invaded by such a
number of Trolls every Christmas-eve that the people of the
farm had to turn out and get shelter with some of their neighbours. He was anxious to go there, for he was very keen upon
the Trolls. He dressed himself in some old ragged clothes,
and took with him a tame white bear that he had, as well as an
awl, some pitch, and waxed twine. When he came to the farm
he went in and begged for houseroom.

"God help us!" said the farmer; "we can't put you up.
We have to clear out of the house ourselves, for every blessëd
Christmas-eve the whole place is full of Trolls."

But Peer Gynt said he thought he should be able to clear
the house of Trolls ; and then he got leave to stay, and they
gave him a pig's skin into the bargain. The bear lay down
behind the fireplace, and Peer took out his awl, and pitch, and
twine, and set to making a big shoe, that took the whole pig's
skin. He put a strong rope in for laces, so that he could pull
the shoe tight together at the top ; and he had a couple of
handspikes ready.

All of a sudden the Trolls came, with a fiddle and a fiddler ;
some began dancing, while others fell to eating the Christmas
fare on the table ; some fried bacon, and some fried frogs and
toads, and other disgusting things : these were the Christmas
dainties they had brought with them. In the meantime some of
the Trolls found the shoe Peer had made ; they thought it must
be for a very big foot. Then they all wanted to try it on; and
when each of them had put a foot into it, Peer tightened the
rope, shoved one of the handspikes into it, and twisted it up till
they were all stuck fast in the shoe.

Just then the bear put his nose out and smelt the fry.

"Will you have a sausage, white pussy?" said one of the Trolls, and threw a red-hot frog right into the bear's jaws.

"Claw and smite, Bruin!" said Peer Gynt.

And then the bear got into such a rage that he rushed at the Trolls and smote and clawed them all, and Peer Gynt took the other handspike and hammered away at them as if he wanted to beat their brains out. So the Trolls had to clear out, and Peer stayed and enjoyed himself on the Christmas cheer the whole feast-time. After that the Trolls were not heard of again for many years. The farmer had a light-coloured mare, and Peer advised him to breed from her, and let her foals in their turn run and breed among the hills there.

Many years afterwards, about Christmas-time, the farmer was out in the forest cutting wood for the feast-time, when a Troll came towards him and shouted—

"Have you got that big white pussy of yours yet?"

"Yes, she's at home behind the stove," said the farmer; "and she's got seven kittens now, much bigger and fiercer than herself."

"We'll never come to you any more, then," shouted the Troll.

"That Peer Gynt was a strange one," said Anders. "He was such an out-and-out tale-maker and yarn-spinner, you couldn't have helped laughing at him. He always made out that he himself had been mixed up in all the stories that people said had happened in the olden times."

GUDBRAND GLESNË.

"There was a hunter in the West-Hills," said Thor Ulvs-volden, "called Gudbrand Glesnë. He was married to the grandmother of the lad you saw at the sæter yesterday evening, and a first-rate hunter they say he was. One autumn he came across a huge buck. He shot at it, and from the way it fell he couldn't tell but that it was stone dead. So he went up to it, and, as one often does, seated himself astride on its back, and was just drawing his knife to cleave the neck-bone from the skull. But no sooner had he sat down than up it jumped, threw its horns back, and jammed him down between them, so that he was fixed as in an arm-chair. Then it rushed away; for the bullet had only grazed the beast's head, so that it had fallen in a swoon. Never any man had such a ride[1] as that Gudbrand had. Away they went in the teeth of the wind, over the ugliest glaciers and moraines. Then the beast dashed along the Gjende-edge; and now Gudbrand prayed to the Lord, for he thought he would never see sun or moon again. But at last the reindeer took to the water and swam straight across with the hunter on its back. By this time he had got his knife drawn, and the moment the buck set foot on shore, he plunged it into its neck, and it dropped dead. But you may be sure Gudbrand Glesnë wouldn't have taken that ride again, not for all the riches in the world."

"I have heard a story like that in England, about a deer-stalker that became a deer-rider," said Sir Tottenbroom.[2]

"Bliecher, in Jutland, tells a similar one," I said.

"But what sort of a place was this Gjender-edge you spoke of, Thor?" he interrupted me.

"Gjende-edge, you mean?" asked Thor. "It's the ridge[3] of a mountain lying between the Gjende-lakes, and so horribly narrow and steep that if you stand on it and drop a stone from each hand, they will roll down into the lakes, one on each side. The reindeer-hunters go over it in fine weather, otherwise it's impassable; but there was a devil of a fellow up in Skiager—Ole Storebråten was his name—who went over it carrying a full-sized reindeer on his shoulders."

"How high is it above the lakes?" asked Sir Tottenbroom.

"Oh, it's not nearly so high as the Rondë-hills," said Thor. "But it's over seven hundred ells high."

[1] "Skyds"—conveyance.
[2] An English sportsman who accompanies Asbjörnsen on his rambles.
[3] "Rygge"—back-bone, *arête*.

THE WALTER SCOTT PRESS, NEWCASTLE-ON-TYNE.

IBSEN'S FAMOUS PROSE DRAMAS.

EDITED BY WILLIAM ARCHER.

Complete in Five Vols. Crown 8vo, Cloth, Price 3/6 each.
Set of Five Vols., in Case, 17/6; in Half Morocco, in Case, 32/6.

"We seem at last to be shown men and women as they are; and at first it is more than we can endure. . . . All Ibsen's characters speak and act as if they were hypnotised, and under their creator's imperious demand to reveal themselves. There never was such a mirror held up to nature before: it is too terrible. . . . Yet we must return to Ibsen, with his remorseless surgery, his remorseless electric-light, until we, too, have grown strong and learned to face the naked—if necessary, the flayed and bleeding—reality."—SPEAKER (London).

VOL. I. "A DOLL'S HOUSE," "THE LEAGUE OF YOUTH," and "THE PILLARS OF SOCIETY." With Portrait of the Author, and Biographical Introduction by WILLIAMARCHER.

VOL. II. "GHOSTS," "AN ENEMY OF THE PEOPLE," and "THE WILD DUCK." With an Introductory Note.

VOL. III. "LADY INGER OF ÖSTRÅT," "THE VIKINGS AT HELGELAND," "THE PRETENDERS." With an Introductory Note and Portrait of Ibsen.

VOL. IV. "EMPEROR AND GALILEAN." With an Introductory Note by WILLIAM ARCHER.

VOL. V. "ROSMERSHOLM," "THE LADY FROM THE SEA," "HEDDA GABLER." Translated by WILLIAM ARCHER. With an Introductory Note.

The sequence of the plays *in each volume* is chronological; the complete set of volumes comprising the dramas thus presents them in chronological order.

"The art of prose translation does not perhaps enjoy a very high literary status in England, but we have no hesitation in numbering the present version of Ibsen, so far as it has gone (Vols. I. and II.), among the very best achievements, in that kind, of our generation."—*Academy.*

"We have seldom, if ever, met with a translation so absolutely idiomatic."—*Glasgow Herald.*

LONDON: WALTER SCOTT, LIMITED, 24 WARWICK LANE.

The Contemporary Science Series.

EDITED BY HAVELOCK ELLIS.

Crown 8vo, Cloth, 3s. 6d. per vol. ; Half Morocco, 6s. 6d.

I. THE EVOLUTION OF SEX. By Professor PATRICK GEDDES and J. ARTHUR THOMSON. With 90 Illustrations. Second Edition.

"The authors have brought to the task—as indeed their names guarantee —a wealth of knowledge, a lucid and attractive method of treatment, and a rich vein of picturesque language."—*Nature.*

II. ELECTRICITY IN MODERN LIFE. By G. W. DE TUNZELMANN. With 88 Illustrations.

"A clearly-written and connected sketch of what is known about electricity and magnetism, the more prominent modern applications, and the principles on which they are based."—*Saturday Review.*

III. THE ORIGIN OF THE ARYANS. By Dr. ISAAC TAYLOR. Illustrated. Second Edition.

"Canon Taylor is probably the most encyclopædic all-round scholar now living. His new volume on the Origin of the Aryans is a first-rate example of the excellent account to which he can turn his exceptionally wide and varied information . . . Masterly and exhaustive."—*Pall Mall Gazette.*

IV. PHYSIOGNOMY AND EXPRESSION. By P. MANTEGAZZA. Illustrated.

"Professor Mantegazza is a writer full of life and spirit, and the natural attractiveness of his subject is not destroyed by his scientific handling of it." —*Literary World* (Boston).

V. EVOLUTION AND DISEASE. By J. B. SUTTON, F.R.C.S. With 135 Illustrations.

"The work is of special value to professional men, yet educated persons generally will find much in it which it is both interesting and important to know."—*The Scottish Weekly.*

VI. THE VILLAGE COMMUNITY. By G. L. GOMME. Illustrated.

"His book will probably remain for some time the best work of reference for facts bearing on those traces of the village community which have not been effaced by conquest, encroachment, and the heavy hand of Roman law." —*Scottish Leader.*

VII. THE CRIMINAL. By HAVELOCK ELLIS. Illustrated.

"An ably written, an instructive, and a most entertaining book."—*Law Quarterly Review.*

London : WALTER SCOTT, LIMITED, 24 Warwick Lane.

The Contemporary Science Series—continued.

VIII. SANITY AND INSANITY. By Dr. CHARLES MERCIER. Illustrated.

"Taken as a whole, it is the brightest book on the physical side of mental science published in our time."—*Pall Mall Gazette.*

IX. HYPNOTISM. By Dr. ALBERT MOLL. Second Edition.

"Marks a step of some importance in the study of some difficult physiological and psychological problems which have not yet received much attention in the scientific world of England."—*Nature.*

X. MANUAL TRAINING. By Dr. C. M. WOODWARD, Director of the Manual Training School, St. Louis. Illustrated.

"There is no greater authority on the subject than Professor Woodward."—*Manchester Guardian.*

XI. THE SCIENCE OF FAIRY TALES. By E. SIDNEY HARTLAND.

"Mr. Hartland's book will win the sympathy of all earnest students, both by the knowledge it displays, and by a thorough love and appreciation of his subject, which is evident throughout."—*Spectator.*

XII. PRIMITIVE FOLK. By ELIE RECLUS.

"For an introduction to the study of the questions of property, marriage, government, religion,—in a word, to the evolution of society,—this little volume will be found most convenient."—*Scottish Leader.*

XIII. THE EVOLUTION OF MARRIAGE. By Professor LETOURNEAU.

"Among the distinguished French students of sociology, Professor Letourneau has long stood in the first rank. He approaches the great study of man free from bias and shy of generalisations. To collect, scrutinise, and appraise facts is his chief business."—*Science.*

XIV. BACTERIA AND THEIR PRODUCTS. By Dr. G. SIMS WOODHEAD. Illustrated.

"An excellent summary of the present state of knowledge of the subject."—*Lancet.*

XV. EDUCATION AND HEREDITY. By J. M. GUYAU.

"It is a sign of the value of this book that the natural impulse on arriving at its last page is to turn again to the first, and try to gather up and co-ordinate some of the many admirable truths it presents."—*Anti-Jacobin.*

XVI. THE MAN OF GENIUS. By Professor LOMBROSO. Illustrated.

"By far the most comprehensive and fascinating collection of facts and generalisations concerning genius which has yet been brought together."—*Journal of Mental Science.*

XVII. THE GRAMMAR OF SCIENCE. By Professor KARL PEARSON. Illustrated.

XVIII. PROPERTY: ITS ORIGIN AND DEVELOPMENT. By CH. LETOURNEAU, General Secretary to the Anthropological Society, Paris, and Professor in the School of Anthropology, Paris.

An ethnological account of the beginnings of property among animals, of its communistic stages among primitive races, and of its later individualistic developments, together with a brief sketch of its probable evolution in the future.

London : WALTER SCOTT, LIMITED, 24 Warwick Lane.

XIX. VOLCANOES, PAST AND PRESENT. By Professor EDWARD HULL, LL.D., F.R.S.

This volume will treat of the form and structure of volcanic mountains, the materials of which they are composed ; of volcanic islands ; of tertiary volcanic rocks of the British Isles, Europe, and America ; recently extinct or dormant volcanic areas ; Etna, Vesuvius ; causes of volcanic action and connection with earthquakes, etc. Besides maps and plans, the volume will contain a large number of illustrations showing structure of volcanic mountains, etc., etc.

XX. PUBLIC HEALTH. By Dr. J. F. J. SYKES. With numerous Illustrations. (*In Preparation.*)

The increased knowledge of the internal and external influences upon health obtained within recent years, and the practical applications of which it is capable in the prevention of disease, gives rise to many interesting problems, some of which are being solved, some are only partially touched, and others remain unelucidated. In this volume an attempt will be made to summarise and bring to a focus the essential points in evolution, environment, parasitism, prophylaxis, and sanitation bearing upon the preservation of the public health

The following Writers are preparing Volumes for this Series :—

Prof. E. D. Cope, Prof. G. F. Fitzgerald, Prof. J. Geikie, Prof. A. C. Haddon, Prof. C. H. Herford, Prof. J. Jastrow (Wisconsin), Dr. J. B. Longstaff, Prof. James Mavor, Prof. Aug. Weismann, etc.

Foolscap 8vo, Cloth, Price 3s. 6d.

THE INSPECTOR-GENERAL

(Or "REVIZÓR.")

A RUSSIAN COMEDY.

By NIKOLAI VASILIYEVICH GOGOL.

Translated from the original Russian, with Introduction and Notes, by A. A. SYKES, B.A., Trinity College, Cambridge.

Though one of the most brilliant and characteristic of Gogol's works, and well-known on the Continent, the present is the first translation of his *Revizór*, or Inspector-General, which has appeared in English. A satire on Russian administrative functionaries, the *Revizór* is a comedy marked by continuous gaiety and invention, full of "situation," each development of the story accentuating the satire and emphasising the characterisation, the whole play being instinct with life and interest. Every here and there occurs the note of caprice, of naïveté, of unexpected fancy, characteristically Russian. The present translation will be found to be admirably fluent, idiomatic, and effective.

London : WALTER SCOTT, LIMITED, 24 Warwick Lane.

Crown 8vo, about 350 pp. each, Cloth Cover, 2s. 6d. per vol.
Half-polished Morocco, gilt top, 5s.

COUNT TOLSTOÏ'S WORKS.

The following Volumes are already issued—

A RUSSIAN PROPRIETOR.

THE COSSACKS.

IVAN ILYITCH, AND OTHER STORIES.

THE INVADERS, AND OTHER STORIES.

MY RELIGION.

LIFE.

MY CONFESSION.

CHILDHOOD, BOYHOOD, YOUTH.

THE PHYSIOLOGY OF WAR.

ANNA KARÉNINA. (2 VOLS.)

WHAT TO DO?

WAR AND PEACE. (4 VOLS.)

THE LONG EXILE, AND OTHER STORIES FOR CHILDREN.

SEVASTOPOL.

THE KREUTZER SONATA, AND FAMILY HAPPINESS.

Uniform with the above.

IMPRESSIONS OF RUSSIA.

BY DR. GEORG BRANDES.

London : WALTER SCOTT, 24 Warwick Lane, Paternoster Row.

SELECTED THREE-VOL. SETS

IN NEW BROCADE BINDING.

6s. per Set, in Shell Case to match.

O. W. HOLMES SERIES--

Autocrat of the Breakfast-Table.

The Professor at the Break-fast-Table.

The Poet at the Breakfast Table.

LANDOR SERIES--

Landor's Imaginary Conversations.

Pentameron.

Pericles and Aspasia.

THREE ENGLISH ESSAYISTS--

Essays of Elia.

Essays of Leigh Hunt.

Essays of William Hazlitt.

THREE CLASSICAL MORALISTS--

Meditations of Marcus Aurelius.

Teaching of Epictetus.

Morals of Seneca.

WALDEN SERIES—

Thoreau's Walden.

Thoreau's Week.

Thoreau's Essays.

FAMOUS LETTERS—

Letters of Burns.

Letters of Byron.

Letters of Shelley.

LOWELL SERIES—

My Study Windows.

The English Poets.

The Biglow Papers.

London : WALTER SCOTT, 24 Warwick Lane, Paternoster Row.